THE STOLEN BRIDE

Also by Jo Beverley
Lord Wraybourne's Betrothed
The Stanforth Secrets

The Stolen Bride

Jo Beverley

Walker and Company
New York

FIC
BEV

First published in the United States of America in 1990 by
Walker Publishing Company, Inc.
Published simultaneously in Canada by Thomas Allen & Son
Canada, Limited, Markham, Ontario

Library of Congress Cataloging-in-Publication Data

Beverley, Jo
The stolen bride/Jo Beverley

ISBN 0-8027-1119-7
I. Title.
PR9199.3.B424S76   1990
813'.54—dc20   90-31292
CIP

Printed in the United States of America
2 4 6 8 10 9 7 5 3 1

I belong to a working group which is of great value to me and I want to thank my friends and fellow writers:

Marianne Avon
Vicki Cameron
Debbie Dumoulin
Linda Wiken

I also want to acknowledge the help I received from Alice Harron Orr, my first editor at Walker, who showed me how to smooth my style and led me gently into the challenging world of the published author.

Thank you, everyone.

=== 1 ===

BETH HAWLEY CLOSED her book and eased her legs. Even in the luxurious Wraybourne carriage, travelling was a tedious business. At first she had found some amusement in exploring the vehicle, equipped as it was with embroidered footstools, rugs, oil lamps, and curtains. In the side walls she had found compartments, one containing wine and spirits, one a small writing desk, one games, and one a well-stocked medicine chest. It would seem the nobility liked to be prepared for all eventualities. Such explorations, however, had not even occupied the first day. At least now, in the third day on the road, the journey was nearing its end. Soon she would see her friend and former pupil, Jane, for the first time since Jane's wedding.

With a smile she wondered how Jane, who had been such a sober, shy girl before her betrothal, had adapted to married life as the Countess of Wraybourne. Very well, she suspected, remembering the way the girl had blossomed and matured during her season in London. And of course, it could not be hard to be married to a man like Lord Wraybourne, especially when one was in love with him.

For a fleeting moment the pain of her widowing pulled at Beth. It was so long ago now, that brief marriage to her darling Arthur, that it was ridiculous for grief to bother her. After all, if he were to appear now in the coach, eyes bright with a new challenge, his hair as always escaping whatever style he tried to impose on it, she would surely think him a callow youth at twenty-two. And he would think her a dry old thing at thirty-three.

She returned to the present and looked out of the window as the coach rolled into the small town of Much Wenlock. It was market day and the High Street was full of stalls and customers.

The groom blew a blast on the horn and the carriage turned under the stone arch into the courtyard of the posting inn. Beth tied on her bonnet, looking forward to a chance to stretch her legs. Perhaps there might also be time for a cup of tea. It had been many hours since lunch and though a hamper of food was provided each day, it could not provide a fresh-brewed pot of tea.

The groom swung open the door and let down the steps.

"We still be a couple of hours from Stenby, ma'am. Mr. Kinnock says you may want to take a break here."

"I do indeed, Grigson," said Beth, pulling on her cotton gloves. "Would it be possible for me to stroll about here?"

"Well, I wouldn't, ma'am," said the groom seriously as he handed her down. "It's market day and busylike."

Beth had to admit the truth of it. Jane had urged her to hire a maid for the journey but that had seemed a great deal of nonsense to Beth. She and the two menservants had got along very well thus far, but now she could have used a companion. Of course Beth was accustomed to going about on her own, but she knew if she attempted it here one of the men would feel obliged to escort her. Doubtless they too needed liquid refreshment.

"Well, at least I can take tea here, I hope," she said. "I am parched to death."

"Aye, ma'am," said the man with a grin. "It's dusty weather, sure enough. Not bad for the roads, but hard on the throat. I'll see to it."

At each stop Grigson had made sure the innkeeper knew the quiet little lady in the plain blue gown and bonnet was the special guest of the Earl of Wraybourne, just in case anyone took it into his head to be insolent. As a consequence, Beth soon found herself in the inn's best parlour with a steaming pot of tea and a selection of cakes before her.

She sat close to the open window to enjoy the refreshment and was entertained by the bustle around the market stalls offering everything from fish to lace. A woman walked along the

2

street with a live goose in her basket, trailed by two young lads sticky from some sugared treat. The dust from the traffic was rapidly turning their hands and faces brown.

Outside a nearby shop a maidservant on business was pretending not to be interested in the blandishments of a uniformed soldier who wanted to buy her some trinket from a stall.

A very large gentleman came striding down the pavement. There was nothing about him of the rural-quaint—he was all Town Bronze from the curly brimmed beaver on his short dark hair to his gleaming top boots—and that was perhaps what made him stand out. That and his size. Well over six feet and built to match he seemed a giant among mortal men. Such size was off-putting to Beth, who could just reach five feet if she had a heel to her slippers, but the maidservant obviously did not think so. She called something to the colossus as he strode past which made him laugh and had the soldier scowling.

Beth had just recognised the gentleman when Grigson came to say they were ready for off again. Her poor stiff body protested, but she knew this was the last stage. She did, however, walk around the parlour a few times before emerging, just to remind her legs they had some purpose.

In the busy yard she waited for a loaded stagecoach to pull in before making her way over to the crested carriage. As she approached, a booming voice was heard.

"Kinnock, by God! You're a sight for sore eyes."

Beth turned to see the colossus approach. The coachman turned from his inspection of the harness and touched his forelock.

"Good day to you, Sir Marius. Be you on your way to Stenby, sir?"

"I am indeed, if I can find the means. My damned rig's split the axle and there's no way to fix it today, they tell me."

Both Grigson and Kinnock looked awkwardly at Beth and she quite understood she had been overlooked. She was accustomed to it.

She stepped out from behind the groom. "Good afternoon, Sir Marius. I am Mrs. Hawley, Jane Wraybourne's governess. We met at the wedding, though you may not remember it."

The hand she extended was engulfed in Sir Marius Fletcher's much larger one. "Of course I remember," he said, though she was not sure of his veracity. "You are on your way to Stenby, ma'am?"

Beth nodded. "Do I understand you to be in need of transportation?"

"You have it. I'd hire a horse except that only the largest beasts can take me and they have no such available. And no other carriage. You don't need to think I'll bother you, ma'am. I'll happily ride on the box."

"Of course not," said Beth, concealing some doubts. The conventional notion that an unmarried lady should not share a closed carriage with a gentleman did not concern her; she considered herself too old for such restrictions. She did wonder, however, whether there was room to share the carriage with this giant. It had seemed very spacious for her alone, but it was difficult to imagine how he would fold himself to fit.

"You must ride inside," she said firmly despite her misgivings. "For the three of you to crush together on the box would be absurd."

It was soon arranged. Sir Marius's baggage was transferred from his curricle to the boot of the coach, his man was given instructions for the care of his equipage, and then the baronet climbed into the coach to take the seat opposite Beth.

It was not as bad as she had imagined, though he did dwarf the compartment.

"I don't care much for closed carriages," he said dryly as the coach rolled out of the inn yard. "I always feel as if I'm going to put an elbow through the wall."

She remembered Jane had found this man rather forbidding when they had first met, then had come to call him a friend. Beth could certainly understand the first part. *Harsh* was the word which came to mind. Like granite. The bones of his jaw and skull were solid beneath the flesh.

She realised she had been staring. "It must certainly be a problem at times, being so large," she said hastily.

"No more of a problem than being so tiny, ma'am," he drawled.

Beth sat up straighter. "Well, really, Sir Marius. There is no call for personal remarks."

There was a teasing twinkle in his eyes. "It was no more personal than the remark you made about me, dear lady."

"It was you, as I recall, who began the topic with talk of elbows . . ." Beth trailed off as she realised she was arguing, in a rather childish way, with a virtual stranger. "I . . . I do beg your pardon," she stammered, knowing she was turning a fiery red. She was a redhead with very indiscreet skin.

"Now don't spoil it," he said with a grin. "I was looking forward to sparring all the way to Stenby."

"Well, I could not contemplate such a thing, Sir Marius," Beth said stiffly, regretting her charitable impulse. She didn't even feel able to remove her bonnet and be comfortable.

He looked at her consideringly and then smiled in a more natural way. "I apologise. It is not good of me to be teasing you when we're in such a situation."

For some reason these words only made Beth feel more flustered. "What do you mean, 'such a situation'?"

He leant back at his ease. "Why, in a closed carriage, Mrs. Hawley. You can hardly escape me short of risking life and limb by leaping into the road. We're going a fair speed too. Kinnock must be keen to be home."

Grasping a safe topic with relief, Beth said, "You must know Stenby well, Sir Marius."

"Very well. David and I have been friends since we were boys. I've spent many a happy summer at the Castle. Is this your first visit there?"

"Yes. Jane invited me during the summer but I felt she and her husband should have time together. Now she has asked me to come and help with Lady Sophie's wedding."

"Well, if you were giving them peace and quiet," said Sir Marius, "you should have taken that minx Sophie out of their orbit. She has a natural antipathy to tranquility."

Beth was beginning to understand the large gentleman and did not miss the fondness behind the comment. "Lady Sophie is lively," she responded, "but she has a kind heart. I'm sure she has done her best not to be a bother to her brother and Jane."

He raised a quizzical brow. "It's certain she hasn't sought their company if Randal's been available."

Beth smiled. She remembered Lady Sophie Kyle and Lord Randal Ashby at Jane's wedding, always together, always smiling, always in some way *connected*. Even though their betrothal had not been officially announced until recently, no one who saw them could be in any doubt as to the state of affairs. "It is only natural for young people in love to want to be together, Sir Marius. And Lady Sophie and Lord Randal are very much in love."

"Sickening, ain't it?"

Beth chuckled. "I can quite see you are not of a romantical disposition, Sir Marius, but you should not begrudge your friends their happiness."

"Why not?" he replied, but with a twinkle in his eye. "It's spoiled a perfectly good summer. My two closest friends have wasted it on mere women."

Beth shook her head. "I fear you are a cynic, Sir Marius. One day you too might come to that dreadful fate."

"Marriage—maybe. Love, never. It ain't in my disposition."

Beth felt the conversation was becoming a little too intimate, and in a way she found strangely disconcerting. "Could you tell me a little more about Stenby Castle?" she asked quickly. "Jane has conveyed some of its history in her letters but I have a very unclear picture. Is it truly mediaeval?"

He settled in his seat and stretched his legs. Beth had to move slightly to ensure her skirt was not in contact with his boots. When she thought of her previous journeys on a crowded stage, her unease with the slightest contact seemed ridiculous.

"That's difficult to say, Mrs. Hawley," he replied easily. She knew he had noted her move and was amused. A truly infuriating man. "Most of the external walls date back to at least the fourteenth century but the Kyles haven't done without their comforts. Arrow-slits have become windows, fireplaces have been improved. Walls have been covered with tapestries, panelling, and wallpaper. Apart from the Great Hall, which is hardly used, the house appears very like any gentleman's seat." He leant forward and she hastily leant back.

He was merely gazing out of the window.

"If you look carefully," he said, "you can catch your first glimpse of the place through those trees."

6

Forgetting her concerns Beth quickly moved forwards to share the view.

"Over on that rise," said Sir Marius close to her ear.

Then Beth saw Stenby Castle in the distance, crenelated grey stone walls softened by greenery and set with glittering windows. As the coach bowled along, she sat and watched the place gradually fall behind a screen of trees. She became aware of Sir Marius's breath warm on her cheek.

Startled, she turned to face him and surprised a look of enigmatic amusement. She drew back into her seat feeling far more flustered than was reasonable.

"A charming prospect," she said hurriedly.

"Decidedly," he drawled. "But not in the common run."

"Of course not. Most earls do not have castles for their principal seats."

"Certainly most people prefer the younger, the more fashionable standard of beauty," he said in a manner she could only take as teasing, though she could not see what there was to joke about.

"Do you think so?" she queried. "I thought there was a decided taste for the Gothic these days."

"Gothic?" he echoed with a grin. "Do you really think that description fair?"

Beth could not remember ever having been so off-balance. She was used to handling events with calm competence and yet this man, in some way, was making her feel dizzy. He was also talking nonsense.

"I know some people use 'Gothic' in a pejorative sense, Sir Marius," she said sharply, "but surely it can be used more exactly. A mediaeval castle must have elements of the Gothic."

"Time will tell," he drawled. "It certainly promises to be an entertaining visit—" He broke off as the horses were suddenly pulled up.

As soon as the coach stopped he swung open the door. "What's amiss?"

"Coach off the road, Sir Marius," said Kinnock. "Grigson's just gone to see if they need help."

Sir Marius turned back. "I'll see what's going on," he said and jumped down onto the road.

Not at all unwilling to stretch her legs, Beth followed. He turned back and moved to help her down.

Beth felt a decided reluctance to allow him to swing her to the ground, but it would be a long jump for her and she could hardly order him to let down the steps. Two strong hands nearly spanned her waist, and she was lifted down as if she were a feather. She was used to being small, but this man made her feel positively childlike and she didn't like it one bit. At least he didn't linger to tease her again but went straight to the other carriage.

It appeared to be a hired coach, not new or smart. It had apparently lost a wheel on the bend and toppled. The driver was struggling with the panicked horse and Grigson moved quickly to cut the tangled harness. Sir Marius went over to the coach and Beth followed.

"What passengers?" he called out to the driver.

"Just an old biddy. Taking her to Stenby. Be she all right, sir?"

Sir Marius knocked on the bottom of the coach. "Ma'am? do you need help?"

There was no answer. He pushed at the coach a little to see how stable it was and then hoisted himself onto the side. There was an ominous crack but nothing drastic happened. He looked in through the window.

"She's unconscious, or dead." He eased to one side and tried to open the door but the fall, or his weight, had jammed it. In the end it looked to Beth as if he tore it off its hinges by brute force. He threw it over into the hedge then swung his legs in and the coach jolted to a different angle.

"She's alive," he called out. "I think it's just a knock on the head and a few glass cuts, but she seems a frail thing. I'll lift her. Get one of the men to take her from the top."

By this time the horse was disentangled and subdued. In fact, now it was out of its panic it was obviously a sorry old nag. At Beth's call, Grigson came quickly to help. The old lady was soon hoisted out of the wreck of the coach and laid by the side of the road. She was haggard and pale and her face trickled blood from a number of cuts.

Beth ran back to the Wraybourne carriage for some rugs and

the medical chest. The dratted vehicle loomed like a mountain, the bottom of the door level with her chest. She was fumbling with the steps, trying to work out the catch when those large hands grasped her again, picked her up as if she were a doll, and placed her inside. She looked down, pleased for once to be a good head taller than he.

"What is it you want?" he asked.

"There are blankets and a medicine chest," she said. "Wait there and I'll pass them down." She did this and then added the bottle of water from the food hamper.

Then, of course, she had to submit to being tossed around again. Actually she was becoming strangely accustomed and there was something very safe about his strength.

Beth pulled herself together and hurried back to the woman.

"I don't think there are any broken bones," she said, after a discreet examination. "Just a bad head wound." She gently wiped the blood away from the woman's face and saw with relief that the cuts there were slight and none were near the eye.

She opened the medicine chest, grateful that she had explored it before. There were tweezers, and she used them to take out a couple of slivers of glass. She then smeared some salve over the wounds and bandaged the cuts on the woman's temple. There really didn't seem anything else to do for the moment.

She looked up to see the men watched her, waiting for her decision. "We had best take her to Stenby," she said. "It was where she was going."

Sir Marius turned to the driver. "Who is she? Did she say?"

"No, sir. Just asked to be taken to Stenby Castle and paid the price."

"Did she have any baggage?"

The driver quickly pulled one leather bag from the boot. It was old-fashioned but of solid quality. It was securely locked.

"I presume she has the key on her," Sir Marius said. "If we're taking her to the Castle, there's no point bothering about it. The sooner she's in a bed and the doctor called for the better."

He turned to pick up the woman but was stopped by the whining voice of the driver. "What'm I going to do with me rig in this state?"

9

Beth looked at the coachman closely for the first time and saw the heavy wear on his clothes, the sallow, gaunt look on his face. He was already on the edge of poverty and was probably facing ruin with his livelihood gone. Her eyes met Sir Marius's and the baronet's lips twitched. He took out several guineas.

"Here, man. With these you should be able to fix this or buy new. Take better care of it next time. If this lady doesn't haul you before the magistrate for negligence, you'll be lucky."

He lifted the woman easily and frowned. "She weighs even less than you," he said to Beth, "and she must be half-a-head taller. I wouldn't be surprised to find she's ill. Why on earth would she be going to Stenby?"

Between them, he and Grigson settled the woman on a seat on the coach and Beth sat beside the invalid to support her.

"Perhaps she's a servant," said Beth. "It's quite likely Jane is hiring more with the wedding coming up."

"A superior kind of servant," he said thoughtfully as the coach set off again, holding a steady pace. "Her gown is of silk, even though it's not new. Her wedding band is very solid and this was lying in the coach. It must have fallen from around her neck."

He held out a locket on a broken golden chain. Its cover was beautifully engraved with the initials E.H. After a moment Beth discovered how to work the catch. Inside there was a lock of curly brown hair and a miniature of a young man, apparently the owner of the curls for they hung fetchingly on his brow. A vague swirling whiteness where his collar should have been was presumably meant to suggest classical draperies.

Sir Marius looked at the picture. "It reminds me of someone, but damned if I can think who."

= 2 =

THE DISTANT VIEW of Stenby on that warm August afternoon had not shown Beth and Sir Marius an impromptu cricket match on the lawns which ran up to the east wall. The rolling green set with ancient, spreading trees was dusted with daisies and ornamented in a more substantial way by ladies and gentlemen in white and pastels. The *thunk* of the ball on the long bat was mixed with laughter and cries of triumph or disappointment.

The Kyles were playing the Ashbys. David Kyle, Lord Wraybourne, captained a team composed of his two brothers, Mortimer and Frederick; his sister, Sophie; his wife, Jane, and an assortment of footmen and estate workers. The Ashbys were captained by Lord Randal Ashby. His team consisted of Tyne Towers' servants and his friends Piers Verderan and Justin, Lord Stanforth.

A beech tree had a seat built around it and it was in this shady spot that the spectators had established themselves. There was the Duke of Tyne, portly and short of breath; his mother, the dowager duchess, tiny, bent but sharp as a needle; and his niece, Chloe, Lady Stanforth.

The Kyles had won the toss and elected to bat, David and his brother, Captain Frederick Kyle, going up first. Mortimer, Jane, and Sophie had taken seats in the shade with the others.

"Well," said the Duke of Tyne heartily. "Here I am with all the beauties. Come and give me a kiss, Sophie." When she obliged he pinched her cheek and she tried not to wince. "Can't tell you how pleased I am one of my rascals finally found a woman willing

11

to have him. Now we'll see some sons. That's what every house needs."

Sophie had suffered this often enough in recent weeks to have become accustomed. She no longer even blushed at all this talk of procreation. It was the dowager duchess who said tartly, "Without daughters in the world you'd be hard pressed to make sons, Arthur. And I would point out you only favored the Ashbys with two sons yourself."

"Two's enough," said the duke with a frown. "If they live and breed, two's one too many."

Sophie hastily moved off and left these combatants to their long-established battle. She rolled her eyes at Jane and saw the countess hard put not to giggle. "Why does he demand a quiverful of sons in one breath and only one in the next?" Jane asked quietly.

It was Chloe who answered. "The duke has an obsession with the continuance of the line. He wants to be sure that sons of his sons will rule here."

"But surely, then," said Jane, "a dozen sons for Randal and Chelmly is what he wants." The Marquess of Chelmly was Randal's brother and the heir to the dukedom.

"Ah, but the duke and my father never rubbed well together," said Chloe. "My father wasn't happy being the second son and has been thoroughly unpleasant to Uncle Arthur all his life. In fact, I think the duke's obsession is actually to be sure my brother, Charteris, doesn't become duke one day. It's this bitter feeling between brothers that leads him to say one is enough."

Jane shook her head at this convoluted reasoning. "At least there's no ill feeling between Randal and Chelmly. They both seem perfectly content with their position."

"Indeed yes," said Chloe. "Chelmly is delighted to spend every minute ensuring the Duchy of Tyne glides along on well-oiled wheels and increases in prosperity year by year. He even runs Randal's estates, you know. Doubtless far more efficiently than Randal could himself. And, since the duchess's death he's run the household as well. He just can't seem to get enough of such things and he certainly can't bear to see anything mismanaged."

"And Randal," contributed Sophie, "is equally delighted to

take the income from his properties and enjoy it. An idyllic arrangement if only Chelmly would produce sons as efficiently as he produces profits. Then Randal could achieve his ambition and join the Hussars."

"Well," said Chloe, "doubtless you and Randal will have a boy one day and if Chelmly continues his misogamistic way your son will continue the line."

Sophie couldn't think a son produced by her and Randal would be suited to filling Chelmly's shoes. "That's no good," she said firmly. "Randal will probably give up all notion of the army if we set up our nursery. No, what we need is for Chelmly to marry and produce the next Ashbys. I don't for a minute suppose he's antimarriage. He just can't tear himself away from business long enough to choose a bride. It's typical that he's dropped out of this match just because of some problem with land over Cock-shutt way."

She plucked a pink-edged daisy from among the grass and twirled it thoughtfully. "I think I will simply choose a suitable woman and put her where he'll fall over her. That way there'll be no chance of a son of ours inheriting." She suddenly looked up at the others. "Have you thought? As things stand now, a simple accident or a purulent fever and *Randal* could be saddled with running the duchy—would be duke one day!"

Jane laughed. "Are there many young ladies in the kingdom who would regard being a duchess with such alarm? Really, Sophie, there's no need to fret over it. Chelmly's healthy as a horse and lives a safe and quiet life. As you say, you doubtless have only to present him with a well-chosen bride and he'll settle happily to filling a nursery."

At the thought of nurseries, Sophie looked over at the Stanforth's first child, two-year-old Stephen, who was making a gallant but fortunately futile attempt to climb the spreading beech tree which shaded his mama. In the mistaken belief that the tree was animate, Stephen stood before it, arms raised, and imperiously demanded, "Up! Up!"

All the ladies laughed. "Stevie, the tree cannot lift you," said Chloe. "When you're older you may climb it but not now."

The boy first looked dubious, then mutinous. Then he gave up on the tree and looked around for other tall creatures. He made his choice and trotted speedily towards the nearest fielder on the Ashby team. He took up his stance and said, "Up! Up!"

Sophie saw Chloe make as if to lunge out of her chair, but her grandmother restrained her. "Let be, Chloe. He don't eat little ones for breakfast."

For Stevie had run to Piers Verderan. This was no great surprise. To his mother's alarm, Stevie had conceived a violent attachment to the tall, handsome man who owned the nickname of the Dark Angel and a very unsavoury reputation to go with it.

Verderan looked down at the child. "No, brat," he said, with no trace of fondness. "And if you're hit by the next ball it'll serve you right."

Instead of setting up a wail as he would have done with his parents, Stevie studied the man thoughtfully and then sat down plump between his legs to gather daisy heads.

Verderan was turning to Chloe to complain when a cry spun him back in time to intercept a ball thoroughly walloped by Frederick heading straight for the child. He threw the ball back to the bowler then tucked the child under his arm, walked over and dropped him ungently by his mother. Without a word he returned to his place in the field.

Chloe took a firm hold of her son's gown when he attempted to follow Verderan again. "No, you bad boy." She turned to her grandmother. "How is it that this child has no discrimination? That man is a dueller. He has killed *two* men!"

"I hear they wanted killing," replied the pragmatic duchess. "I gather that as much as his money kept him out of the hands of the law." She laid a hand on her granddaughter's arm. "Neither we nor the Wraybournes are overly keen to have the man in our homes, but he is one of Randal's closest friends. As long as he is willing to behave correctly we can accept him. You can hardly say he is working to attract the child."

"I don't understand it," complained Chloe. "His father spoils Stevie. The duke dotes on him and all the staff at the Towers are slaves to his dimples. Yet the person he haunts is Verderan who just scowls at him and tells him to go away."

"Perhaps that's the secret of his charm," said the duchess

cynically. "With women at least. There's many a woman can't stand to see a man ignore her."

At that point Frederick was caught out and Sophie bounced to her feet. "At last," she said. She hastily pinned back her rose-sprigged muslin and hurried out to bat. When she found she was facing Randal as bowler, she grinned cheekily, confident of a soft toss—especially as she'd pinned her skirt to show a good few inches of her calves.

True enough, the ball was popped gently down and she swung mightily, sending the footman fielding deep nearer the coppice off running. With a cry of triumph she hitched her skirt a little higher and ran down the pitch and back, crossing her brother, David, both ways.

When she stopped before the footman had reached the ball, David Kyle called, "Run again, Sophie!"

"No," she said pertly. "I prefer to be in to bat. Randal wouldn't send *you* soft balls."

David turned to his friend. "Are you going to stand for that, Randal?"

"And how would you bowl to Jane, then?" was the amused reply.

David laughed and looked over at his wife, sitting awaiting her turn at bat, long hair in a braid and hat carelessly abandoned by her side. She blew him a kiss . . .

Randal poked him. "I have bowled, Sophie has walloped it, and you're supposed to be running." David hastily sprinted down the pitch, then refused to run back, despite Sophie's shouts.

"I have to get a turn somehow," he called.

"Are you perhaps avoiding me?" murmured Lord Randal to his betrothed, now at his end of the strip of grass. "Always trying to keep to the other end of the pitch."

Sophie felt his lips brush softly at her nape and turned suddenly, but he had already gone. It was always the same. Brief promises that never amounted to anything.

She watched him hungrily, the sheer beauty of the man a painful pleasure. In loose canvas trousers and an open-necked white shirt he was still the most elegant man in the world. His bright yellow curls were naturally windswept and yet some would pay a coiffeur a fortune to achieve the effect.

He turned and ran back, tossing a hard, fast ball at his friend, who turned it, but not far enough for a run.

"I don't think I am the one doing the avoiding," said Sophie sharply as Randal strolled back past her.

He stopped and rubbed some dirt off the ball against his trousers. "Don't pick a fight here, Sophie," he said gently. "It's rather public."

"Since you avoid being private with me—" But he had gone and was preparing to make his run. She could have screamed.

The bowling changed without David scoring and Sophie found herself nervously facing Piers Verderan. He deserved his nickname of the Dark Angel for he was nearly as beautiful as Randal but what is commonly called a "black Irish." His curls were dark, his eyes were a startlingly deep blue, and there was something devilish about him.

Though Verderan had behaved with perfect propriety over the past few weeks he made Sophie nervous. She saw the way he smiled at her and knew this would be no easy toss.

She was right. It was hard and straight. She got the bat between it and the stumps but only to deflect it into her beloved's waiting hands. "Out," said Randal with satisfaction.

She walked past him towards the seats. "If you wanted me out, why didn't you bowl harder?" she said.

He spoke for her ears alone. "I am learning to do without what I want, Sophie. At least for a little while."

She looked at him. Was that a promise for the future?

"At least now," he said sternly, moving away even as she stepped closer. "You can go and unkirtle your gown so the whole county isn't admiring your ankles."

Sophie stuck her tongue out at his back.

She returned to the spectators and slumped down on the shaded bench to look darkly at her beloved husband-to-be. The man was going to drive her mad. She had thought her every dream had come true when Randal offered for her hand but now things were not as she would want them at all. She had dreamed of long walks together, the sharing of souls and kisses but instead he almost seemed to be avoiding her.

She had known Randal since childhood and adored him just as long. How had they come to this pass? Her mind slid back irresistibly to the time when she realised what he meant to her.

She had been just fifteen that summer and still of an age to play tomboy when Randal would let her. They had gone fishing in the river which marked the boundary between her family's land and his, at a special spot they called the Magic Pool. Her brother Frederick and Randal's sister Cecilia were with them but had taken positions a little further along the bank, out of earshot. It was a hot day and Randal and Frederick both took off their jackets and waistcoats. Sophie boldly stripped off her cotton stockings and laced slippers despite Cecilia's protests. Randal and Frederick, called upon to exercise authority, merely laughed.

The angling was good and there were a number of trout in the creel when Randal decided to try for a large pike known to haunt this spot. On his first cast, however, his hook snagged on some weeds. After watching him try to pull it free, Sophie hitched her skirts up high and waded out to clear it. When she turned, triumphant, she saw the first seriously disapproving look Randal had ever given her.

"For heaven's sake, Sophie, you're too old for that sort of thing. Don't your governesses teach you anything?"

She was bruised a little by her idol's displeasure, but answered with her usual pertness, "Not if I can help it."

His frown didn't lift. "Get out of there and rearrange your skirt."

Abashed, she obeyed. "Why are you angry, Randal? You never used to mind me wading."

"You weren't fifteen then," he said tersely. "It's time you grew up, minx."

She blinked away tears. "I'm not sure I want to if I'm not allowed to have any fun and everyone is angry with me."

He smiled then and came over to wipe away a tear with a gentle finger. "Never fear, little flame. You'll take to being a woman like a duckling takes to the river."

Something stirred within her, softly, tentatively, like a new and fragile leaf pushing up out of the ground. She looked up and his familiar beauty—his fine-boned face, his clear blue eyes, and chick-soft buttercup curls—took on a new and frightening glamour. "What will happen when I'm a woman?" she asked with conscious naivety.

He turned away slightly, but she saw his lips twitch. "You won't be able to take your stockings off in public for a start."

"Is that all?"

He turned back and there was a strange expression on his face. Was it only the sunlight falling speckled through the leaves which made him look wistful? "No, of course not. Hundreds and hundreds of men will gather around you like moths, little flame, and one of them, one lucky man, him you will choose to burn."

The leaf unfurled to the sunlight and grew, and swelled. But it was a strange and frightening process and Sophie flinched away. "Why would I want to burn anyone?" she asked.

He grinned, and was the old Randal again. "Now *that* proves you're not a woman yet, minx. Why don't you catch me something to use as bait?"

Mind spinning with a host of new and strange ideas, Sophie obediently cast a small baited hook and pulled in a dace. She speared it live onto his hook without a shudder, because he'd trained her that way. Head bent to her task, Sophie struggled to make sense of it all.

Her feelings were unformed and poorly defined but she knew. In her childish adoration she would unhesitatingly have fixed herself upon the hook had he asked. But in an emotion much deeper and more potent she wanted to put some sort of hook into him, to capture and hold him. . . .

It had taken time for Sophie to truly absorb that she was in love with Randal, and what it meant, but from then on she had planned her life with that in mind.

When she had gone to London this spring to make her debut she had been sure that Randal would finally see her as a woman and claim her as his own. Her heart had broken when she had realised this wasn't to be.

It had been that dreadful night which had changed everything—the night when Sir Edwin Hever had been confronted by her brother, David, and accused of being the rapist who had preyed upon the women of the city for months. Sir Edwin had taken her hostage and her very life had been in danger until Randal had risked an almost impossible shot to save her.

Even now, sitting in the warmth of the sun, Sophie shivered at the memory. Sir Edwin had been quite, quite mad. She had fainted, she remembered, and only come to her senses in her bedchamber, in Randal's arms. He had held her as she recovered from the shock. Her brother had found them there. The next day Randal had formally offered for her and been accepted.

Any gentleman found in a maiden's bedchamber, with said maiden in his arms, was bound to offer marriage. Why had that not occurred to her for months? Why did it haunt her now?

Randal seemed so cool at times. He positively avoided being alone with her. Despite words of love, had he been trapped into this betrothal? Sophie could not bear it if that was so. In fact Sophie's love for Randal was so deep and selfless that if freedom was what he wanted, she would give it to him.

But that only left her the two weeks before the wedding to make such a terrible decision.

Shadows were lengthening across the rolling lawns when the high-born members of the teams wandered back to the Castle while the servants cleared away the stumps and chairs. They found the family coach just pulling up to the *porte cochere*.

Jane hurried forward as the steps were let down.

"Beth," she exclaimed happily, then stopped in surprise as Marius Fletcher stepped down first and turned to help her friend.

"We met Sir Marius stranded on the way," said Beth as she went to embrace Jane. "But we have another passenger too, I'm afraid."

"Why afraid, Mrs. Hawley?" asked David as he came forwards to shake hands.

"Well, my lord, she's a bit of a mystery," said Beth as Sir Marius lifted the unconscious woman out. She quickly recounted the events.

"We were expecting no one today except you," said Jane, "and I haven't hired any staff from far afield. We must put her to bed, though, and call the doctor."

This was soon arranged. Beth was relieved of responsibility

for the invalid and taken to her own bedchamber to freshen herself after the journey. She almost felt she should protest at being given what was obviously a choice guest room—after all she had only been Jane's governess—but it was clear neither Jane nor her husband would hear of any objection.

It was the loveliest bedchamber she had ever had for her own. A deep rich carpet was spread on the oak floor and red damask curtains hung at the long windows and from the canopy over the large bed. As Sir Marius had said, the Castle might be hundreds of years old but the Kyle's didn't stint themselves of comfort.

One of the casement windows was open to the evening breeze. Beth went to the seat which filled the embrasure and gazed with delight over the lake to rolling hills set with stands of trees. Swans and ducks placidly cruised the water while peacocks stalked the lawns nearby, occasionally giving their plaintive screech.

Beth turned at a scratch and called, "Enter."

Jane came in and hugged her friend. "I am so pleased to have you here at last, Beth. Isn't Stenby beautiful?"

"It is indeed, Jane. You must be happy in your home."

Jane sat on the chest at the foot of the bed. "So very much. David likes to stay here most of the time, you know, and I have no argument with that. In fact, to be honest, I'll be delighted when the wedding is over and we can go back to the quiet times of the early summer."

"It must be a great deal of work. I remember your wedding, and that was a quite affair."

"I really don't mind," said Jane. "The organization is merely a challenge, and one I enjoy. The tangle here is Sophie and Randal. He has become a glutton for propriety, unlikely as that may seem, and when they are here I have to spend more time than I can afford playing chaperone. It's not a role I'm comfortable with at the best of times. I am hoping," she said with a winning smile, "that you will take the task off my hands."

"If Sophie wants someone to play propriety," said Beth, "I will be happy to oblige."

"Since propriety seems to be the price for Randal's presence," said Jane dryly, "Sophie wants propriety. Those two are enough to drive me distracted. Anyway, the real reason I came is to tell you about our mysterious visitor."

"Do you know who she is, then?"

"No," said Jane. "Perhaps I should have said 'to tell you how little we know about our mysterious visitor.' The maid found a secret pocket when she undressed her. It contained quite a lot of money and the key to her valise but there's no indication as to who she might be. She has a card case in her reticule but it's empty. There's a letter addressed to Edith, but there's no address on it so it must have been part of a packet."

"How peculiar. And yet she seems a lady."

"I think so. There's the money—she's carrying nearly a hundred pounds—and her clothes are good quality even if not new. There are a few pieces of jewellery, all very good. Her wedding ring is solid and she wears a new mourning ring of silver set with jet. No one can imagine why she was coming to Stenby, even though she had the announcement of Sophie's wedding torn from the *Gazette*."

"Good heavens," exclaimed Beth. "Surely she is a relative, then. There must be people on the fringes of the Kyles who are forgotten."

"That is possible," said Jane dubiously. "But Mortimer acts as family archivist and he's sure there are no Ediths that he has ever heard of. Another strange thing is that she was carrying a pistol, powder, and shot."

"Well," remarked Beth. "A woman travelling alone might think that wise."

"That's what David said. He took it, though, in case she is out of her senses when she recovers."

"A mystery and an adventure," remarked Beth, with twinkling eyes. "And I've always lived a quiet life."

"Indeed," said Jane, "but I could have done without excitement just now. The doctor says the blow to the head is not serious but that the woman seems weak as if she had been ill. We are likely to have her on our hands for ages if we can't identify her and find her relatives, and I will need her room for wedding guests. And her family will be concerned. David is having enquiries made about her on the coaching routes." With a practical shrug she abandoned a problem which could not be helped. "Now, I must go and dress for dinner. And before you say a word, Beth," she added quickly, "you are dining with us. I warned you to bring at least one evening gown so you have no excuse."

"The rigours of the journey?" queried Beth dryly.

Jane was immediately contrite. "How thoughtless of me. Of course you will have a tray here."

"Oh no," said Beth with a laugh. "If I'm to ape the aristocracy I may as well start now. You know I am not easily tired, Jane, and yes, I did bring not one but two presentable gowns."

Jane kissed her friend. "Wonderful. Now all I have to do is make a match for you. Randal's father is a duke, though elderly and rather frail. . . ."

"Jane," warned Beth in her best schoolroom tone.

"Or Mortimer, perhaps," mused Jane mischievously. "Oh no, I forgot. He doesn't believe in marriage."

"A parson who doesn't believe in marriage?"

"For himself. He believes in a celibate priesthood."

"Goodness!"

"I have it," said Jane as she opened the door. She smiled naughtily as she looked back. "Sir Marius is just the man for you."

Before Beth could voice the objection on her lips, Jane was gone. Beth knew she had turned pink. What was it about the dratted man? The notion was ridiculous on every count. Apart from inequality of rank and fortune, they would be a laughing stock when her head hardly reached the middle of his chest.

Still, for some quite ridiculous reason, the memory of being swung to the ground as if she were a tiny child returned and brought a disturbing sensation. Sternly, Beth disciplined herself. Jane had been teasing and Beth wasn't at Stenby in search of a husband. She would enjoy a little interlude among High Society and then return contentedly to her brother's home and her role of favourite aunt.

== 3 ==

THE PARTY WHICH met in the drawing-room before dinner that night consisted of all who had been at the cricket match as well as Sir Marius, Beth, and the Marquess of Chelmly. The marquess bore a distinct familial resemblance to Lord Randal, Beth noted, but lacked his beauty. He was both more solid and softer and his colouring was muted as if a layer of dust covered his brother's brilliance, turning golden curls to ashen and bright blue eyes to grey.

The drawing-room was panelled in richly carved birch and contained a magnificent modern marble fireplace. It could have been a room in any grand house. The dining-room, however, was another matter. Beth was fascinated to see that the walls were still unadorned stone, many feet thick. The stone fireplace looked large enough to roast an ox in and the two doors were solid oak hinged with heavy black metal. Beth looked forward to exploring more of this wonderful old building.

First, however, she had to survive eating amongst the high and mighty. She was pleased to note that her gown was adequate for the occasion. In the county dress was moderate. The pale green silk Beth had made up with the help of her sister-in-law held its own, especially as they had employed an embroideress to decorate the neckline and hem. She had even been given a maid who had managed a charming arrangement of her ginger curls. Beth was feeling very grand.

And, despite the presence of a duke and duchess, the gathering was not formal. The fourteen people who sat down at the long table were all friends or relatives and the talk was general.

Beth's self-assurance took a knock, however, when she found herself seated between Sir Marius and the devilishly handsome Mr. Verderan. With his lean tanned face and short, crisp, dark curls the latter needed only the horns, thought Beth, to make devilish exactly the right word. Even she had heard of Verderan's wicked ways and she had no desire to become acquainted. As for Sir Marius, who knows what the man would take it into his mind to say next?

She would have to have words with Jane about this sort of thing and demand more suitable companions. The Reverend Mortimer Kyle would have been an unalarming partner, for example, for he was a quiet, studious gentleman. Or even his brother, Captain Frederick Kyle. He was a high-spirited young man making the most of a brief furlough from the Peninsula but Beth felt able to handle that type.

She wouldn't have minded, even, being set between the Duke of Tyne and his heir, the Marquess of Chelmly. Despite their high rank the former was obviously just a man in poor health, and the latter was a quiet, sober gentleman. When introduced before dinner Beth had received the impression that he was in some ways a limited man lacking a quick intellect and a sense of humour, but both kind and conscientious.

For this meal, at least, she was fixed between a rake and a teasing colossus and she had to talk to one of them. To her surprise she found she would rather address the rake. What to say, though? An infallible way to open a conversation was to ask the gentleman about himself, but she doubted there was much about Mr. Verderan she cared to know. She took a long drink from the claret in her glass and turned to him.

"You are an old friend of Lord Randal's, I believe, Mr. Verderan."

She didn't know what she had been expecting but the rake turned to her with a polite smile. "Yes, Mrs. Hawley. We were at Eton together. And Christ Church."

She was struck by the fact that though the two men were presumably the same age Lord Randal's looks still had something of boyish smoothness about them while Mr. Verderan's were thoroughly matured. The price of dissipation? She forced herself to stop thinking in such an intimate way. His features were no business of hers. "School friendships are often the longest lasting," she commented.

"Please, Mrs. Hawley," he drawled with a quite charming smile. "Spare me a dissertation on the innocence of youth."

Beth felt a little flutter inside and reminded herself that a gazetted rake must have some attractive features. She commanded herself to be wary but her nerves made her retort tartly, "I can't say *innocence* was the word which sprang to mind."

As soon as the words were out she looked at him in alarm, wondering if she would get a set-down but he was laughing. "Don't worry, dear lady. I am delightfully happy being wicked, you see, so I'm not likely to bite when it's spoken of."

Sophie addressed them across the table. "I don't think you truly can be wicked then, Verderan. Mortimer is always preaching that wickedness is certain to lead to misery. What is it, Mortimer? 'There's no peace for the wicked'?"

Her brother, seated on the far side of Verderan, was obviously uncomfortable with calling across the table but replied, " 'There is no peace, saith the Lord, unto the wicked,' Isaiah 48:22. Mind your manners, Sophie."

"Who on earth would want peace?" asked Verderan of no one in particular.

Sophie wrinkled her nose at her brother. "At least I attend to your sermons now and then, Tim."

"If you took them to heart, I'd be more gratified," he retorted.

Sophie was about to respond to this sibling taunt, but Randal turned her head and laid a finger on her lips to hush her. "Behave yourself," he said with a smile.

"Behave yourself, behave yourself!" Sophie hissed. "That's all you ever say to me these days."

Silence fell and the whole table turned to listen.

Randal looked at his betrothed, unperturbed. "Do you know that the hippopotamus bleeds itself?" he said.

"What?" Sophie gaped.

"If it has overindulged on grass," said Randal, lounging back in his chair, "or fish, or whatever a hippopotamus eats, it pierces itself with a sharp reed. When it has bled enough, it patches itself

25

with mud. Read it somewhere. May I help you to more carrots, Sophie?"

"You're mad," said Sophie, rather flushed. "What has all that to do with anything?"

"I said something to you other than 'behave yourself,' " he pointed out with a teasing smile. He kissed a finger and brushed it lightly over her lips.

"Randal, behave yourself," said the duchess firmly, causing a general laugh as everyone picked up their conversations.

Beth however viewed the lovers with concern. She understood Jane's uneasiness. Something was certainly not right in that quarter and though it was easy enough to put it down to prenuptial nerves, she felt uneasy. She took another long drink from her wineglass.

Sir Marius spoke softly to her. "Now, Mrs. Hawley, if you trace that conversation back, I think you will find it was all your fault."

She turned to glare at him. "No such thing, Sir Marius, and I do not see why you cannot attempt to be polite to me."

"But I can't be bothered to be polite any more than Verderan can be bothered to be virtuous."

Mr. Verderan emitted an audible sigh. "It is clear you haven't been here for the past fortnight, Fletcher. I have been applying myself to virtue most assiduously. I swear the last really wicked thing I did was before I came north."

To her horror, Beth only just stopped herself asking what that had been. She began to think she was unsuited to this kind of company. She took another fortifying drink of claret then, as a slight dizziness washed over her, began to wonder if that was a wise thing to do.

"Don't pay attention to Ver, Mrs. Hawley," called Lord Randal. "He's no more wicked than Marius is rude."

Beth was skeptical. She was willing to admit that Sir Marius's manners were within the range of tolerable. That was not the impression she had of Verderan's morals.

When she glanced at the rake his deep blue eyes flashed with humour. "You are quite correct, Mrs. Hawley. Randal is trying to whitewash me. Since he has taken to the paths of sanctity, he don't much care to be acquainted with anyone as wicked as I. I, however, am moved as the prayer book bids us, to acknowledge and confess my manifold sins and wickedness."

"Please don't," said Beth firmly and he laughed.

Those blue eyes were fringed with outrageous lashes, and warm with endearing humour . . . Good heavens, thought Beth with alarm, this was surely exactly the sort of man she had been taught all her life to flee from and yet she was fascinated.

She found herself consumed with curiosity to know precisely what he did that was so wicked. He didn't look like a bully, and he appeared too healthy to be totally given over to debauchery. She had once met an opium eater and the poor man appeared merely pathetic. Was it just women? But many men had mistresses and were not shunned. . . .

She was not aware she had been staring until he said, a little sharply, humour gone, "Do I perhaps have a smut on the end of my nose, Mrs. Hawley?"

Beth knew she had turned fiery red. It dawned on her that she was a little inebriated. It was the only way to account for her behaviour. She just hoped she could survive the meal without everyone becoming aware of her disgrace. "I do beg your pardon, Mr. Verderan. My mind was wandering."

"I generally find that when a person is looking at something or someone, the individual's wandering mind is travelling that road, Mrs. Hawley."

She really couldn't tell if he was seriously annoyed or not, but now he truly made her nervous. There was something about him, beneath the superficially correct manners . . . Then she recognised it. This man was dangerous. She didn't think she had ever met a dangerous man before. He acknowledged no rules. If it suited him he was capable of anything. Regardless of what he did, it was that unpredictability and people's knowledge of it, which gave him his reputation.

He immediately illustrated her revelation. She had been staring again and he took her chin and turned her head sharply away, not particularly gently. Silence spread around the table and Beth wanted to crawl under the tablecloth. His action had been intolerably rude but so had hers. And all because of *drink*.

"I do beg your pardon, Mr. Verderan," she said quickly. "I know how distressing it is to be stared at."

People looked away and conversation resumed.

"Behave yourself, Verderan," said Sir Marius quietly and it wasn't a joke.

"I always do what I damned well please, Fletcher," said Verderan without heat. "Short of shooting me, there's no way to stop me."

"That can be arranged," said the baronet laconically.

Beth dared to raise her eyes from her plate and saw a light flicker in the younger man's eyes like a flame. "That couldn't possibly be a challenge, could it, my dear man? I've been suffering from the most terrible ennui."

Beth's rare temper flared and burned free in alcoholic liberation. "No, it could not!" she said fierce and low before Sir Marius could respond. "I don't care how wicked you are, you stupid boy. If you ever dare to embroil me in any kind of imbroglio, I will shoot you myself!"

She had spoken louder than she intended. Silence fell again but Beth didn't care. She meant it.

Verderan's lips twitched, then he laughed out loud. He picked up his glass and turned to the end of the table where Jane sat watching in horror. "My dear Lady Wraybourne, my congratulations. I thought you'd brought the lady here to act as Sophie's chaperone, but I see now she's supposed to keep me in order. I concede. My behaviour will be pattern-card perfect from now on."

When the ladies finally retired to the Crimson Chamber, Sophie came straight over to Beth. "Well, Mrs. Hawley, aren't you the dark horse! Fancy bearding Verderan."

"Lady Sophie, please don't tease me," said Beth. "I don't know what came over me." But she did, and she could still feel the effects of the claret. A certain lightness in the head and a numbness around her mouth. She prayed earnestly that it wasn't obvious.

"Aren't you the slightest bit attracted to him?" asked Sophie, curiously. "He's wonderfully handsome, and there's something about a truly wicked man . . ."

Beth looked at the young woman with concern. Surely she

couldn't be casting eyes at Lord Randal's close friend. "He's a trifle young for me," she said, adding pointedly, "and I am not a foolish believer in the power of a good woman to reform a rake."

"Well, I've managed to reform Randal," said Sophie so morosely that Beth was hard put not to chuckle.

Beth decided it would be wise to bend the rules of propriety a little. "I think you'll find in two weeks, Lady Sophie, that he's not reformed beyond redemption."

Sophie coloured but looked pathetically grateful for this crumb. "Do you think . . .? But then it will all be settled won't it? There'll be no going back."

Beth considered the troubled girl. There was no sense to any of this. "Lady Sophie, I know this can be a nerve-wracking time for anyone. If you truly have doubts, however, do not commit yourself yet. I thought he was your choice, but Lord Randal will not be the easiest husband . . ."

"Of course I want Randal," said Sophie, flushing with colour. "But he . . ." She made a gallant attempt to smile. "As you suppose. It is all just bridal nerves. What do you think of our mysterious guest, then? Perhaps she's a skilful thief, come to murder us all in our beds."

Beth let the girl turn the conversation but something was wrong here. She remembered the happy lovers who had danced at Jane's wedding. Their love and closeness had been a tangible thing, spreading warmth to all around. Now they seemed more like squabbling siblings. She suspected she had not been invited to a sinecure after all.

When Jane came to sit beside her she said as much.

"It is worrying," said Jane. "Sophie adores Randal and I'd swear he feels the same way and yet they are so awkward together. . . . But then," she said with a teasing look at her friend, "they are not the only ones who have me in a puzzle. You're the first person I've heard say a cross word to Verderan."

Beth blushed. "And I should not have done so," she said firmly. "I'll ask you not to put me between the two most notorious men at table again, young lady."

"But, Beth, I was sure you could handle them," said Jane, laughing. "And Verderan does present a problem. Lady Stanforth has taken against him because of her child's misguided devotion. Sophie is inclined to flirt with him, which I think dangerous. The dowager can manage him very well but she wanted to sit by Mortimer and discuss some matter of genealogy. I thought you managed wonderfully. And Verderan will behave himself now, you know. He does keep his word. As long," she added with a frown, "as he doesn't lose that dreadful temper, that is."

"Is he so bad?"

Jane shrugged. "He's supposed to have taken a whip to someone recently and half killed him, but no one will tell me what for. I really don't know what to make of him. He certainly has women and there have been duels. Randal swears they were honourable, though, and even the men he killed deserved to die. You know men," said Jane, who a few short months ago had not known men at all. "Even David has been out, though he's never injured anyone seriously."

"I wouldn't want to have much to do with Mr. Verderan," said Beth. "With or without a temper, one would never know what he might do next. He is . . . uncivilised."

"Uncivilized?" echoed Jane in surprise. "He's extremely well educated and has beautiful manners when he cares to use them." She took a few thoughtful sips of tea. "But yes," she said. "I do see what you mean."

"Is Sophie attracted to him?" asked Beth directly.

"No, of course not. She has eyes for no one but Randal. If the silly man would just take her into the garden and kiss her soundly, we'd all be better off."

Beth choked on her tea on this pragmatic advice. There was no trace of her shy innocent pupil in the Countess of Wraybourne.

"Perhaps you should tell him that," said Beth.

But Jane shuddered slightly, and looked much like her old self. "Oh no. I tried to advise Randal about Sophie once . . . When I think of the things I said I could crawl into a hole. It's only two weeks to the wedding. We shall all just have to endure."

Beth looked over to where Sophie was standing alone, looking out of a long window. The two weeks till the wedding seemed a very long time.

Beth's thoughts were interrupted by the arrival of the gentlemen in high spirits. Or at least, Lord Randal was in high spirits, aided and abetted by Verderan and Marius, without much restraint being applied by any of the rest—though the marquess looked a little disapproving. Beth thought wryly that she was not the only one to have overindulged in drink, but that did not make her offence any the better.

"Do you remember," asked Randal of David, "the time we sneaked off to the Wem fair and tried to catch the greasy pig? Such a mess we were both in and you got the brunt of the trouble, being older."

"Feelingly," said David with a pained expression. "My father believed I was too old to beat but after the tongue-lashing he gave me I'd rather have had the whipping. He seemed to feel I was leading the younger ones astray. And after you had escaped from your tutor and ridden over with the wonderful idea. There's no justice."

"Well," said Randal, the picture of innocence. "It was taking Sophie along that really tore it."

"Are you seriously suggesting that was *my* idea?" protested David. "What brother has ever desired the company of his little sister?" He accompanied this by a teasing wink at Sophie and settled beside his wife to take a cup of tea.

Randal strolled over to Sophie, warmly smiling. He raised her hand and kissed it just by the diamond ring he had given her. "She cried so prettily to be taken along," he said, looking into her eyes. "Irresistible."

"I found her resistible," said David firmly. "Tangled hair and a snotty nose. Woe to you if you're going to let her bear-lead you all your life with tears. And she ended up with a black eye which was what incensed my revered father so."

"I remember," said Sophie. "I ran into a tree."

Beth could see Sophie blossoming under Randal's lighthearted attentions and her concerns about the pair began to fade.

"Why don't we go to the fair?" asked Sophie eagerly. "It would be such fun."

"Yokels and strong ale?" queried the Marquess of Chelmly dismissively. "I don't think you'd enjoy it now you're more than five, Sophie."

31

"Randal and David enjoyed it at much past five," Sophie retorted. She looked around for support and fastened on Piers Verderan, lounging in a chair rather apart from the rest. "Would you like to go to the fair, Ver?"

He looked at her and seemed to read her mind. "I always hold that a touch of squalor makes us appreciate our good fortune," he drawled.

"Is that your excuse?" queried Marius dryly. Beth stiffened. The antagonism between the two could be felt. Over her? It was impossible surely that these two men could be bristling like hounds over little Beth Hawley.

"I never need an excuse," replied Mr. Verderan. "It's so boringly bourgeois to be forever justifying one's actions."

Before Sir Marius could respond, Mr. Verderan got support from an unexpected quarter. "Damn me if you ain't right," barked the Duke of Tyne.

"Good," said Randal, seemingly oblivious to ill-feeling. "Then, if we need no excuse for enjoying proletarian pleasures, I vote for the fair. I never did catch the greasy pig, after all."

Sophie clapped her hands and her brother, Frederick, let out a whoop.

"You can't be serious, Randal," said Chelmly, and Sophie scowled at him dreadfully.

"If I can't be serious," said Lord Randal blithely, "then I won't be. I think I'll pass on the greasy pig, but I'll break pots for trinkets."

He turned to Sophie with a decidedly mischievous twinkle and turned her so her back was to him. He undid the chain around her neck and drew away the pearl and diamond pendant she wore. "Sophie can't be going around in costly stuff like this," he said, slipping it into his pocket. "It will quite turn her head. Pinchbeck and glass is what she needs if she's to be a frugal housewife."

Sophie turned around and put her hands on her hips. "Indeed!" She moved her left hand and studied the magnificent marquise diamond. "Yes, I see it's a worthless bauble."

"What else?" he agreed. "I'm an impoverished younger son." He took her hand and turned it. The precious stone flashed fire from the candles but he appeared unimpressed. "But I could have done better than this, all the same." He kissed her hand again. "I shall win you a better, sweeting. Something with more colour."

"Oh, good," said Sophie, her eyes nearly as bright as the diamond at this delightful nonsense. "I haven't liked to complain, my dear—I'm sure you were pressed for the ready at the time—but something yellow, perhaps, or red, would be nice. And much, much larger. I can hardly hold my head up in company with this paltry thing."

Beth saw the two lovers lose themselves for a moment as the world disappeared for them and they gazed into each other's eyes. Then Randal recollected himself and drew Sophie back into the center of the room.

"Dare I hope they have pistol shooting at this fair of yours?" asked Verderan.

"Of course not," Randal replied. "Strictly stones thrown at chipped pots."

"I'll need to practice then," said the Dark Angel, with a deliberately wicked look at a display of Middle Eastern pottery in one corner. Beth gasped and Sophie gave a nervous giggle. David got speedily to his feet and stood in front of his valuable collection, but his lips were twitching.

"Some of them *are* chipped," said Verderan innocently. "Lady Wraybourne, I appeal to you. Do you not have some common pieces we can hurl stones at?"

"Now?" asked Jane blankly.

"Come on, Jane," said Sophie. "I'm sure the kitchen must be full of stuff they'd be glad to see the back of."

Beth saw Jane flash a look at her husband, but he must have given his approval for she began to enter into the spirit. "But you're not breaking pots in here, or anywhere in the house for that matter. In the garden, I think. Nor am I asking the servants to do extra work this time of night. You," she said, pointing at Verderan, "and you," she pointed at Randal, "can come with me and carry."

The party divided in two at this point. The duke, the duchess, the marquess, and the Stanforths decided to return to the Towers and the earl went to see them on their way. The rest, caught in an adventurous spirit, invaded the kitchen in search of pots.

It was perhaps fortunate that the Stenby staff had a parlour to sit in so that the arrival of the ladies and gentlemen in the kitchen did not throw anyone into hysterics. Mrs. Jolley, the cook, soon arrived to protect her preserve but Sophie's words proved true. She remembered a box in the back of one of the storerooms where her predecessor had put discarded pottery twenty years before. There were bowls and jugs with tiny chips or cracked glazing, and pieces of pottery with awkward handles or dribbling spouts.

"Never could bear to throw a thing out, she couldn't," the woman remarked. She turned with a frown. "Now, now, Master Randal," she said to that gentleman, who was exploring with fascination the line of earthenware pots on a sideboard. "Keep your fingers to yourself, if you please."

He stopped with the look of an angelic child caught in a rare moment of naughtiness.

Obviously, that was the impression Mrs. Jolley received for she clucked slightly and lifted down a large crock. She opened it to reveal crisp, golden Shrewsbury biscuits. The ladies and gentlemen, despite having had a perfectly adequate dinner, fell upon them as if starving. The cook shared an indulgent look with Beth, who had not joined in the business. Then she turned to the others.

"Many's the time you young ones have come here looking for my Shrewsbury biscuits," Mrs. Jolley said. "Now don't you eat them all, though, or there'll be none for tea tomorrow."

It was in a spirit of hilarity that the party made its way to the gravelled driveway, arms full of pots and many a pocket full of biscuits. Even the staid Reverend Mortimer strolled beside Beth, fondly remembering kitchen raids of his youth. Lord Wraybourne caught up with them, stole some biscuits from his sister, and took Marius on a side trip to the kitchen garden to gather stones.

Frederick and Mortimer volunteered to fetch two chairs and a board on which to stand the pots. Jane requested Verderan and Beth's assistance in investigating the ancient box of discards. Beth looked back for a moment at Randal and Sophie, who were left standing alone in the moonlight. Ah well, they'd be better for a little privacy.

"No work for us," said Randal lightly. "Perhaps we should stay almost-married for the rest of our lives."

"No, thank you," said Sophie sharply.

"No," he said softly. "Not a terribly good idea. 'If it were done when 'tis done, then 'twere well it were done quickly.' " He turned her head with a finger on her chin and lowered his lips softly to hers. Those lips and that finger were the only point of contact and yet Sophie's head began to swim. She kept her eyes open and thought she saw an expression of pain in his.

She drew back resolutely. "Do you wish it were not to be done?" she asked.

"What?"

"That quotation. Macbeth doesn't really want to kill the king."

"Very wise," he said flippantly. "Look what happened when he did—ghosts and witches and walking woods." He moved to join Jane, Beth, and Verderan.

Sophie grabbed desperately at his sleeve. "Were you saying you don't want to marry me?" she asked.

He looked at her with humorous amazement and peeled her fingers off the cloth. "Don't be silly, Sophie. Serves me right for quoting Shakespeare. If there was any sense to it, surely, it was that I wish we had been married months ago. And that," he added, with an indulgent touch of her chin, "is certainly true."

By then the others had returned and he moved away to help set up the board and place items upon it. Then they cheerfully, ladies as well as gentlemen, hurled stones at the pots to shatter them.

Sophie did remarkably well but Beth wasn't really surprised as she appeared to be taking out some bitter feelings on those pots. What had occurred between her and Randal? Beth had noticed that brief kiss and hoped it augured well. Judging from the anger Sophie was directing at the pottery it was not so.

Sophie was about to hurl a final stone at a singularly dull and ugly urn with a large chunk out of the rim when Lord Wraybourne's shout stopped her.

He ran over and picked the pot up with reverence. "For God's sake. It's the Rakka Pot. It's been missing for years." He rubbed away some of the dirt and cobwebs, and they could see the raised design on the clay. "This is priceless!" He looked sharply at Verderan. "Surely you must have seen this was not kitchenware?"

The Dark Angel was the picture of innocence. "I'm no authority on such matters," he said.

The earl made no further comment but Beth saw the expression in Verderan's eyes.

"He knew," she said softly to herself. "He just left the matter in the hands of fate."

Sophie heard. "Is that the way, then?" she asked.

Beth could tell it was not an idle question and had no notion of how to answer. "Some say we cannot change our fate, Lady Sophie, no matter how we try."

"But can we be sure," asked Sophie, "that someone will come between us and shattering disaster?"

She walked away slowly and Beth had no idea what that short exchange had been about.

= 4 =

BETH AROSE THE next morning to a quiet household. Only Jane and her husband, Sophie, Beth, Captain Frederick, and Sir Marius remained. Soon after breakfast Lord Wraybourne took Sir Marius and Frederick off on some manly pursuit, leaving the ladies to handle the household.

"There is, I'm afraid," said Jane, "still rather a lot to do. Despite the fact that the staff here is excellent, the Castle has lacked a woman's touch. We're expecting the whole clan—all David's aunts and uncles and not a few of the cousins as well as many friends. The staff can take care of cleaning all the bedchambers we will need, but I'd like to ask you and Sophie to check the linen and fixtures to make sure everything is as it should be. And Sophie, perhaps you can consider who would be suited by some of the less usual quarters."

Beth agreed to this willingly enough, though Sophie could not be said to be enthusiastic. She did agree to guide Beth around the huge place, however, and soon became more animated as she related stories of the Castle.

"This is called the Nun's Walk," she said with relish as they climbed a short staircase to find another unpredictable passageway. Beth decided it would be very easy to get lost in Stenby. "I think we will put my cousin Maria Harroving and her brood in here. She deserves to meet the tortured nun."

"The tortured nun!"

"Yes. One of my ancestors—oh, I don't know how many greats ago, turned Catholic. Under Elizabeth, would you believe? Well, actually, I think she converted under Mary and then stuck with it, foolish woman. The second earl, her brother, handed her to the authorities for attending Mass, and she was crushed to death because she wouldn't make a plea. She's said to walk here, dripping blood."

"Lady Sophie, are you teasing me?"

"No, honestly," said Sophie. "My aunt Elizabeth claims to have seen her and she's the most down-to-earth person. She's married to the Bishop of Winchester and certainly has no sympathy for popish martyrs. There're lots of tales of knights in armour walking over near the Great Hall too."

Beth had to admit that if any house was likely to have spectres, it was Stenby, with its quaint corridors, its thick and ancient walls. "Well," she said briskly, "ghosts or not someone will have to sleep in this part and it may as well be the Harrovings as anyone. Let us see what state the rooms are in."

As Jane had said, they were freshly cleaned, but the servants had paid little heed to the finer points. One bedchamber, for example, had no chairs at all. Beth made a note on the tablet she carried.

"They must have been moved elsewhere," said Sophie, peering idly into a wardrobe. "I don't think anyone has slept in the Nun's Walk since David's christening. The king came to that, you know."

"It's to be hoped he wasn't put in here," said Beth dryly, "or the Kyles can hold themselves responsible for his mental instability."

"Oh no. He had the Royal Suite. Come on, I'll show you."

Before Beth could protest, she had sped away and Beth felt she might as well follow. Up and down staircases and along a myriad of passageways they came to heavy, ancient oak doors which Sophie flung open. "It's not called the Royal Suite because of Farmer George," she said. "I think Henry VIII was the first to use it and most of the others have at one time or another. It was refurbished for David's christening, but keeping the sixteenth century style."

The Royal Suite, in one of the oldest parts of the Castle, was magnificent. The walls were hung with blue silk damask embroidered with gold crowns. The same design was used in the fringed hangings over a huge bed and in the covers of the heavy oak chairs and benches. There was a dressing room with a curtained bathtub, and two anterooms where attendants could wait and sleep. There was also the King's Gallery, a long narrow saloon with a massive fireplace and tall windows giving a view of the lawns.

"Who on earth gets to sleep in here?" asked Beth. "Or is the regent invited?"

"Well, he is, actually. One has to, you know. But he is unable to attend, thank goodness. He doesn't much like coming north. Brummell is coming, though," she said with a grin. "Perhaps he would like all this, especially as no one but a monarch is supposed to sleep in the great bed." She went to flop on it. "I can't say it's very comfortable. This mattress feels like the original."

It soon became clear to Beth that Sophie was unwilling or unable to put her mind to organised employment and was much more of a hindrance than a help. With a flash of inspiration, she sent the girl off to discover the condition of the invalid and see to her comfort. Sophie happily agreed, obviously finding something appealing in the mystery. With a sigh of relief, Beth went off to find some member of the staff to guide her.

Easier said than done. When another staircase she had thought familiar brought her to another strange passageway, she stopped and uttered a very unladylike, "Oh drat!"

She heard a chuckle behind her. "My dear lady," said Sir Marius. "Could it be that you are lost?"

Why on earth did she have to blush? she wondered as she turned. "That is correct, Sir Marius. May I hope that you will guide me?"

He strolled forwards. Casual country buckskins suited him, she realised, and in this solid, old building, his scale seemed somehow right. He would have done very well as a knight in armour.

"Could I refuse a damsel in distress?" he asked. "Where is it that you wish to go?"

"I don't know . . ." she said accurately, then realised that it sounded very silly.

"In that case," he said with a grin. "I suggest we sit and consider the problem."

"I merely meant that I don't know the names of all the rooms, Sir Marius," she informed him. "Everything here has a special name—the Large and Small Crimson Chambers, the Knight's Hall, the Great Hall, the Nun's Walk . . ."

"You want to go to the Nun's Walk, Mrs. Hawley? I wouldn't have supposed you to have a taste for the macabre."

"Of course I don't," she snapped, wondering why conversations with this giant always seemed to spin out of control.

He came over to her, took her hand, and gently led her to the window seat. To her surprise, she went. He sat down beside her. "Now, let us talk calmly and find out what it is you have in mind."

"I am perfectly calm, Sir Marius," she said with some heat, snatching her hand out of his.

His lips twitched. "Just like when you challenged Verderan to a duel?"

Beth knew she was bright pink. "I do not care to be reminded . . . And I did not," she said, meeting his eyes. They were, she discovered to her surprise, rather fine. "I threatened to shoot him in cold blood."

"And called him a stupid boy."

"Which he is."

"No," he said seriously and took her hand again. "A word of advice, Mrs. Hawley. He is unpredictable. Last night, for some reason he took your words well. Don't presume on that. He is a very dangerous man and I would not like to see you hurt."

"Even the infamous Dark Angel wouldn't assault a lady," she protested.

He shook his head. "There is nothing he would not do if it pleased him at the time, and when his temper is roused he is likely to do things that don't please him at all. In actual fact I like the man, but I tread very warily near him and I would suggest you do the same. If you cannot avoid him entirely."

Beth became aware of her hand in his large warm one and withdrew it. "I would be delighted never to meet him again," she said firmly.

"Well," he said with a lazy smile, "I hardly thought you were setting your cap at him. He's too young for you for one thing."

"Setting my cap!" said Beth leaping to her feet and moving away. "Really, Sir Marius."

"Are you going?" he queried, rising lazily to his feet. "I thought you wanted a guide."

"Since you are not in the mood to be serious," she retorted, "I will fadge for myself. I can hardly get lost beyond recall."

After a few steps, his voice stopped her. "No, but if you go that way you'll end up out in the garden by the sundial and it's a devil of a walk from there back to the front entrance."

She turned to look at him with narrowed eyes. "Which way should I go, then?" she asked.

"We come back to the question, Mrs. Hawley. Where do you want to be?"

"The front hall will do nicely, thank you, Sir Marius."

He lazily pointed to a door. "Through the Tapestry Chamber, turn right. Take the second stairs and I don't think you can miss it. If you don't appear for luncheon, I'll organise a search party."

Beth flounced off and was hard put not to slam the door. Really, what was it about that man? She couldn't be five minutes in his company without degenerating to behaviour more fitted for a schoolroom, and a poorly governed one at that, than a lady's chamber.

She must have still been scowling when she descended the wide staircase to the main entrance hall, and met Jane crossing it.

"Why, whatever has happened, Beth? Is it Sophie?"

"Sophie?" echoed Beth. "No, of course not. I've sent her off to attend to the invalid. It's Sir Marius."

"What has he done?" asked Jane.

"Oh, nothing," said Beth, wishing she'd not mentioned it. "He seems disposed to tease me."

"He's very kind really," said Jane, surprised. "I can't think he means to overset you."

"Oh, really," snapped Beth but then hurried on. "What I need, Jane, if I am to be of any use, is some member of the staff to guide me and run errands."

Jane soon arranged for a maid and footman to accompany Beth and saw them off on their labours. Then she stood in thought for a moment with a little smile on her lips. Beth and Marius? Well, why not?

Sophie knocked softly on the door of the modest bedchamber given to the injured lady, then entered. A maid had been set to sit with the woman and do mending. She rose and dropped a curtsey.

"Has she recovered consciousness?" Sophie asked.

"Yes, milady. She understands what we say to her, but she's not said anything to the purpose. The doctor dropped by this morning and says she's well enough. Just needs a good rest."

"You may go and do something else for half an hour," Sophie said and went to look at the patient.

Not so very old, she thought. Not like Randal's grandmother at nearly eighty. More like her own mother, aged and worn down by grief. Had no one taken care of her? At least the Dowager Lady Wraybourne ate reasonably, took exercise, and pursued mild interests. This woman looked half starved and had the pallor of living indoors. Heavens, what if she'd been in a prison or an insane asylum?

The parchment-like eyes fluttered and the woman looked around with hazy confusion.

"Don't worry," Sophie said quickly. "You are safe at Stenby Castle. Would you like a drink? There is some barley water here for you."

The woman nodded and so Sophie raised her, noticing how frail she was, and set the glass to her lips. The invalid drank and then settled back.

"If you could tell me who you are," said Sophie gently, "we could summon your family. They must be concerned."

The eyelids drooped and Sophie thought she had lapsed into unconsciousness but she spoke in a dry, raspy voice. "Who I am?"

"Yes. There is nothing in your possessions to say who you are, you see."

The eyes remained shut but Sophie knew the woman was conscious. "I don't know," the woman said at last.

"You don't know what?"

"Who I am. Where did you say I am?"

Sophie looked down with a frown. This must be the result of the blow on the head. She supposed they would have to advertise. "Found, on the road in Shropshire, one middle-aged lady in frail condition . . ."

"You are at Stenby Castle, seat of the Earl of Wraybourne. You were on your way here when you had a carriage accident and suffered a blow to your head. If you rest, I am sure you will soon recall why you were coming here."

The eyes opened again. They were a pale blue-grey, a faded, weary colour. "And who are you, young lady?"

"I am Sophie Kyle."

Something flashed in those eyes.

"Does that name mean something?" Sophie asked quickly. "You were carrying an announcement of my forthcoming marriage in your reticule."

The woman's face was blank again. "For a moment . . ." she said faintly. "But I don't think we have ever met."

"Nor do I, ma'am. Perhaps you had better sleep and it will all come back to you."

"I am not sleepy," said the woman. "Weary, yes. But I have been weary a long time I think. If you were to talk to me, Lady Sophie, I think it might help."

Sophie sat in the chair. "If you wish. Of what shall we speak?"

"Why not of your marriage? It is to be soon?"

"Two weeks," said Sophie, all her doubts about Randal returning in an instant. Two weeks was both too far away and far too soon.

"You do not seem happy," said the woman.

"I am extremely happy," said Sophie, knowing her voice was unconvincing.

"And who are you to marry?"

"Lord Randal Ashby. He is the second son of the Duke of Tyne."

"A good and suitable match, then."

Sophie thought of her brother's doubts as to the wisdom of matching two such volatile people and smiled slightly. "Not necessarily. He's a bit of a rake, you see."

The woman's eyes were no longer vague. She fixed Sophie with a stare. "You deserve better than that, my dear."

Sophie was a little embarrassed by what she had said. It was like talking to oneself, this conversation. She glanced at the woman and caught a look of such intensity that she drew back. "Oh, Randal is a reformed rake," she said lightly and rose to her feet. "I don't fear he'll be off wenching and gambling."

"What then do you fear?" asked the woman softly in a tone that sent shivers down Sophie's back. Or perhaps it was just the question.

"Nothing," said Sophie firmly, looking away at an anonymous portrait which graced the wall above the small fireplace. "Nothing at all. We will be happy as no others have been since time began." Once those words could have been spoken honestly but Sophie could hear the brittle uncertainty behind them now. She glanced back at the invalid. How was this woman drawing truth from the recesses of her mind? "I am afraid I have duties elsewhere, ma'am. Please excuse me. I will send the maid back to attend on you."

"There is no need. I am not so sick as that and I have a bellpull here by the bed. But come to visit me again, my dear, if you would be so kind. You seem almost like my daughter . . ."

"You remember your family?" asked Sophie quickly.

"No," said the woman faintly. "You just make me think I might have had a daughter like you. And do not worry, my dear. Soon all your worries about your wedding will be a thing of the past."

Sophie hurried from the room. Why had the poor sick lady made her feel so uncomfortable, so suspicious? She stopped abruptly as she clearly remembered the woman saying, "If you were to talk to me, *Lady Sophie*." She had not introduced herself thus, so how had the woman known her title?

After a moment she gave a little laugh. The maid undoubtedly told the old lady when she first awoke the names of those in the Castle. Sophie feared her mind was becoming unhinged if she was to see such a thing as suspicious. Everything the woman had said had been proper; it was just that Sophie did not like the thoughts she had stirred.

She stopped not far down the corridor to look at her flashing diamond ring. Everyone said that soon all her troubles would be over. She would be married to Randal, they would be deliriously happy. . . .

She could just believe in that and leave it to fate. But what if he had regrets? She could bear it if that were ever so.

= 5 =

AT LUNCHEON JANE asked, "How did you find our patient, Sophie?"

"She has recovered consciousness, but not her memory. I would swear though that something about my name caught her. I suppose she must be a distant relative. Do we have any black sheep?" she asked of her brother as she flipped through the letters lying by her plate. The post bag had just been opened and there were four letters for her.

"Apart from you?" he teased.

Sophie scowled. "Under Randal's influence I am positively bleached, brother. I should have married Trenholme."

"Well, that's what I said all along," her brother reminded her, and she laughed. One of the letters had no frank, and so no indication of the sender. Curious, she picked that one up first.

"I think I'll ride over to the Towers this afternoon," said Sophie as she broke the seal. She watched her brother to see if he would object.

"If you wish," he said calmly. "But go in the carriage and take Mrs. Hawley. I'm sure she'd like to see it."

Sophie smiled at Mrs. Hawley. She had no trouble with that plan for she liked Jane's old governess. She spread open the letter and gave a little cry. "How positively horrid!"

Her brother took up the paper and read it. " 'Be brave, Sophie, and shed no tears. Your marriage will never come to pass.' Where the devil did this come from?" He looked again at the sheet but there was no indication.

"What does it mean?" Sophie asked, pale faced. She turned to Jane. "It reminds me of that nasty note you got from Crossley Carruthers, but this is worse."

The earl put the letter in his pocket. "It's just as meaningless," he said firmly. "Some malicious prankster. But from now on, Sophie, I will open your correspondence. There's no need for you to be bothered by stuff like this."

Sophie told herself it was true, that the letter was a very unpleasant joke, but she couldn't quite put it out of her mind. What did it mean, "Your marriage will never come to pass." Did someone suspect her doubts and fears? She was extremely glad to soon be setting off to the Towers and Randal, where the unpleasantness of that letter would be washed away.

As they settled in the open landaulet, parasols tilted against the warm sun, Beth said, "You must not allow that silly note to distress you, Lady Sophie." She wanted to wipe the shadow from Lady Sophie's lovely blue eyes.

"But what if it means something?" Sophie asked.

"What could it possibly mean?" Beth went on quickly to ask, "Is Lord Randal expecting you today?"

It worked. Thought of Randal wiped away other matters. "He'll expect me to come," Sophie said with a secret smile. "Tomorrow there's a picnic planned near the old abbey. On Thursday a visit to the fair at Wem." She looked at Beth with humour, but it had a bitter edge.

"He is perhaps trying to make these last days pass, Lady Sophie," said Beth gently. "Anyone can wait two weeks for anything."

She saw a flicker of exasperation pass over the girl's lovely face and revised her opinions. At Carne Abbey, Jane's old home, Beth had realised Lady Sophie was not the silly ingénue she occasionally appeared. She was, in fact, deceptively deep and it would be as well to remember it.

Beth looked down and traced the design on her lustring gown as she said, "We are not well acquainted, my lady, but sometimes a stranger is a better listener than family. If you have concerns I would be honoured to try and help you."

She looked up and Sophie's eyes met hers directly and honestly. "Thank you. I may . . . But you must stop 'my ladying' me, then, you know. I refuse to discuss my love life otherwise."

"Well then, Sophie," said Beth quietly, so as not to be overheard by the coachman, "what has you so out of tune? I could not help but see that you were out of sorts before that letter."

"Megrims, follies," mused the younger woman. "Everyone could be right and it is just the waiting. . . ."

Beth decided she would have to probe. "Is it perhaps that you find you do not love Lord Randal as much as you thought?"

Sophie smiled. "Good heavens, no. How could anyone *not* love him?"

The blindness of love, thought Beth. No one would deny Lord Randal's spectacular beauty, but many had managed to resist infatuation.

Sophie spoke again, "But do you think he truly loves me?"

Was this the problem? wondered Beth. "I really don't know, Sophie, but there is every indication that he adores you. Why would you doubt it?"

"I think it's so unfair," said Sophie sharply, "that a gentleman cannot withdraw from an engagement to marry. What choice has he? How am I to know?"

Beth felt greatly relieved. This *was* a silly megrim and very similar to one Jane had suffered from. "He is old enough to know his mind," she said firmly. "If he asked for your hand, you may be sure he wanted it."

It hadn't quite worked with Jane either, Beth remembered now. Sophie's smile was only courteous as she said, "Of course you are quite correct." For the rest of the journey she kept up relentlessly superficial social chat and Beth knew she had failed badly. It really shouldn't matter. It was just a case of getting through the days. Yet she wished she had done better.

Tyne Towers sat square and glistening in the sun, its many windows and ornate little towers and chimneys typical of the reign of Queen Anne. The carriage wound through carefully laid-out gardens set with pools which could sprout fountains from the statues in the middle when someone took the trouble to arrange it.

By the time they entered the cool marble hall, Lord Randal

was there to greet them. Beth wished Mr. Verderan was not by his side, though. Reflection had made her more ashamed than ever of her outburst at dinner.

Randal had known Sophie would come, Beth decided. Had known and depended on it. He did and said nothing in particular and yet it was as if happiness danced with the dust motes in the sunbeams. How could Sophie doubt she was loved?

"Mrs. Young's turning out the old china because of all the guests we're expecting," he said lightly, taking his betrothed's hand. Beth suspected he could no more help touching her than he could stop breathing. "You'll never believe how ugly some of it is, Sophie. We should practice pottery-breaking again. Come and see."

Beth thought of hanging back, of going in another direction even if it meant enduring the company of the Dark Angel. As if he divined her thought, however, Randal glanced back and she knew that without her the expedition would be cancelled. There was more than one stupid boy around, she thought testily.

"I know, I know," murmured Mr. Verderan by her side as they followed the betrothed couple. "I, too, would like to knock his head against the wall if it would do the slightest good."

She looked up at him and decided he seemed to be in a straight-thinking mood. "Have you spoken to him?"

"And what am I supposed to say to him, Mrs. Hawley?" he asked dryly. "Your bride needs to be at least half seduced or . . . or what? Is Lady Sophie Kyle going to jilt him? No. Is she going to run off with a groom from the stables? No. Is she going to drown herself in the river? Hardly. She will just be unhappy for a week or so, and I don't care to risk one of my few friendships over that."

At the tone of his voice Beth looked at him curiously. "Do you not like her?"

He raised a brow. "You cannot expect me to answer such a question."

"You don't," said Beth, surprised beyond manners. "She is high-spirited but has a warm heart, a keen mind, and courage. What terrible fault do you find?"

Verderan just looked at her and refused to answer.

Beth gave up her pointless attempt to change his opinion. It hardly mattered anyway. "You are quite right, though," she said with a sigh. "Nothing terrible is going to happen. I don't know why I feel so uneasy about it. . . ." She swallowed and decided to get a distasteful duty over with. "I must apologise as well for my behaviour last night, Mr. Verderan. More nervous fidgets, I'm afraid. My excuse must be that this is not the life or company I'm accustomed to."

He looked at her with faint surprise. "I will claim then that my rudeness was just to make you feel more comfortable, Mrs. Hawley, knowing you had got as good as you had given."

It was doubtless as close to an apology as she could hope to get from this man. Beth looked up to meet a spectacularly charming smile and instinctively responded. Goodness, one could come to like him, and that would probably be most unwise.

Then she took herself to task. This habit she was developing of imagining that gentlemen were out to seduce her was doubtless proof of approaching senility. She was long in the tooth and nothing out of the ordinary, and they probably all thought of her as a comfortable maiden aunt.

Whatever his motives, Verderan set himself out to please, proving true Jane's words that he did have beautiful manners when he cared to use them. He drew Beth out to talk of her life at Carne as Jane's governess and her time since in London at her brother's house. He spiced the dialogue with interesting anecdotes from his less disreputable adventures. She knew herself to be blossoming, conversing with animation and frequently genuinely amused.

She could not be unaware, however, that ahead of them Sophie and Randal were quietly arguing.

Sophie was growing too desperate, too pushed for time for subtle approaches, and that note had somehow increased her sense of urgency. "Randal, I need to spend time alone with you," she said. She saw the refusal on his face and continued, "If you fear you will be overcome with lust, I promise to scream when you start ripping my clothes off."

"Sophie, behave yourself," said Randal, colour touching his cheeks and making him even more beautiful.

Sophie's teeth gritted painfully. "If you say that to me once more . . ."

He gave a little laugh and tweaked an auburn curl. "I apologise. But really, Sophie, I can't see why you've got this maggot in your head. In little over a week we can be as alone as we please, for as long as we please. It seems worth waiting to me."

The picture he had conjured up sent fire through her veins but she brought her feelings ruthlessly under control. "What on earth do you think I'm demanding?" she asked. "Look, we could walk into the picture gallery and leave Verderan to show Mrs. Hawley the china. That gallery has windows all down one side and is lined with your watchful and forbidding ancestors. It would be perfectly proper and," she said as enticingly as she knew how, "we could be together, just you and I, Randal."

They had come to a stop between the door to the gallery and the one to the Etruria Room where the ducal china was displayed. He wound his fingers through hers. It was something, she supposed, draining every drop she could from the feel of his skin. She could almost imagine their blood crossing that thin barrier, weaving them together, heart and soul. It wasn't enough. It just created a greater hunger.

"And you would slip into my arms," he said softly as his thumb gently rubbed the back of her hand. "And you would want to be kissed. And I would kiss you . . ." His hand tightened painfully on hers as his voice took on an edge. "And I don't think my grandfather's haughty disapproval would matter a damn."

That was hunger she saw in his eyes. She locked her fingers in his and made to pull him in the direction of the gallery, but he was stronger and the door to the Etruria Room was closer.

Beth and Mr. Verderan had tactfully dawdled while the lovers talked. Beth, at least, had hoped that something to the purpose was being said. When they entered the Etruria Room, however, Randal was opening a cupboard to display a singularly horrendous blue Chinese elephant which was used to cool wine. Sophie had a bitter line to her pretty lips and the moistness of tears in her eyes.

After viewing the china, they strolled in the gardens and then went to the cool blue Adams Room for tea. They were joined there by the marquess, by Lord and Lady Stanforth, and by the Stanforth offspring and his nurse. With a blissful smile, the child toddled straight to Verderan with an offer of a carved horse.

"No thank you, brat," said the man coolly. "I have better of my own."

"Horsy," Stevie informed him seriously.

"Only in the most general sense." Stevie thrust the wooden toy at him insistently and Verderan sighed. "If you look behind you, young man, you will see a valuable crystal bowl full of fruit. Why don't you throw it to the floor and stamp the subsequent mess into the Aubusson carpet."

Chloe Stanforth came dashing over. "Mr. Verderan!" she exclaimed, picking up the squirming boy. "I will thank you not to corrupt my child!"

As she turned away, Stevie set up a screech of deprivation.

"Seems to me he's hell-bent on perdition," murmured Verderan quite audibly.

The child's father was clearly hard put not to give in to amusement but he said, "Ver," in a warning tone. The Dark Angel looked over, laughed and raised a hand in a gesture of surrender. He removed himself to the far side of the room.

Beth herself knew her lips were twitching. The child had been pacified by his father's watch, but his eyes kept travelling across the room to the tall, dark man like one besotted. They said something about children and animals being fine judges of character, but she had to think this infant was sadly misguided.

Beth had to give up her study of the cherub and the angel when the place beside her was taken by the Marquess of Chelmly. She found herself slightly nervous. He might be an ordinary kind of man but he was still the heir to a dukedom, and Beth was not accustomed to this kind of company.

He proved, however, to be very unalarming, talking pleasantly enough of ordinary affairs and drawing her out to talk of herself a little. It was the same polite behaviour as Mr. Verderan had shown but from him it had seemed natural and had become enjoyable. Here the effort was showing.

She found herself wondering how the marquess felt about his

high estate. Would he perhaps have been happier as a simple country squire? How silly it was to expect these highborn aristocrats to be any different at heart from anyone else. The Marquess of Chelmly was obviously a little shy.

"You must love your home here," she said at one point and was rewarded by a genuine smile.

"I do indeed. My father is after me all the time to go to London and find a bride, but I hate that kind of Society life. When I marry I want a bride who will be happy here in the country."

"I think a great many debutantes only visit London in search of a husband, my lord. Some, I'm sure, would be happy never to go there again. I confess, after so many years in the country at Carne Abbey, I find the city rather noisy and dirty."

"And crowded," he agreed. "It's scarcely worth taking a riding horse there."

"Do you stay here all year round?" she asked. "You must have other estates."

He laughed. "Far too many, Mrs. Hawley. Plus the fact that Randal wheedles me into overseeing Fairmeadows and Conifer Hall for him. He has no taste for estate management."

She had become comfortable with him. "I don't think you would let yourself be wheedled if it didn't suit you, my lord," she said.

He smiled ruefully. "In a sense you're right, ma'am. I can't stand to see a place being neglected and I fear that's what would happen if I didn't take a hand. Randal is a butterfly and never holds to a task once it has lost its novelty. But he can charm anyone, you know, so I would doubtless do it even if I was unwilling." He looked over at his brother with indulgent affection. "He has the Ashby charm."

"The Ashby charm?" queried Beth.

"Don't you know of it? The bearer attracts people, willy-nilly." They both looked over at Randal, who was seated on the carpet, easily distracting Stevie from Verderan.

"I don't understand it," said the marquess, "but I think it has something to do with attention. If we feel someone is really interested in us, it pleases us. It is completely unconscious, though, and largely out of Randal's control. He finds it a bother and I certainly consider myself well suited to have been spared the gift."

He rose to his feet. "It has been a pleasure to speak with you, Mrs. Hawley. If I may be permitted to say so, you have a gift yourself. You make a person feel comfortable. Now, though, you must excuse me. I have an appointment to discuss some boring agricultural matters."

Despite those words, as he left Beth could see a spring in his step. Time away from the estates was time wasted to the marquess. She pondered his flattering words. Another high-ranking swain? Goodness, but her head would soon be turned. The heir to a dukedom, even. She'd never have thought him so adept at flattery. It was doubtless again just a piece of polite behaviour drilled into them.

She imagined a dry and stern-faced tutor, birch in hand. "Remember, gentlemen. Always leave a lady with a compliment. Always."

She disciplined her mind to the task in hand. It was Randal and Sophie who were her main concern and watching them together, her concern grew rather than diminished. Sophie watched Randal constantly and Randal ignored Sophie—except for the occasional stolen glance that showed something deep and almost dangerous. It was passion of some kind and it was under iron control.

A butterfly? Beth doubted that.

Was it just propriety? Beth could not believe that Lord Randal Ashby was holding himself so aloof from his bride-to-be, far more aloof than Society would demand, because of propriety. And was Sophie disturbed simply by lack of kisses? She thought the girl beyond that kind of petty impatience and the earlier conversation suggested deeper motives.

Had that malicious note had any meaning? Who would send such a thing and what could anyone possibly do to prevent a marriage only two weeks hence?

Beth suddenly became convinced, however, that it was essential that Randal and Sophie reach a firmer understanding.

When she found herself alone with Lord Randal she made herself remember that. He had been escorting Beth and Sophie to their carriage when Sophie had recollected a request to be made of the Towers' housekeeper and sped off, leaving them alone together.

Beth had never been *tête-à-tête* with the handsome young man before and she looked for the magical Ashby charm. She didn't detect it. He was extremely good-looking and very graceful in his manners, but that was all. She steeled herself to speak to him on Sophie's behalf but he had swung effortlessly into smooth social conversation. Beth soon decided to have done with it.

"Do you know," she said when she had the chance, "I really do appreciate good manners but I am growing a little tired of relating my boring life to bored gentlemen."

He grinned with understanding. "Social conversation. I know. Hate it myself. But . . ."

"But it's difficult to know what to say to a stranger of another station in life entirely."

"Something like that," he said easily. They had arrived at the side entrance where the carriage waited. He perched boyishly on a wall there, letting the slight breeze stir his curls. "It's not snobbishness, you know, though sometimes people think it is. It's just the difficulty of being different."

"Me or you?" she asked, becoming alarmingly aware of something which could be that fatal charm. Her senses told her that he was enjoying a rare and welcome moment of intimate conversation with a soul mate, while her head struggled to remind her that he was just politely passing time with a social inferior.

"Both, of course," he said. "I can talk naturally with my friends and you with yours. Together, however, we have nothing to say that has meaning unless we become uncouthly intimate, like this." The words could have been offensive but a smile robbed them of sting. "I'm sure it was even worse talking with Chelmly. He hides behind formality. He's been taught from birth to expect people to encroach on him and as a result he fears strangers."

"You don't fear people taking liberties with you, Lord Randal?"

"I can handle it. People say that I have charm and Chelmly doesn't. The truth is, though, that I'm not afraid to be approachable because I'm ruthless enough to deal with the consequences. Chelmly isn't."

Beth took a fortifying breath. "Then I suggest you use your gifts on Sophie," she said calmly.

He stiffened and then turned on her a look full of generations of cold arrogance. "Now that, Mrs. Hawley, *is* presumption."

Beth stood up to him. "I know it, and even worse, it is an attempt to stand your friend, Lord Randal. Whatever is wrong with Sophie, however, is far deeper than a need for lover's kisses. She needs you and you ignore that at your peril." Even as she said the words, they seemed melodramatic to her and yet she would not take them back.

He frowned in puzzlement. "What do you fear?"

Beth shook her head. "I don't know, my lord." Making a quick decision, she told him of the note Sophie had received.

"Damnation," he muttered, then apologised. "It's nonsense, of course, but . . ."

"But," interrupted Beth firmly, "every instinct I have tells me things would be a great deal simpler if you would surrender whatever vow of propriety you have made, my lord."

Sophie appeared at the far end of the hall and Lord Randal jumped down from his perch. "You are the most extraordinary chaperone I have ever come across," he said with a cool courtesy which built a wall between them. "I'm sure that note was upsetting. I'll have a word with David about it. But you are too concerned, Mrs. Hawley. You're quite correct, though, in one thing. I have made promises to myself that seem worth keeping and I will do so."

He led Sophie over to the carriage and said farewell with a kiss on the cheek. As he courteously shook Beth's hand, she knew she had as much chance of being alone again in conversation with him as Sophie did of a moonlight tryst. He could indeed handle presumption.

Randal wandered back in search of Verderan, feeling guilty about freezing out the little governess, and yet irritated at the same time. All his life people had been preaching propriety at him and now, when he had embraced it, the most unlikely people were luring him towards wickedness.

He thoughtfully pulled out a letter he too had received that day. "You will have no chance to besmirch an innocent. Your reprobate ways and worthless idleness are known. Sophie Kyle is not for you and you will die before you ever wed her." He easily shrugged off the threat, but some of the words wove in with doubts he felt, doubts about his ability to be a good and steady husband. At the thought of Sophie receiving drivel from the same source, however, he just felt burning rage.

He found Ver in the billiard room and they started a game but it soon palled. He put his cue down restlessly. "There's supposed to be hawks in the woods over near Stillbeck. What do you say we take some guns over there?"

Verderan looked closely at him. "Of course," he said. "Killing things is very soothing to the nerves."

"And what the devil's that supposed to mean?"

Verderan laughed. "Man sublimates the urge to mate in killing. Or is it vice versa? There's nothing like frustration to bring out destructiveness. Why go in search of hawks? You could always pick a quarrel with me."

Randal laughed and didn't tell his friend the reason for his restlessness; there was enough truth in Verderan's words anyway. "We made a schoolboy pact never to call each other out . . ."

"Being the best shots around," supplied Verderan. "I have no objection to bloodying your nose."

"Do you think you could?" asked Randal, the light of challenge in his eye.

"I'm more ruthless than you. I didn't say I'd fight by any rules."

Randal weighed it and then shook his head. "I've no mind to go to my wedding with a black eye."

"The hawk's fate is sealed, then," said Verderan.

They changed into buckskins and boots and collected guns. Then they set off across the park.

On the crest of a rise Randal stopped and loosened his cravat. He felt a strange uneasiness, as if he were being watched. Was he letting that silly note affect him? It must just be the heat. He looked at the cloudless sky. "Damn, but I didn't realise how hot it was. Do you want to go back?"

Verderan looked ahead towards the stand of trees. "It will be cooler among the trees. Let's go on."

The weather was fine and dry. Randal smiled to himself when he thought how everyone had started to complain of the heat. Never satisfied. Even the animals, though, had decided it was all a bit much. In the next field cows huddled in the shade chewing the cud and there were few birds around. Flowers rioted in the bright light however, buttercups and cowslips, red poppies and purple foxgloves.

He felt an unaccustomed pang of fondness for the very land, an appreciation of its bounty. A sense of pride, perhaps. It was not in himself, for he had nothing to do with this except the luck to be here. That note had been correct in one thing—worthless idleness had marked his life thus far.

From the rise he looked around at the neat patchwork of fields put to crops both golden and green, saw the fat cattle and tubby sheep and the village down near the river, sound, solid, and prosperous. He gave thanks for Chelmly and the others of his sort who worked so hard to make it all so good.

A rabbit bobbed up and raced across the field. Randal lazily raised his gun to take a shot at it, but it was soon gone and he wasn't displeased. Despite Verderan's words, he was enjoying the simple pleasures of life too much to want to kill. Looking back to where the rabbit had leapt from the ground he thought he glimpsed a larger shape and his nerves tightened again. He shook his head. Doubtless a fox and he certainly couldn't shoot a fox.

He wished Sophie was here at such a perfect moment. He'd like to laze back in the shade with her in his arms and enjoy the countryside, share with her his sense of blessedness. But they must wait. He was far too uncertain of his control for such an interlude.

Recollecting himself he glanced at Verderan, but his friend was standing idle, allowing him silence and time with his thoughts. Randal was grateful but he moved on. They should get out of the blazing heat.

Since his betrothal he found himself wishing he was different, someone more like Chelmly—a solid post around which to build a marriage and a family. Despite the fact that they were friends, David had doubts about the wisdom of the marriage. Because they were friends David knew him well and probably had

58

excellent reasons for his concern. Sophie was a darling but she was high-spirited and mischievous—not that he'd have her any other way. Randal was doing his best to be sober and responsible, to assure David that he could keep his sister safe, but it was hard and that was perhaps the most dismaying fact of all. With Sophie nearby the last thing he wanted to be was sober and responsible.

He'd become aware years ago of the first warnings that Sophie was more to him than an adopted sister and he'd ruthlessly suppressed those feelings. He was not the stuff of which good husbands are made and Sophie deserved only the best. He'd been prepared to watch his little flame make her debut and choose a husband, standing guard merely to make sure the man was worthy. He'd never for a moment intended claiming her for himself, even when she'd shown signs of having a silly infatuation for him. He'd cursed himself for the carelessness of that though. He should have know better and kept his distance.

Seeing her in danger from that swine Hever, however, had splintered something in his mind and changed everything. From that moment he had known he could not bear to trust her to anyone else, that he had to cherish and protect her himself. He had not consciously compromised them in her bedroom; he had merely been doing his best to take care of her. As soon as David had walked in, however, he had recognised the situation and taken gladly what fate had given him. Had he been unfair? He would do anything to make her happy. He would become the sort of man she deserved.

As Verderan had predicted, the Stillbeck Woods were a little cooler. In the torpid heat there was no sign of the reported hawks, but the two men wandered over the leaf-molded floor, enjoying the temperature.

Verderan stopped.

"What's the matter?" Randal asked.

The darker man shrugged uneasily. "A prickling between my shoulder blades. Is this wood haunted?"

Randal looked around more alertly. If Ver felt it too, perhaps it wasn't just his imagination, this feeling of being watched. "Not to my knowledge," he said. "It's very quiet, but that's doubtless because of the heat and the fact we've invaded." His nerves settled. The woods were totally still. No other creature was so foolish as to be out on such a day. "There's a stream over here," he said. "I could do with a drink."

They found the fast-flowing water, laid their guns against a log, and made their way down the shallow bank. Both men used their hands as cups and drank.

Randal perched on the raised root of a tree and rubbed his damp hands around his neck. "I'm all in favour of fair weather but this is excessive. Might as well be in Italy. I hope it breaks before the wedding."

Verderan leaned against the trunk of an ash tree. "What are your plans for after you're wed?" he asked lazily.

"Apart from the obvious, my imagination doesn't stretch that far," said Randal dryly. Verderan laughed.

"Will you live on your estates?" Verderan asked. "You've made the Towers and the London house your base up till now."

"Fairmeadows will be our home," said Randal, idly throwing buttercups to float on the stream. "I'll even have to settle down and manage the place."

"How very dull," drawled Verderan.

Randal looked at him. "You manage Maiden Hall."

"I enjoy being a tyrant and cracking the whip over my wretched serfs."

Randal laughed. He knew that Verderan's people did rather well out of him and only worried that one day his luck would fail and he'd lose everything on the roll of a dice.

"What of your military ambitions?" Verderan asked.

"Hopeless unless Chelmly marries. My father takes a fit, literally, whenever the matter is mentioned. It could be the death of him and I daren't risk that. I suppose if I have a string of boys . . . But I doubt I'd want to go off to the wars by then." Having rid his immediate area of blossoms, he pulled up some grass and cast that upon the stream. "I wouldn't want to drag Sophie after the drum, anyway. She thinks of it as a great adventure, but she doesn't realise what it would really be like."

Randal looked sharply behind Verderan and the other man turned.

"What?"

"I thought I saw something move. There's no deer hereabouts, though."

Verderan looked closely at him. "Your nerves are shot to Hades, my friend, and my healthy instinct for dangers is clamouring like a fire bell. Would you mind telling me what is going on?"

After a moment Randal pulled out the letter and passed it over. "It's utter nonsense," he said.

Verderan read it. "Can you be sure? Who wishes you ill?"

Randal laughed but looked around carefully. "No one."

"It could come from a disappointed suitor of Sophie's," suggested Verderan.

"They are legion, but none so demented as this."

"Seriously, Randal. Have you caused anyone to hate you? Have you injured anyone?"

Randal shook his head, but he remembered Edwin Hever. He'd killed him, though, and it had all been covered up, made to look like a suicide, as much for the man's family as for Randal's sake. He'd been a villain, but once he was dead there had been no point in dragging his name through the dirt.

Verderan shrugged and returned the letter. "Despite your obvious lily-white innocence, Randal, I feel a pressing need to leave this place and have strong stone walls around me. Come."

Their sense of danger was alert and they watched the wood carefully as they picked up their guns and retraced their steps. Nothing moved. It was silent. Too silent.

They both breathed easier when they left the woods and were in the open again, though they were not particularly safer if there was any danger. All the way back to the Towers Randal felt as if he had a bull's-eye pinned to his back and forced himself to ignore the feeling.

If he ever discovered the author of that damned note, he'd kill him.

= 6 =

THE NEXT DAY, the day of the latest picnic arranged by Lord Randal, proved an embarrassment to Beth.

Everyone from Stenby was riding to the old abbey which was the chosen site, but Beth had to admit that she could not ride. She nervously refused to even consider the gentlest slug in the stables while awkwardly aware that she was being difficult.

No one would accept her suggestion that she stay home and so it would seem that the carriage would have to be brought out just for her.

"Well," said Sir Marius. "Why don't I drive you in my rig, Mrs. Hawley? If I know anything this is going to be an ambling kind of ride, and in that case I'd rather drive, and I'd appreciate the chance to test it after the repairs."

She accepted gratefully. It was only later that she wondered if she wanted to be by his side for a whole half hour. When she climbed into his curricle, she wondered if she wanted to be behind his horses. The muscular matched chestnuts had obviously recovered well from the journey north and they champed at their bits and shifted their weight from hoof to hoof as if longing to be off at a gallop. The ground seemed a long way down and Beth clutched at the rail by her hand.

"Nervous, Mrs. Hawley?" drawled the Corinthian as he gave the horses the order to go. "I won't overturn us."

"I'm sure you won't, Sir Marius," lied Beth gallantly. "I am just unaccustomed to an open carriage other than a simple gig."

"I'm delighted to be able to enlarge your experience, dear lady.

I'm sure we can find other new experiences for you during your stay at Stenby."

For some reason Beth found nothing to say to that but was conscious of a strange flutter of excitement at the prospect. "Do you know where the picnic is to be held, Sir Marius?" she asked quickly.

"If not, how could I take us there, Mrs. Hawley?"

Why, thought Beth, do I always end up saying something goosish to this man? "I mean, do you know anything *about* it. Sophie referred to it as the old abbey."

"So it is," he said. "There's not much to it, though. Not like Fountains, for example, or some of the other great ruins. Just some low walls covered by ivy. Very appealing though to the modern taste for the picturesque. And the Gothic."

There was something in his tone which started the flutter again. "But I thought you had no taste for the Gothic, Sir Marius," said Beth.

"Oh, I've decided it grows on one remarkably. In fact," he said casually, "I am thinking of making a change in my home along Gothic lines."

"Really? Pointed windows and battlements?" she asked.

He rumbled a deep chuckle. "Not precisely. Something more internal."

"Carved woodwork with points and spires," said Beth sagely. "But I do feel, Sir Marius, that if one already owns a house of character and charm, it is a shame to alter it merely in pursuit of fashion."

"How true. One day I hope you will tell me if my house has character and charm, dear lady." Before Beth could make any objection to this he carried on, "I hope not to have to make substantial changes, however. It is more an addition I contemplate—in the drawing room, and in particular in the master bedroom."

Beth imagined a huge new bed with cathedral-like carving on headboard and tester. Not to her personal taste but of course it was no concern of hers. She felt the silence called for a comment, however. "I'm sure you know best how to ensure your comfort, Sir Marius."

"Oh, I do," he said with a smile. "And I'm most particular and determined when it comes to my comfort in my sleeping quarters."

Which, Beth thought, was a perfectly unexceptionable thing to say. So why did she feel colour heating her cheeks? Since arriving at Stenby not three days ago she seemed to be turning into a different person all together and her mind was becoming positively flighty.

She quickly raised the subject of Sophie's letter, as a much less personal topic.

Sir Marius was inclined to discount it, however. "I have to admit that Randal has had his share of devoted females at one time or another. That letter was doubtless the work of one such, driven crazy by jealousy. If David checks the post from now on, there is no need for concern."

Beth couldn't help but be reassured. Sir Marius was a very reassuring gentleman. She couldn't help thinking how wonderful it would be to have a man like Sir Marius to take care one.... She forced the thought away and kept the conversation determinedly on politics for the rest of the drive. There was plenty to discuss in the increasingly optimistic developments on the continent and the declaration of war on France by Austria. Sir Marius followed her lead tamely enough.

When they arrived at the picnic site, the abbey was as he had described it—often not more than grassy humps with occasional stone walls rising higher. For the rest it was smooth grass well populated by people. Grooms were taking care of horses and other servants were setting out food. About fifty guests strolled around the ruins or down near the river, and sat on rugs laid under the trees. There was a handful of children running around under the supervision of nurses and governesses. Master Delamere, however, was by far the youngest. Beth couldn't help feel that his mother's fondness for Stevie's company, though doubtless admirable, was perhaps unwise.

Even as she walked over to join Jane beneath an oak tree, Beth saw Stevie tugging his nursemaid off towards the river. And Verderan. She sat beside Jane on a rise of ground ideally situated to watching events around them as they sipped appreciatively at chilled sangaree. The afternoon was turning very hot and a cloudless sky offered little hope of relief.

Beth hoped she was not going to develop one of her sick headaches for she was prone to them in the heat. After being such a problem to transport to the picnic, she would die with mortification to have to be especially taken home again.

Sophie, she saw, was firmly by Randal's side and it was clear from the way they moved together that he would have it no other way. Though this affair might be less than Sophie would like, it must be a delight to her to be with him for a whole afternoon.

They and some other young people wandered down to the river and began to play ducks and drakes. The stones went skimming across the water with quite remarkable skill. Fascinated, Beth went down to a rise closer to the river to watch.

Most of the young ladies lacked the skill, but some were not averse to learning, especially as their swains had to encircle their bodies to show them the correct flick of the wrist. Sophie, perhaps to her disappointment, needed no such lessons. She was holding her own with Randal, Verderan, and another young man called Tring.

"Care to chance your arm?" said a voice close to her ear and Beth started around to see Sir Marius behind her. "I'd be pleased to instruct you."

"I'd need to see your talent first, sir," said Beth. Then realised that could be seen as a challenge, and one with a forfeit attached.

She heard the conversations, applause, and small splashes as she looked nervously into those fine eyes. Then he smiled and looked away. "You've caught me out. 'Fraid it's not one of my skills. Some lack of flexibility in the wrist, or so they tell me. Same reason I'm no great hand with a sword."

"I'm too old anyway for such things," she said.

"Nonsense," he replied, almost angrily.

Sophie was about to attempt another spin when a small figure dashed by her legs, knocked her to the ground, and flung a tiny wooden horse out onto the water.

For a two-year-old the action wasn't at all bad. Unfortunately, Stevie's follow-through was too good and he threw himself into the water to lie there facedown, half submerged.

It was as if everything were slowed down. The careless nurse-maid set up a screech; Beth began to run forwards but she was a fair distance away; Randal went straight to Sophie, who was already sitting up and looking cross. It was Verderan who walked into the shallow water and picked Master Delamere up by the back of his cambric dress.

He looked at the still child and gave him a hard slap on his padded behind. Stevie immediately screamed. The erring nurse-maid came running up red-faced and had the damp bundle dropped in her arms, presumably with a caustic comment for she went even redder. Chloe and Justin hurried over to add to the mayhem. Stevie screamed even louder.

By the time Beth had reached the riverbank it was clear to all that Stevie was not screaming in fright, or in outrage because of the blow, but because his horse was now bobbing in the wide river. His mother promised him a new one; his father told him it was his own fault for throwing it there; someone even tried to tell him it was a sea horse and much happier in the water.

Stevie screamed on and the horse bobbed into the deep water. There were no boats in sight.

"Someone should throttle that child," muttered Sir Marius and Beth felt a touch of sympathy with the remark.

Lord Randal said, "Ver!" in a tone both shocked and hilarious. Beth turned and saw that Piers Verderan had stripped down to his cotton small-clothes and was wading out into the river. A few ladies emitted mild screams. There were not a few sighs, how-ever, at the sight of that magnificent tanned body. When he was deep enough he slipped into a smooth, athletic stroke and cut through the water to the bobbing object.

Stevie abruptly stopped screaming. Quite clearly in the watch-ful silence he said, "Ver. Horsey." Then he started sucking his thumb.

Horse in hand the man flipped easily around and stroked smoothly back. When he rose majestically from the water his clothes clung to every inch of him. There were a few rather more genuine screams and a couple of mothers turned their fascinated daughter's eyes away.

The Dark Angel walked over to the child and gave him the toy.

"Not a bad first throw, brat," he said lightly. "I must thank you for giving me the chance to get into the water. The only civilized place to be on such a hot afternoon."

He then turned, waded back into the river, and went swimming.

Sir Marius broke into laughter. "The man's a genius. Damn it if I don't wish I had the nerve to follow him!"

Beth could see not a few of the men had the same longing, and perhaps some of the ladies too. Though she had never swum in her life, the notion of lazing in cool water on such a hot afternoon was very appealing. She looked curiously at Lord Randal, surely the other man present most likely to follow his friend.

If he was tempted he showed no sign, merely called over a footman and told him to find some kind of towel and dry underclothes for when his friend emerged.

He walked back to Sophie's side. She was watching Verderan thoughtfully.

"Care to tell me?" he asked.

"What?"

"Your thoughts," he prompted. Sophie blushed. She'd been wondering if Randal's body would look like that when she saw it fully exposed. She hoped so. She could tell by his tone that he guessed. She didn't particularly mind. A bit of jealousy wouldn't do him any harm at all.

"Do you swim?" she asked.

"Yes."

"I don't."

"I know."

"Will you teach me, after we're married?"

"Yes," he said softly. "After we're married I'll teach you anything you want."

Sophie felt as if her lungs had shrunk and were totally inadequate. 'After we're married . . .' But why then would he not teach her anything now? Was he really saying, 'When I've no choice anymore I'll make the best of it.'?

She laid her head on his chest. "Why must we always wait?" she asked.

He pushed her away gently. "Because it's time for tea," he teased and led her towards the rugs and the food.

Sophie resisted. "Do you have any idea how much I hate it when you do that?" she snapped.

He looked at her as if she were a conundrum. Suddenly he drew her closer and placed a firm, yet gentle kiss on her lips. He kept his lips against hers so she felt them move as he murmured, "Little more than a week, Sophie. That's all."

A promise and a threat. Sophie was trying to frame the question she must ask, one that allowed him no space for soothing platitudes, when they were interrupted by administrative details. Randal went off to handle a case of bad wine. Sophie gave up and went to join Jane.

As she crossed the grass, one of the footmen came up to her. "You must have dropped this, my lady."

Sophie took the letter. It was the one she had received yesterday. David must have dropped it. She opened it with fingers that trembled a little and saw it was not the same. "Be brave and steadfast. Remember your true love. The debaucher will soon be no more." What on earth was that supposed to mean? How could she forget her true love, Randal? Who was the debaucher? Verderan was the only one who sprang to mind.

Beth saw Sophie standing frozen with a letter in her hand and hurried over. "What is it?" she asked.

"Nothing," said Sophie quickly. Then she shook her head. "It's just another note, as silly as the last."

Beth took it and read it. "Indeed it is," she said reassuringly. "But you must show it to your brother. We need to know how it came to be delivered."

The earl was clearly angry and Lord Randal was furious. The footman was questioned but could add nothing. He had found the letter on the ground with Lady Sophie's name on it and assumed she had dropped it.

They all tried to dismiss the matter, but there was a cloud of concern over the party as they settled to eat.

The meal was halfway through when Verderan strolled back, dry, clothed, and enviably cool. He was the hero of the hour, praised for his rescue of the valued toy. Beth found herself wondering how much he had been motivated by mischief and how much by the simple desire to swim. A complex man, she thought, and not one to judge simply on the surface. The thought came to her to wonder whether he could be mischievous enough to send those letters to Sophie but she instantly dismissed it. That wasn't in the man's style at all.

After the meal it transpired that local wedding customs had been a topic of conversation. There was another betrothed couple present besides Randal and Sophie and they had decided to try "Handing." After a bit of teasing, Randal and Sophie were persuaded to take part.

All the ladies present stood in a circle. Randal and the other young man, Mr. Richard Stevens, were blindfolded. They were to walk around taking each pair of hands in turn. When they thought they held the hands of their true love, they were to kiss them and remove their blindfold.

Beth looked around the circle. She wondered how easy it was to distinguish a pair of hands. Some of the ladies would present no problem, being much older or plumper than the two brides-to-be but many would surely feel much the same. She saw that Sophie had mischievously slipped off her diamond ring; now why would she want to make it more difficult for Randal? A few ladies laughed and entered into the spirit of the thing by either removing their own rings or moving a ring to their wedding finger.

It was a positive conspiracy of deception. Beth would go odds, though, that if any couple in the world could identify each other just by the touch of their fingers, it was Randal and Sophie.

"What happens if they choose amiss?" Beth asked of the lady standing next to her.

"In the olden days they say he had to forfeit his bride," was the amused answer. "We're not so severe today. He has to buy free of the one he has mistakenly chosen by a gift of a pair of gloves, and pacify his true love with a kiss."

Beth could see now why Sophie had agreed to play the game and why she was trying to fool Randal into choosing amiss. In fact she wouldn't put it past the young lady to have instigated the game in the first place.

Mr. Stevens took Beth's hands for a brief moment and passed by. She wasn't surprised. Her hands were noticeably smaller than both brides'. Lord Randal too passed by after brief contact.

The gentlemen could go around the circle as often as they wished before making their choice and poor Mr. Stevens was obviously nervously undecided. Beth looked at his bride and saw tension there. Mr. Stevens knew his betrothed and knew she would be upset at his failure.

Sophie, she saw, was positively wishing failure at Randal.

But in the end he stopped in front of her without noticeable uncertainty, raised both hands for a kiss, and removed his blindfold.

"How did you know me?" she demanded.

"How could I not?"

Which was perhaps an unfortunate comment as Mr. Stevens had just chosen a laughing Countess of Wraybourne. His bride, however, was soon pacified by a very hearty and much applauded kiss. Sophie looked cross.

"Now I wonder if I could tell a particular lady's hands," said Sir Marius as he was escorting Beth to the curricle for the drive on to the Towers. The adults had been invited back there for dinner and an informal hop. "Yours, for example."

"Surely the idea is that the hands are special to the man in question," Beth retorted.

He captured one of her hands and considered it, turning it this way and that. "A small and delicate hand. I'd lay odds not as weak as it looks."

Beth tugged unsuccessfully. His large, rough thumb rubbed over her palm. "Good strong lines. A gypsy would say you have a determined personality."

"Do you tell fortunes?"

"I could give a fair try at yours, my dear."

"Really?" Beth queried skeptically, but unwillingly amused. "What would it be?"

"Oh," he said carelessly. "The usual. An unexpected meeting with a tall, dark, handsome stranger. Love, marriage, and happiness ever after."

Beth raised her brows. "Very unlikely in my case, I'm afraid."

"Time will tell." He rubbed the ball of her thumb. "This is interesting," he said.

"Why? Do you really know anything about such things?"

"A little," he said with a secretive smile. "A nice, firm, plump mound here is very significant."

"What of, pray?"

He looked up and released her. "I'll tell you one day, dear lady. One day soon."

Beth was left with the feeling yet again that the obvious conversation was not in fact what had been going on at all. A woman of sense, she decided, would avoid the teasing baronet on all future occasions. Why did she feel she wasn't a woman of sense?

At least the meal that evening provided no problem for she was seated between Arnold Tring and young Mr. Stevens. They were both pleasant companions and the type of unassuming people she was accustomed to. Afterwards they all repaired to the ballroom and sets were formed for dancing. There were too few people for the grand room, a matter which appeared to concern nobody.

The ducal household included two footmen and a maid of musical talent who were trained by the duke for just such an occasion. They played tolerably well on the piano and violins and the company threw itself merrily into a succession of country dances.

At first Beth was inclined to refuse invitations both on the grounds of age and status. It was Lord Randal who persuaded her onto the floor. He didn't point out, as he might have done, that many of the ladies prancing in front of her were older, or that her rank could not be considered inferior to that of the curate's wife. He merely said, "If you don't dance with me, Mrs. Hawley, I'll conclude you can't forgive me for being so elevated with you yesterday. I'll sink into a melancholy and drown myself in the Stenby moat. And then what will poor Sophie do?"

Beth had as much chance of not taking part in the next set as the candle in the wall sconce had of surviving till the morrow.

As they walked towards the set he added to his apology, saying ruefully, "It's just that I'm growing tired of being pushed in the direction everyone's been pulling me back from all my life. I do know what I'm doing, you know."

Beth was not above doing a little manipulating. "I'm afraid to say anything, Lord Randal."

As the music started and they bowed and curtsied, he flashed her an amused look from those very blue eyes that could appear as innocent as a cherub's. "I doubt that," he said blithely. "But speak away, Mrs. Hawley. Preach the work of the devil. Tempt me into the pits of hell. I can withstand it all!"

The dance then required him to twirl her around which he did with such verve she felt dizzy. Beth gasped, "Lord Randal, you have a way of carrying things to extremes!"

He stopped dead and swung her smoothly into another move. "It's my nature," he declared, as he put his hand on her waist. He looked down at her with a glittering smile that seemed to invite her to share with him the glorious absurdity of life. "Aren't you going to harangue me into debauchery, dear ma'am?"

Beth gave up. As a means of ridding himself of interference this madcap effervescence was more effective than the chilling hauteur.

She happily surrendered to the pleasure of the dance. She hadn't danced like this since her husband died, though she had kept up her skill when teaching country dances to Jane. She remembered those strange performances, just the two of them pretending they were eight and singing the tunes as they went through the moves. It had been inadequate teaching but great fun.

It was even more fun in a set, with real music and a skilful partner.

Lord Randal was an excellent partner. He was always graceful, of course, but he was also in control of every move. His hands on hers, or on her waist, were firm. On the occasions when she forgot a step and faltered, he guided her smoothly on so that she was sure a watcher could never detect her hesitation.

When their set was over, and he had procured a glass of lemonade for her, she said, "Thank you, Lord Randal. That was most enjoyable. You are a fine dancer."

He laughed. "Now, Mrs. Hawley. It is I who should say that to you."

Beth blinked. With his colour heightened and his eyes shining with uncomplicated enjoyment, he was stunning. Did Sophie perhaps feel nervous at taking this much desirability into her keeping? Beth silently admonished herself for stupidity. It was not a matter to concern most women, least of all a nineteen-year-old. She wouldn't be surprised to find that Sophie's notes were written by a jealous young miss with a taste for Gothic novels.

She sipped the cool, refreshing drink. "But I am not a fine dancer," she replied to his comment, "and I'm sure you would never offer me Spanish coin."

His eyes brightened still more. "Foolish certainty!" He dug into a pocket and spun a gold coin. "Here, Mrs. Hawley. For you."

She shook her head. It was like trying to handle quicksilver. When she studied the coin he had given her she saw it was a Spanish doubloon. "I grant you the point," she said with a smile. "But I can't possibly take this, Lord Randal. It must be valuable."

"Not particularly. It is just a lucky piece."

"Then I definitely must not take it."

He closed her hand over the coin and his smile steadied to something warm and genuine. "Please, Mrs. Hawley," he said. "What need have I of luck, when I'm to marry Sophie next week? And you have, I think, a genuine kindness towards me. Take it, and may it make you as fortunate as I."

He went to his next partner and Beth looked at the coin, bemused. She had no objection to a little luck, but hardly thought the coin would bring her wedded bliss. Perhaps, she thought pragmatically, she should buy a lottery ticket.

As Lord Randal had persuaded her onto the floor, she lacked an excuse to use with other gentlemen, nor did she wish for one. How many other dances would she attend in her life? Soon Sir Marius led her out. To her surprise her dance with him was ordinary and decorous. He was too large a man, of course, for prancing, but still she had come to expect a little teasing and perhaps one of those amused, secretive looks. She found herself quite disappointed.

Then, as they stood together afterwards, she saw one of those amused, secretive looks and a shiver went through her.

"You look rather sad," he said as he commanded wine for them.

"Could it be that you are disappointed, Mrs. Hawley?"

"With what, pray?" asked Beth.

"Perhaps you hoped to dance the waltz here?"

"Not at all," said Beth, wondering what it might be like.

"Perhaps the wine is too dry, then?"

"On the contrary," she said. "It is delicious, Sir Marius."

"Then it must be the heat. I fear we will have a storm one day soon."

Beth became aware that the fickle breeze had disappeared with the sun and there was nothing now to cool the heavy air. The ballroom formed the ground floor of one wing. Windows and doors on both sides stood open but little air passed through. In her light muslin Beth was not too uncomfortable, but she suspected the men must be feeling the heat in their jackets and cravats.

Sophie suddenly appeared at her side and offered a fan from a dozen or so she held in her hand. Beth took it gratefully. She opened it to find it was a simple thing made of wood and paper, prettily decorated with flowers and the ducal coat of arms. "They order them by the gross," said Sophie lightly. "Never know when they will be of use."

She turned to Sir Marius. "Would you like one, Marius? You're looking a little wilted."

He considered her offering dubiously. "Do you have a larger size?"

She laughed and flitted off. Beth plied her fan gratefully in such a way that some of the breeze played on him.

"Thank you," he said. "I'm wondering whether to go and have a word with Verderan. If he were to shock everyone by removing his cravat, perhaps we could all follow suit."

Piers Verderan, however, seemed to be the only person unaffected by the heat as he danced indefatigably through the evening.

As the Stenby party prepared to depart Beth felt a tremor of nervousness at the thought of driving home with Sir Marius. There was a clear full moon, but still to be alone with a man in the middle of the night was an unusual situation.

He showed no inclination to tease, however. Perhaps he

realised how tired she was. When she yawned, and apologised, he said, "Why not lean against my shoulder, Mrs. Hawley?"

"I could not possibly do such a thing," she protested.

"I won't tell anyone if you don't," he teased.

And so she did and almost dozed off before they got back to the Castle.

"Would you like me to carry you in?" he asked softly when he drew his horses up at last.

That stiffened Beth's spine like a ramrod. "Of course not," she said sharply. A groom assisted her down from the seat and she made her way quickly into the house. It was only when she reached her bedchamber that she realised that in her flight she had been less than gracious, whereas he had been kind, perhaps more than kind, all day.

She had to acknowledge that she was coming to regard Sir Marius Fletcher in a particular manner which was doubtless unwise. In the privacy of her bedchamber she tried to argue herself out of her wanton foolishness but her heart was not amenable to reason.

=== 7 ===

DESPITE HER TIREDNESS, sleep did not come easily to Beth that night, and she roused the next morning feeling dissatisfied with herself and anxious about life in general. There was certainly much to fret about—Sophie and Lord Randal, those strange letters, Sir Marius . . .And to think she had anticipated a pleasant sojourn in the country. When Jane asked her to check on their invalid, saying she had no faith in Sophie's supervision, Beth was pleased to have something to take her mind off her problems.

The woman was sitting in her bed, drinking tea, looking much improved. A frilled nightcap covered most of her bandage and her cuts were healing. There was even a little colour in her haggard cheeks.

When Beth introduced herself, the lady smiled. "I understand from the maid that you were the Good Samaritan who brought me here. I must thank you."

"I could do nothing else. This was, after all, your destination. Do you still not have your memory?"

"I am afraid not," said the lady with a sigh. "It is a very strange state of affairs. You have no idea . . ."

"You must not concern yourself," said Beth briskly. "In such a large household, you are no great burden."

"But with the marriage coming so soon."

Beth took a seat by the bed and smiled reassuringly. She could understand how very awkward the lady must feel. "Even with that."

"Lady Sophie seems a delightful young lady. Her husband will be a very lucky man."

"Indeed yes," said Beth simply, having no intention of gossiping.

The woman put down her cup and saucer and looked closely at Beth. "I hope he is a sober, reliable gentleman," she said.

Beth instinctively drew back slightly. Why was this woman so concerned about strangers? "He will make her a good husband," Beth responded carefully.

"Is their attachment of long-standing?" the woman asked. It was not so much the question as the avidity in the older woman's eyes, which disturbed Beth.

"I am not an intimate of the family, ma'am," Beth said repressively. "I was merely the countess's governess. Lord Randal and Lady Sophie have known each other all their lives, I understand."

The invalid responded to Beth's tone and looked away, but there was the tightness of irritation on her face. Was her curiosity just a natural desire for information, any information? Beth remembered the woman had come here with Sophie's marriage announcement in her reticule. . . .

"Lady Wraybourne visited me yesterday," the woman said, with a social smile. "She's very handsome. What kind of man is the earl? Does she have a happy marriage?"

So it wasn't only Sophie who invited the woman's prying. Beth was having no part of it. "They are very well suited," she said firmly and rose to her feet.

"Please," the woman said quickly. "Do not be offended. You must try to understand. I cannot speak of myself, as I know nothing. I am naturally curious about those around me."

Repugnance was replaced by guilt and Beth sat down again. She could not imagine what it must be like to awake with no knowledge of one's identity or history, dependent upon the goodwill of strangers.

"But it would be unseemly, ma'am, to gossip about people's personal lives. Perhaps if I arrange for the newspapers to be brought to you something might trigger your memory."

"Thank you," said the woman meekly, laying a hand briefly over Beth's. "You are very kind. And I wonder if you know what became of my portmanteau?"

Beth checked the wardrobe and found the bag there. The

clothes it had contained were put away but it was obviously not empty. She took it over to the bed.

The woman took it as if it were precious but made no move to open it.

"Shall I replace it?" Beth asked.

"No," the woman said. There was a hesitation and then she opened the bag and took out a flat wooden box. She raised the lid almost eagerly and then stopped. Beth looked. The box was the case for the pistol she'd been told of. The pistol, of course, was missing.

"How strange," the woman said. "Is this mine?"

"So I understand."

"Then where is the pistol?"

"I believe it was taken in case . . ." Beth sought for tactful words.

"In case I was deranged? Or suicidal?" the woman queried dryly. "I assure you I am not, for all that my memory appears to have gone on furlough." One dry finger traced the empty, velvet-lined socket. "I wonder if it would be possible to have the firearm back. I feel a flickering of memory when I look at this. . . ."

"I will ask Lord Wraybourne," said Beth. She had to admit to feeling uneasy about the woman having a gun, and yet it was foolishness to think of such a frail lady running amok with a pistol. Even if she did so, she would have only one shot and was doubtless untrained in the art. The gun would have belonged to some male relative and could hold fond memories. It might well help.

Beth would put the matter to Lord Wraybourne and let him decide. She assured herself that the invalid lacked for nothing and took her leave.

She relayed the request for the return of the pistol to Lord Wraybourne.

He took the heavy, old pistol out of a drawer. "I don't suppose she's going to try to wipe us out with this," he said dryly. "I certainly wouldn't care to try to hit the side of a barn with it. Perhaps if you were to take away the powder flask, that would be wise."

Beth took the heavy firearm and detoured to the library to pick up some recent magazines and a newspaper. She added a small selection of books and made her way back to the invalid's room.

The woman was warmly grateful for all Beth brought, but Beth noted her hand lingered lovingly on the pistol.

"Does it stir any memories?" she asked curiously.

"Little flickers," said the woman, frowning. "It is like trying to remember a dream. Always just beyond grasp." She opened the case and placed the gun carefully into its place.

Feeling just a little awkward, Beth reached forwards and took the powder flask. "The earl thought it best if this was removed," she said.

The woman seemed merely amused. "Does he really think I'm going to stalk the corridors looking for someone to shoot? I can hardly leave my bed and I'm not even sure I know how to handle this thing."

"Then you will be safer without the explosive," Beth said firmly. "I understand firearms can be extremely dangerous if mishandled."

"I'm sure you are right," said the woman. She thanked Beth again for her kindness and settled to read the *Morning Post* of a few days past.

Beth left, feeling strangely as if she had escaped. If Sophie was reluctant to visit the lady, Beth had some sympathy with her even though the woman seemed harmless and unfortunate.

Randal sat by the window in his dressing room and pulled out the sheet of paper. It had come in the post bag and one glance had shown him it was another of those damned letters. He'd made sure Chelmly and Ver hadn't noticed it.

'Make your peace with God. A pistol ball is all you deserve and then poor Sophie will be safe forever.'

He was not a coward but this faceless, irrational hatred would shake anyone. It was easy enough, after all, to kill, especially with a gun. A steady hand and a still target was all that was needed.

And what of Sophie? Should he perhaps take her away into hiding until the wedding? As soon as the thought coalesced he dismissed it. She had been distressed by this maniac but not threatened. It seemed likely the culprit was a disappointed suitor and so she should not be in danger of injury. Not that David was intercepting her correspondence she should be left in peace.

Randal stood abruptly and crushed the paper in his fist. He'd be damned if he'd be driven to panic by this drivel. That was doubtless the intent and the perpetrator would be waiting glee-fully for just such a reaction.

With steady hands, Randal took out his tinder box and lit a candle. He burnt the note to blackened ash and dusted off his fingers. Then he dressed for the trip to the Wem Fair.

The trip to Wem was made in three open carriages and so caused Beth no embarrassment.

Moreover, with Lord Wraybourne and Sir Marius along Beth felt relieved of responsibility for the younger members, for which she was profoundly grateful when Sophie and her brother Fred-erick began to kick up their heels. The two youngest people shied for coconuts and rode the swing boats, insisted on looking at the freak show and playing penny toss for hideous pottery orna-ments.

Matters were not improved by the outfit Sophie had chosen to wear. It was a cheerful gown of green and blue with a bodice *à la soubrette* laced up the front. Very rustic but somehow suggestive. Fortunately a cambric chemisette made the very low neckline decent, but in true country style the skirt was a good two inches shorter than usual and showed her ankles. She had tied her flat leghorn bonnet jauntily to one side.

Beth considered her own simple, demure blue muslin, delicate white shawl, and straw bonnet ornamented by only a bunch of silk flowers. She was surprised by a spurt of dissatisfaction that was definitely related to Sir Marius Fletcher. She simply mustn't allow herself to lose her head over the man. However, when he took her arm as if it were inevitable, Beth found herself going with him to tour the fair.

Sophie watched Beth, so quiet and proper, and knew she probably should try to behave like that herself but the raucous atmosphere of the fair was like heady wine, and there was Freddy to encourage her. She kept an eye on Randal all the time, hoping he would do something—either try to restrain her or join in.

Hay bales had been stacked to provide stepped seating for the greasy-pig contest, and she and Freddy climbed to the very top to watch. They laughed uproariously at the sight of contestants trying to hold onto the slippery animal. Sophie began to feel a little sorry for the frantic beast, however, especially when its fate was doubtless to be slaughtered and salted by the winner.

She turned away and realised Randal and her brother were standing beneath her perch, unaware of her presence.

"Where's Sophie?" David asked.

"Up to mischief somewhere," said Randal carelessly. "Freddy's with her."

"I did have hopes you could keep that hellion in order."

"She's not my responsibility yet, David. You go rein her in."

"At times like this I'd like to lock her up for a week."

"Could make life somewhat simpler," drawled Randal, "but I don't doubt I'd feel obliged to rescue her."

It would almost make being locked up worth it, Sophie thought wistfully. She wriggled over to sit on the edge of the bales over an eight-foot drop. "Randal!" she called. "Catch me."

He looked up sharply and started to speak but she gave him no chance and dropped. He staggered slightly as she fell against him, grasping her strongly to make sure she did not fall. Sophie closed her arms tightly around him and looked up.

She knew her eyes pleaded and saw him catch his breath. His eyes went strangely dark as he murmured something too soft to hear. Then his hand came up to cradle her head and he set his lips to hers hungrily. Her fingers splayed across his back and she felt his tongue deliciously tease her lips.

Someone whistled.

Laughter burst from the crowd.

With a curse, he wrenched back from her, his fine skin flushed. With embarrassment? Or need?

"This is hardly the place . . ." he said, pulling her away.

Beth, feeling her role as chaperone, moved forwards to help smooth over the awkward moment. She heard Sophie say, "Name your time and place, Randal," and shook her head. "Sophie . . ."

she began to expostulate, but neither Randal nor Sophie heard.

"God help us all, Sophie," he said with a laugh. "Do you want seconds too?" His hand reached out to her, but before Beth was forced to intercept further mayhem, the movement deflected and Randal brushed a curl back from the girl's flushed cheek.

"August the twenty-eighth," he said softly. "Fairmeadows. The large front bedroom which looks out over the rose garden . . . Are you prepared to meet me there, little flame? Alone?"

Feeling as if she had intruded upon a very intimate moment, Beth stepped back and came up against a large, hard body. She turned, knowing herself to be flushed, to look up at Sir Marius. "Don't take your duties too seriously, Mrs. Hawley," he said in a deep rumble of a voice which seemed to vibrate through her. "Nothing too terrible is going to happen here. Come and give me your opinion on the horseflesh."

"I know nothing about horses," Beth protested.

"Does that matter?" he asked, and Beth knew that moment between Sophie and Randal had spilled over to them. Nothing sane and normal mattered anymore. She placed her hand on his arm and went with him.

Sophie looked up at Randal. Prepared? A wave of hot desire burned through her at his words. "If I get any more prepared than this, my lord," she said, "it will be positively indecent."

He laughed even as he turned her and gave her a push. She landed in Piers Verderan's arms.

"Ver," said Randal. "You look after her. You may be the only one up to the task." He quickly moved away to speak to Lord Stanforth.

Sophie looked after him in astonishment. He'd pushed her into Piers Verderan's arms?

Sophie stood for a few seconds like a statue. Randal had abandoned her to the tender mercies of one of the most notorious womanisers in England.

"Well, Verderan," she asked tartly. "Are you up to handling me?"

"With one hand behind my back on a bad day, Lady Sophie," he assured her with dry amusement. "You wouldn't like it, either."

Sophie stared at him. If she wasn't totally devoted to Randal, she thought, she could be very interested in Verderan. He was such a challenge. "Are you sure of that?" she asked with a sideways look.

He met it with sardonic humour. "I'd make sure you didn't like it, young lady."

Sophie gasped but then gave up bandying words. It had occurred to her that Randal deserved a little jealousy for his cavalier treatment. What she needed was to be off with Verderan, out of Randal's sight. "Then come and put your stone-throwing practice to use and win me a fairing," she said with her most appealing smile and pulled him along. "I positively lust after one of those yellow china cats."

He won one for her easily.

"Now some of those coltsfoot drops," she demanded.

He put the cat into her hands. "I'll win them if you promise to eat them," he remarked. She looked up at him, surprised by a tremor of nervousness. Despite his pleasant demeanour, she wouldn't put it past him to force-feed the dratted things to her.

"Perhaps you should fight the local bruiser," she said pointing to the huge man who was taking all comers for a purse of five guineas. She'd rather like to see Verderan with a bloody nose.

"Hardly sporting," he responded. "I spar with Jackson."

Sophie reminded herself of her main purpose in life and glanced back at Randal who appeared to be completely enthralled by a sweetmeats stall. Wasn't he the tiniest bit jealous? If he was wandering around with the female equivalent of Verderan, she'd turn green.

Sophie took off her flat-brimmed bonnet and fanned herself. "It's so hot. I think I'll stand in the shade of that tree." She knew Verderan would have to escort her. For all the fun of the occasion it would be unpardonable to leave a lady unattended among all these yokels, many of them already the worse for ale. Once under the chestnut tree they would be out of Randal's sight. What would he do about *that*?

Verderan obliged without cavil, and when they were in the shade he took her hat and plied it for her.

"Thank you," she said. In an impulse of sheer naughtiness she leant back against the rough bark to make the most of the daring bodice of her gown, watching Verderan from beneath her lashes.

A light flashed in those deep blue eyes and Sophie wasn't sure if it was lust or something more unpleasant. It gave her a tremor of uneasiness. "I am willing enough to play the gentleman," he drawled, "if it is at no cost to my comfort."

Sophie opened her eyes wide. "Is that perhaps a warning?"

"If you care to take it as such," he said. He lowered his eyes and deliberately and insolently let them stroke the upper curves of her breasts, only veiled by the gauzy chemisette. "I've no objection to being used to shake Randal out his ill-suited reformist stage, Lady Sophie, but I won't hazard his friendship."

Sophie straightened hurriedly and rather wished she had a substantial shawl to drag around herself. "You've revealed a little too much, sir," she said tartly. "Friendship is not a matter of comfort."

"Perhaps you've never been without friends, Lady Sophie."

It caught her attention. Was it possible that the Dark Angel was sometimes lonely? "For heaven's sake call me Sophie," she said, in an impulsive but genuine offer of friendship. She laid her hand on his arm. "I'm soon to marry Randal. That should mean something. Perhaps we will be friends-in-law."

He smiled but she couldn't feel it was friendly. "Perhaps we will." A slight turn of his wrist and her hand was sloughed off, rejected. "Do you think we have tested Randal's forbearance enough?" he asked coolly. "Since I am his friend he might well feel you are safe with me, you know."

He put her bonnet in her hands and stepped back, as if he wished to avoid contamination. So much for kindness, thought Sophie. No wonder the man had few friends. "And am I safe?" she asked crossly as she retied the ribbons beneath her chin, wondering if they were crooked. With any other man she would have unself-consciously asked assistance.

Before he could answer, they were startled by a series of loud bangs and an outcry from the center of the fairground. Forgetting minor matters, Sophie looked to Verderan. "What was that?"

"Sounded like a pistol," he said and they both moved off towards the commotion. Everyone else seemed to have the same idea, however, and soon Verderan had to hold Sophie close to protect her. She felt no embarrassment. She was plagued instead by a totally irrational fear for Randal.

"I think we should get out of this mob," he said and pulled her to the side.

"No," she protested. "I have to see what's going on!"

"Don't be a spoiled brat," he snapped and virtually carried her out of the crowd to a peaceful spot.

Sophie struggled madly and even managed to scratch the side of his face. Her struggles stopped, however, when she heard cries and screams coming their way. She turned to see the crowd of which they had recently been a part reverse its flow, panic-stricken. A child tumbled beneath rushing feet and Sophie moved from his relaxed grip to run forwards. Verderan held her back ruthlessly.

"We have to do something!" she cried, trying to prize his arms from around her.

"Not yet," he said tersely.

The cause of the panic was soon apparent as three horned cows rushed wild-eyed along the path, trampling anything in their way. They passed within feet of Verderan and Sophie then broke free of people. In a moment, the mood of the crowd altered again. The uninjured called an halloo and set off in pursuit. Quite a number of people, however, were left on the ground.

Verderan and Sophie made their way cautiously forwards to help but found there were plenty of hands for the job and, fortunately, no serious injuries. The child Sophie had seen fall had scraped his leg and was looking sorrowful. She gave him a ha'penny to buy a sucket.

Then she looked at Verderan and found him dabbing at his scratched cheek with his handkerchief. The look he gave her was not friendly.

"Well," she said, smothering guilt, "you shouldn't have bullied me like that." Before he could reply she turned to the child's mother. "What caused the commotion in the first place?" she asked.

"Someone fired some shots off near the cattle stalls," the woman said angrily. "That's what. Heard tell someone got hurt.

85

I dunno what the world's coming to. Wouldn't be surprised if it's French spies!"

Shots? All Sophie's unease returned. She knew it made no sense, but she would not know a moment's peace until she saw Randal hale and hearty. Ignoring an angry exclamation from Verderan, she turned and ran towards the stalls, searching the crowd. She couldn't see Randal anywhere.

Verderan grabbed at her arm, catching only the short sleeve. "Sophie, for God's sake!"

Randal. Randal was the injured one. She broke free, ignoring the sharp rip, and ran frantically through the crowd, calling his name. She was buffeted by fat paunches and boney elbows, assailed by smells of sweat and ale and spicy meat. Everyone seemed to be shouting or laughing. How could anyone laugh?

She saw her brother and screamed his name. He turned, searching for her and she pushed forwards. A sudden movement of the crowd showed her David standing over a body and Jane kneeling there in the dust ministering to somebody. Beth and Sir Marius stood nearby also looking down with concern. Then the crowd shut again in front of her.

Terror made Sophie careless of everything. She fought her way by people, pushing and kicking, screaming, "Let me by! Let me by!" She lost her bonnet and felt her chemisette half dragged from her shoulder.

She landed breathless against David.

"Sophie, what on earth's the matter?"

She looked down. The body at his feet was that of an older man, conscious but looking sorry for himself. How could she ever have thought it was Randal?

Her heart was pounding, she felt sick and dizzy and clutched his supporting arm even as Beth Hawley came over, full of concern. What an utter fool she had made of herself. As Beth took her in her arms, Sophie looked at David to explain and found he was looking death at Piers Verderan. Verderan had stopped long enough to retrieve her bonnet and was knocking the dirt off it, seemingly unaware of his danger. The bloody scratch was clearly visible on his cheek.

Sophie hastily dragooned her wits into order and grabbed her brother's sleeve to snare his attention. "I wasn't running from him," she said. "I heard someone was injured. I thought it was Randal. I don't know why."

David relaxed slightly and looked at her. "Randal?" he said. "He's nimble enough to avoid a cow. He's off looking for you. Here he is."

Sophie turned quickly. Even with David's words her fear had lingered until now, until she saw Randal safe. As he took her hands she sensed Randal had felt the same dread. His startled glance made her aware that her bodice was hanging loose at one shoulder and her chemisette was disordered. She was perilously close to revealing all. She was immensely grateful when Beth Hawley draped her light shawl over her shoulders.

"Are you all right?" Randal asked. "I thought I saw you in the crowd." He flashed a guarded look at Verderan and Sophie knew even he was suspicious about how she had got into such a state.

"Verderan took care of me as you predicted," she assured him. She tightened her hands on his, letting the knowledge that he was safe seep into her and drive out that terrible panic. For the first time Sophie wondered how she would cope with being a soldier's wife. How could she endure seeing him ride off into battle?

"You look upset all the same," he said.

"I was frightened for you," she confessed.

"For me? Why?"

"I don't know." She looked up at him. "Do take care of yourself, Randal."

His lips twitched in a wry smile. "I thought you wanted a life of high adventure, minx."

Sophie swallowed her anxiety. Despite her fears, she must never tie him down to the safe paths. "Of course I do," she lied firmly. "I won't mind any danger as long as we're together. What happened here?"

"Fireworks in the cow byre," he explained, "and this poor gentleman didn't move quickly enough. He's banged his head and cracked a few ribs. We're just arranging to get him to his home."

Sophie became aware of yelps and howls from within the

crude barn and looked a question at him. He grinned. "I suspect a pair of young hellions won't sit for a week. Have you had enough rustic excitement, Sophie? I think it's time we took our leave."

Verderan came over and gave her bonnet to Randal and again Randal looked at him thoughtfully. Sophie saw the coldly furious look the Dark Angel gave her and bit her lip. What could she say? If everyone was suspicious despite her assurance, it was because of his dubious reputation.

= 8 =

BECAUSE OF THE heat, that evening the Stenby party ate on the west terrace of the Castle, joined by Randal and Verderan. Dusk was falling and lamps were set around to give extra light. There was potted shrimp and salad, grouse from Scotland and lamb from Wales, rabbits shot by Sir Marius, and a fine pike caught that morning by Frederick. For dessert there were custards and ices and the earl's favourite damson pie.

There were wines to drink, but in the heat the most popular refreshment was effervescent lemon.

Sophie sat by Randal on her best behaviour, planning her strategy. Tonight, one way or another, she was going to get him alone and push him a little further. She had set the stage by asking her brother's secretary, Walter Carby, to arrange a treasure hunt for after supper. If Randal could arrange events to suit himself, so could she.

It was hard to sit still with anticipation bubbling inside her more fiercely than the juice in her glass. It was almost impossible to eat. She tried hard, though, for Randal was sure to notice a poor appetite and be suspicious. It wasn't as if she really doubted him, she thought, aware of every breath he took beside her, of the warmth of his body so close to hers. . . . It was that she had to be sure if she was to have any peace of mind.

It was like waiting for an expected letter. It wasn't enough to know it was coming—it had to be received. Lost in her plans she was quite oblivious to the others.

Not so Beth who was aware of the tension between Lord

Randal and Mr. Verderan all, no doubt, because of Sophie's antics. For all that he hadn't seemed to pay attention, Lord Randal had been tight as a strung bow during Sophie's absence that afternoon with Mr. Verderan and her return so dishevelled, no matter how reasonable the explanation, had hardly helped matters.

After all the excitement was over, Beth had seen him and Verderan go apart. It hadn't been a heated discussion—that was not the style of either man—but Beth had seen the one cold glance Verderan had shot at Sophie afterwards. She wouldn't have crossed the man now for a fortune.

After the meal Sophie announced her entertainment. It was agreed to enthusiastically and she went off to check matters. Everyone else wandered about informally, waiting for the event to begin. Beth definitely wanted to avoid Lord Randal and Mr. Verderan, but Jane and her husband were having a *tête-a-tête* near the fish pond and Frederick Kyle had gone off to assist Sophie. Beth found herself with Sir Marius, aware this was entirely too much to her liking.

Everyone had displayed their fairings on a table and they went off to admire the spoils. Sir Marius inspected the crocheted jacket Beth had won in a lottery when she had merely been attempting a charitable donation to the almshouses.

"It must have been Lord Randal's Spanish coin," she said, and at his query, she explained.

"Fancy him giving up that piece," he remarked. "But look at the rewards. You will look charmingly in it, dear lady." Despite his attempts, his lips were twitching with amusement.

"It *was* the top prize," she reminded him, "and it is very fine work."

"Wonderful," he agreed. "The way those . . . er . . . pink ruffles have been worked down the front . . ."

"Very clever," she said firmly.

"Perhaps you should put it on so we can judge the better," he suggested blandly.

Beth tightened her lips. "It would hardly go with the green of my gown," she said.

"Do you think not?" he queried. "But there is some green in it."

Beth gave in and chuckled. There was everything in it. The spencer was a coat of many colours with ruffles down the front and roses worked on top of the cuffs. It was dreadful.

"I intend it as a gift for my sister-in-law," she said firmly.

"Lucky lady," he said with a cough. "But if we are establishing a tradition of passing on our fairings, I think I will gift you with these," he said and took up some handkerchiefs. They were fine Indian cotton exquisitely embroidered white on white and edged with tatted lace.

"Sir Marius, I couldn't possibly accept," she protested. A gift of handkerchiefs was not outrageous, but it was his tone of voice that was sending warnings to her brain. "They are too beautiful," she said firmly.

"You mustn't put your value so low," he said teasingly. "Anyone worthy of that jacket . . ."

"But the jacket is for my sister-in-law," said Beth sharply. He could surely have no interest in her and yet . . . Did he think because she was a widow she was of lax morals?

"A gift of handkerchiefs is hardly an assault on your virtue, Mrs. Hawley," he retorted. "To imply otherwise is to insult me."

He was genuinely angry. "Oh, good heavens," said Beth in distress, looking away. "I am making a fine botch of everything. There will scarcely be a person left willing to talk to me."

His large hand came over hers. "What have you been about, my dear?" he asked gently.

They were virtually alone on the terrace now. Aware of that endearment and his hand warm on hers, Beth looked up at him doubtfully.

He frowned. "I do wish you would stop looking at me as if I were an ogre, Mrs. Hawley."

"Aren't you?" she asked and then could have bitten her tongue off. She leapt to her feet. "Oh, I never realised how unnatural we were at Carne Abbey. Never meeting strangers, certainly not gentlemen. I am full of admiration for Jane for surviving her Season. Here I am, plunged into Society and going from one catastrophe to another!"

"Hardly that," he said comfortably, drawing her back down beside him. "You did very well with Verderan, as it happens, but that was three-quarters luck. I wouldn't try it again. Especially not now."

"He's in one of his tempers, isn't he?" she asked. After being largely silent throughout the meal, the Dark Angel had gone to stand alone on the far end of the terrace.

"Not precisely," Sir Marius said. "He hasn't smashed anything yet."

Beth looked at the solitary figure with impatience. "A man his age should have more control."

"I didn't say he didn't *want* to smash something, dear lady. So who else have you offended? I suppose it must be Randal."

Beth nodded. " 'Fools rush in where angels fear to tread . . .' " Then she looked down at Verderan and a laugh escaped. "That could almost be a very poor pun."

Sir Marius winced at the thought. "Let us change it to Shakespeare then. 'The world is grown so bad that wrens make prey where eagles fear to perch.' I think the birds fit well."

"A wren?" Beth queried, rather hurt.

"A charming, gentle bird, said to bring leaves to cover those benighted in the forest. Yes, dear lady, I see you as a wren. You deserve some credit for trying to talk sense to Randal. It's more than anyone else has been brave enough to do."

"He's the son of a duke," Beth said in despair, "and I . . . Well, he said I was encroaching and it was all too terribly true." She put her hands up to her flaming cheeks. "Why can I not learn to mind my own business?"

He pulled her hands gently down. "You care," he said simply. "If he gave you his doubloon it was probably for that very reason. Among the great there are all too few who really care, my dear. Don't stop."

She looked up at him and something moved in the world, everything shifted and changed. Her senses became heightened and she could hear a cricket and a distant nightingale; could smell the musky evening perfumes from a nearby flower bed. "I'm going to get a crick in my neck," she said helplessly.

He laughed but she never found out what he would have said to that because Sophie bounced out onto the terrace. "We're all ready!" she announced.

"We're to go in three teams," said Sophie, "each with a list of things to collect." She looked around at the scattered people—Beth and Marius up at one end of the terrace; Jane and David by the pond just being joined by Frederick; Randal near her by the door. "I think we've pretty well established our teams. Verderan, you had better come with Randal and me."

There was heartbeat during which everyone seemed to hold their breath, but then the Dark Angel sauntered across to her. "Of course," he said and took one of the lists. "Saltpetre?" he queried dryly. "Do you really think you need extra explosive power?"

There was a flush on Sophie's cheeks when she came over to give Beth the list for her and Sir Marius. Her and Sir Marius! Beth realised and looked up at him.

"We're bound to win," he said with a twinkle. "I can reach the high places while you do the low."

Beth surrendered to moon madness. She hadn't felt like this for so many years. She wasn't sure she'd ever felt like this before. With Arthur there had been none of this danger and excitement, the thrill of the forbidden. Nothing lasting could come of this but, goodness, it was fun. She resolutely put the unholy triad of Sophie, Randal, and Verderan out of her head. She and Sir Marius went off across the dusky garden to find a rose hip, the first item on their list.

Jane looked away from Sophie and the two men and up at her husband. "Do you think . . . ?"

"I think they're all old enough to cope," he said firmly. "If it comes to pistols I'm willing to lock Verderan in the dungeons till after the wedding, but short of that they can manage for themselves. Let me see that list. A pinecone? At this time of year? Come on."

"Well?" said Sophie brightly to Verderan. "What's first on the list?"

"A switch," he said.

She grabbed the piece of paper. "What? That's not . . ." She looked at him and across to Randal who, damn him, looked amused.

"I'd leave you to your own devices, young lady," said Verderan with an edge on his voice like a blade, "which is doubtless what you want. But that would offend Randal's virginal modesty. I give you his advice, though. Behave yourself."

The startling thing, thought Sophie, edging towards Randal simply for protection, was that Verderan might well beat her. He *was* in a rage, she saw, though he had himself well in hand. If she crossed him he doubtless would put her over his knee. And she hadn't even had any such Machiavellian thoughts as his abandoning them; she'd just hoped his proximity would stir a little jealousy in her husband-to-be.

"We," said Verderan tightly, "have to find an earthworm and you, young lady, are going to carry it." He set off towards the kitchen garden with his long fluid stride, leaving Sophie and Randal to follow.

"Don't involve Ver in this game," said Randal softly but firmly as they walked behind. "He can't afford the stakes."

"What do you mean?"

"Rightly or wrongly, his reputation has him living on the edge of an abyss, Sophie. I honestly don't know if he cares if he falls or not but I wouldn't like to see him pushed."

"It's you I'm pushing, Randal, not him," said Sophie desperately.

"I think you may have it in mind to use him as a prod. Don't."

"Is that an order?" she demanded, realising that with Verderan a few yards ahead in the tricky half-light this was as close to privacy as they'd had since that night in her bedroom.

"If you like," he said and put his arm around her waist, but only to hurry her after his friend.

They easily found a worm, and Sophie carried it, though she insisted in putting it in a flowerpot full of earth so it wouldn't die. Verderan was nonplused by the need for a seashell until the local pair showed him a bank of earth full of them.

"The scientists say this land was under water once," said Randal as he picked out a smooth, pink shell. "Next?"

"A piece of orange thread," said Verderan. "Your department, Sophie." She led the way back to the house and up to the sewing room.

Having found the room she shrugged. "I don't know this place any better than you," she said. "Let's all search."

All they found, however, was red and yellow. Sophie was also searching for some way to capitalize on the situation she had created. She didn't find that either. She had intended to flirt a little with Verderan but in his present mood she simply didn't dare.

Her best tactic doubtless would be to get rid of him somehow.

"We had better try Mama's embroidery box," she said and led the way swiftly to the far wing. Could she try to divide the party? Send Verderan for something. She tried to remember the list that he was carrying.

"Hold on," called Verderan as they passed through the music room. "We need catgut too. Will there be any here? If we keep tearing around like this I, for one, will be worn to a shadow."

"That's what you get for a life of dissipation," said Sophie pertly and he laughed. It wasn't a very warm laugh but it was better than nothing.

She went to some cupboards and soon found the catgut. She wound it round her finger into a tight little coil. "Who gets to carry this?" she asked. Without waiting for an answer, she went over to Randal and slowly tucked it into his jacket pocket.

She heard his breathing change. He looked at her in a way that sent a shiver down her spine and raised her hopes sky-high.

It was going to work if she could only get rid of Verderan.

"What else do we need?" she asked him.

"A lustre from a chandelier, for heaven's sake. Are we supposed to wreck the thing?"

"Of course not," said Sophie, heading for the Blue Drawing-Room. "You've obviously never had the task of washing them. They are hooked on. You'll see."

The chandelier, hanging up near the cloud-painted ceiling, had to be let down with pulleys to be in reach.

"How much does that thing weigh?" Verderan asked dubiously.

"I think four men let down the one at the Towers," Randal remarked.

This situation should do very well indeed, Sophie thought.

"We need a couple of sturdy footmen," she said and placed her worm pot carefully on a piecrust table. She turned to Verderan to give him directions. "The bell would bring Burbage, but if you were to go—"

A sound alerted her and she spun around to see Randal already leaving on the errand.

"Damn that man!" she cried as her hopes came crashing down.

Sophie's own temper snapped. It was so bloody unreasonable. He was like a nervous spinster—and to abandon her to the tender mercies of the Dark Angel . . . She forgot his earlier words of warning. The complacent fool deserved everything he got.

Sophie flung herself into Verderan's arms and said, "Kiss me!"

He was turning from watching Randal and off balance, so they both went sprawling onto the carpet. He instinctively caught her and rolled to take the worst of the fall. Sophie found herself sprawled on top of him inches from two of the most furious eyes she had ever encountered.

Even as she scrambled to get off him and escape, he surged fluidly to his feet, carrying her with him. She tried to run but his hand shackled her wrist and dragged her against him as if she were floss. He locked her to him and backed her up against a heavy table.

Terrified, Sophie tried to kick and bite but he controlled, as he had said he could, with one arm, and grabbed her chin with the other hand.

"Oh no, you spoilt bitch," he snarled. "You will get what you wanted from the Dark Angel!"

He hurt her. His fingers pinched as he forced her mouth open. Their teeth clashed achingly and he thrust his tongue deep and ground his body against hers. Then he stepped back and threw her away so she bruised her hip against a corner of the table. She felt raped.

"Randal will kill you for this," she whispered rubbing at her tender mouth with the back of her hand.

The disgust in his eyes shrivelled her. She couldn't face him. She couldn't face Randal just yet. Aware of tears gathering and that she would not give him the pleasure of seeing her cry. Sophie turned and fled from the room. . . .

Verderan was lounging full length on the long sofa when Randal returned with the footmen.

"Where's Sophie?"

"Having been left with the wrong man," said Verderan smoothly, "she took umbrage and abandoned me." He swung to his feet and picked up a pot from the floor. "Fortunately she left the worm, so I had suitable company."

=== 9 ===

FLEEING TOWARDS HER bedchamber Sophie heard the voices of Mrs. Hawley and Marius and turned down a narrow set of stairs to avoid a meeting. She came to the room of the mystery guest and ducked in there for sanctuary.

The room was dark and she thought the woman would be asleep but the dry voice said, "Is that you, Lady Sophie?"

"Yes," said Sophie, coming close to the bed. "I hope I didn't wake you."

"No. I have been lying here since someone brought me supper, trying to remember. I must be a great trouble to you all."

"No, of course not," said Sophie. She surreptitiously rubbed away the few tears which had escaped, grateful for the obscuring gloom. "Do you want me to light some candles?"

"No, no," said the lady. "With the moonlight I have no need of them and it's safer without. I hoped you would come again."

Sophie realised guiltily that she hadn't given the invalid a thought and put her anguish about recent events behind her. She took a seat by the bed. "I hope you have everything you want, ma'am."

"Everyone is very kind," the woman said. "But you, my dear. Have you everything you want?"

"Who ever does?" asked Sophie softly. In this dim greyness there was no reality to this conversation. "I thought once I had the moon and stars in the palm of my hand . . ."

"And now?"

"And now," she said sadly, "I have bruised lips and disgust."

The woman sighed and reached out a hand. Sophie placed hers in it, though it was in fact unpleasantly dry and clawlike. She silently chided herself for her repugnance when the poor woman had been ill.

"You came to me for refuge, my dear," said the woman, with a squeeze. "Your instincts did not play you false. I will hold you safe."

"I don't know what to do," Sophie said, hardly hearing the woman's words as she thought of Randal and Verderan and the mess she seemed to be making of everything. She'd threatened to tell Randal about that assault. After all, Verderan ought to pay for what he had done. It had been vile, far worse than a beating. She still felt nauseated. But could she face the consequences? They were both crack shots. They'd kill each other.

But what if Verderan told Randal himself? He was quite capable of it and might even make it all seem Sophie's fault. She was honest enough to acknowledge that he wouldn't have to distort the truth very much to do that.

"I don't know what to do," she repeated.

"It would be better to tell them all," said the woman as if she knew all about it. "They would not be so very harsh with you, surely, and everyone would know where the real blame should lie. A man like that—a libertine, a debaucher. He's doubtless diseased."

"Oh, I don't think so," said Sophie, shocked. It was difficult to imagine a disease bold enough to attack Verderan—which is what she'd just done, she thought with a touch of hysteria. "How on earth do you know what happened?" she asked.

"My dear, I haven't been spying on you," said the woman gently. "I can hardly leave this bed as yet. I just know who is involved and can guess the rest."

"Well, I don't think I'm up to telling anyone the truth of the affair," Sophie said, rising to her feet. "It would upset too many people and serve no purpose."

The lady sighed softly, like rustling leaves. "Never mind, my dear. It will soon be irrelevant, you will see."

Irrelevant? thought Sophie blankly. And then had a revelation. Yes, Verderan *was* irrelevant. She paced the bedchamber a few times, oblivious of the invalid. He'd called her a spoilt bitch and he'd been right. How terrible to try and involve him in matters between her and Randal. She shuddered as she imagined what would have happened if Randal had walked in during that awful kiss.

She remembered the lady in the bed. "I must leave now," she said abruptly, adding more gently, "Good-night. You have been a great help to me."

Sophie hurried off to try to mend the damage she had caused.

The invalid lay back thoughtfully. Things were come to a pretty pass indeed, thought Edith Hever, when her dear daughter in God's eyes was at the mercy of a debauched libertine such as Lord Randal Ashby. Matters should have been taken care of long before this.

When she'd first regained her wits and found herself in Stenby Castle with no one aware of her identity it had seemed the work of the Lord. Now she fretted at her continued weakness and wondered what her servant, Jago Haines, was about that he could not snuff out one life before now.

The death by suicide of her darling son, Edwin, had left Edith ill for many months and the cruel way her nephew had thrown her out of her home had added to her burden. She had begun to give up on life until she had learned of the terrible plans in hand for Edwin's dear Lady Sophie.

During his stay in London, Edwin's letters had been full of Lady Sophie Kyle and it had been clear she was his chosen bride. A sweet, well-born, sensitive creature. Why then had he shot himself? When the Gazette had conveyed the news that Lady Sophie was betrothed to another—and to one well-known for his libertine ways—she had understood at last. A broken heart and despair over his beloved Sophie's fate, had driven Edwin to take his life.

That was beyond her correction, but Sophie was not beyond her aid. How desperate the poor girl must be, having lost Edwin and being forced into union with such a debaucher. In all ways that mattered the child was Edwin's bride. Without a plan but trusting to Providence, Edith had set out for Stenby to protect her.

On her way she had sent a letter to Sophie. In case the girl's correspondence was monitored she had given her servant, Jago, another letter to pass to the young woman in some discreet way. Edwin's bride must know she was not alone in her ordeal lest she be driven to the same dreadful act of despair.

Edith had also sent a letter to the libertine, Lord Randal Ashby, with another for Jago to post at a later date. It was only fair that the villain receive notice of his fate; a condemned criminal was given the opportunity to make his preparations for the hereafter. She had made it clear that he was not to be killed without this warning but she had not intended Jago to be so laggardly. The wedding day was rapidly approaching and see how poorly Sophie was guarded that she be open to insult.

It was not so hard a business, thought Edith angrily, to snuff out a life. Perhaps she shouldn't have told Jago to make it look like an accident. Or perhaps he lacked the nerve.

If Jago lacked the resolution, Edith did not. She would do the job herself now she had her weapon. She smiled as she thought of the removal of her powder flask. She had had the forethought to pour a portion of the gunpowder into another container. When opportunity presented, as it surely must, she would be ready.

Dead, Lord Randal Ashby would no longer be able to force his loathsome attentions on sweet Sophie.

Sophie went quickly to her bedchamber and checked her appearance. Though her jaw felt bruised and her lips stung, she could see no sign of it. She washed her face to get rid of any trace of tears and hurried down to find the rest of the party.

Randal and Verderan had gone, however. Sophie swallowed. "Were . . . were they all right?" she asked David.

"Should they not have been?" he queried with a suspicious look.

"Of course . . ." said Sophie but she could not meet his eyes.

"Sophie. We are all making allowances at this time but I'm not averse to keeping you in your room on bread and water for a week if it becomes necessary."

"If you hadn't made us wait three months, none of this would have happened!" Sophie cried.

"If you can't behave moderately for three months there's little hope for your future," he riposted.

Sophie stared at him. "Did you say something like that to Randal?" she asked.

He looked away and then said, "Yes."

Sophie opened and shut her mouth a few times, simply unable to enunciate her fury at the mess that had been made of her dream. Then she ran out of the room.

Sir Marius and Beth discreetly resumed their conversation as the earl looked ruefully at his wife. "I didn't put a vow of perpetual celibacy on them," he said.

She laughed and touched his hand reassuringly. "Of course not. It was just another challenge for Randal, like racing to Brighton and going out with the free traders. He'd never tried self-control and decided to. None of us realised what effect it would have on Sophie."

"What should I do?"

"Nothing. There's only eight days to go. I just wish Mr. Verderan wasn't involved. That does make me nervous."

"He has more sense than anyone gives him credit for. He won't let Sophie destroy his friendship with Randal."

"But what about Randal? Self-denial can be a fertile ground for jealousy, I would think."

His hand slipped around to rest on her hip. "Perhaps we should go and take a preventative against jealousy, Tiger Eyes."

Jane looked around. Frederick had gone early to bed for tomorrow he was off for a few days with an old friend. "Should we leave Beth here with Marius?"

"Are you going to play chaperone for your chaperone?" he queried with a grin.

"Well . . ."

"I applaud your sense of decorum," he said, "but have no patience with it at all. Come along."

Beth watched them slip out of the room with alarm and a tremor of excitement. "Do you think that means we won the treasure hunt?" she asked Sir Marius.

"Or lost," he said dryly, causing her to colour.

"No," she said softly. "I think Sophie lost."

"And there you may be very right," he said, "However, I find the insane manoeuvrings of the younger set leave me cold. Would you be willing to indulge me in a game of chess, Mrs. Hawley?"

"Of course," she said, "though I am not a very deep strategist."

"Neither am I," he said with a lazy smile that made her feel warm all over. "I'm more a man for cards, myself."

"Do you know," said Beth, very daring. "I have never, ever gambled in my life."

"You, ma'am, are a barefaced liar."

Beth stiffened. "I beg your pardon?"

"This very afternoon you risked a shilling on the chance of winning a fine jacket with pink ruffles."

Beth giggled. There was no other word for it. She heard herself and it was definitely a giggle. "That is not the same thing."

"You want me to lead you into a life of vice," he declared in surprise.

"Well . . ." Beth hesitated. "I just thought it might be interesting . . ."

"Oh, it would," he said softly and with meaning. Beth swallowed.

"To play a gambling game," she said hurriedly. "Bezique, or piquet, or something."

"Something," he repeated gently. He took her hand and pulled her up and out of the room.

"Where are we going?" she squeaked.

He stopped suddenly and she collided with him. "To the library," he said innocently. "Where did you want to go?"

He was huge and warm and Beth felt dizzy. "The library will be fine but . . ." She gave up and allowed herself to be swept along. She couldn't believe it, but the thought actually flickered across her mind—if he offered to set her up as his mistress, should she accept?

That sobered her. She was Elizabeth Hawley, widow and staid companion, too small and lacking the abundant curves so appealing to gentlemen. She had carroty hair, freckles, and a skin that showed every emotion and she was thirty-three years old. Sir Marius Fletcher was just amusing himself until a more likely lady turned up, which would doubtless happen next week when the wedding guests began to arrive.

That wasn't to say, though, that she couldn't have the tiniest little adventure before then, was it?

When they reached the large, book-lined room, he let go of her and lit a branch of candles. He flung open two windows and a faint breeze refreshed the hot, dusty air. "In the desk, I think," he said as he went through drawers.

"Sir Marius," Beth objected. "Do you think you ought?"

"There's nothing personal in here," he said offhandedly, "Ah, Got 'em."

"What?" Beth asked, a hundred bizarre notions passing through her disordered head.

"Dice," he said. "If you want a dissolute life, there's nothing like dice."

He shook the ivory cubes out of the dice box a few times. "Fall true. David had a crooked set once."

"Lord Wraybourne played with loaded dice?" Beth queried aghast.

"Lord no," he said, looking at her as if she were mad. "Just a curiosity, though I'm not sure he didn't take them off someone rather forcibly. You know," he said sitting at a games table, "one of the men Verderan killed was fleecing young Devizes with weighted ivories, and Devizes lacks a good share of his wits."

"Am I supposed to admire Mr. Verderan for it?"

"The force was maybe a trifle excessive," he admitted carelessly, "but there was doubtless more to it than that. I don't see Verderan killing just to stop a half-wit losing his all."

"It's a better reason for killing than most I've heard," said Beth firmly.

He looked at her and shook his head, smiling, "Try for a little consistency, my dear lady," he said, "or we are going to have a tortuous affair."

"Affair?" Beth gasped and nerves all over her body started to quiver.

"In a manner of speaking," he said casually and rolled the dice again. "Look. You throw the dice so. They have to roll properly to show you're not cheating."

Beth's nerves settled. She must stop reading salacity into

everything he said. He couldn't possibly desire someone like herself. "Sir Marius, I would never consider cheating," said Beth firmly. Curiosity about the game drew her closer to the table.

"Admirable, dear lady. What are we going to play for?" Beth fixed him with what she hoped was a discouraging eye. "You have a very suspicious mind, Mrs. Hawley," he said with a grin. "*Would* you play for kisses if I asked?"

Beth gathered her wits and stepped back. "Sir Marius, I really think I ought to retire . . ."

"Or retreat," he said, with an irresistible smile. "Come, Mrs. Hawley, I promise to behave. Don't abandon me here at this early hour. We'll play for paper points." He took a sheet of paper and a pencil from the desk. He drew two columns and wrote their names at the top and underneath each, a thousand guineas.

"A thousand guineas!" gasped Beth.

"On paper only," he said, looking up at her with those fine grey eyes. He gestured to the chair on the opposite side of the table. "Play with me, Elizabeth," he said in a tone that loaded the question with a host of wicked meanings.

Sensible Mrs. Hawley, widow and governess, fled screaming, but Beth sank slowly into the chair. "I am generally called Beth," she said.

"I will call you Elizabeth," he said calmly.

They looked at each other and smiled. A servant could come in and discover them. There might be talk. But Beth had no intention of seeking employment again, nor did she need to preserve her reputation for a fine marriage. She was a free woman.

"So how do we play at dice?" she asked.

"Hazard. We should put our stakes on the table but we'll write them down. I stake fifty guineas. Are you going to match it?"

"Should I?" asked Beth, thinking that her vast savings which guaranteed her freedom amounted to less than the thousand guineas written on the paper.

"Don't be a chicken-heart. It's all in fun. Match me." Again his words seemed to have a double meaning.

"Very well," said Beth softly. "Who wins?"

He smiled at her across the table. "Time will tell. We haven't started playing yet, Elizabeth." Then in a brisker tone he said, "I cast the dice to establish a 'main.'" The dice both showed threes. "The main is six."

"What does that mean?"

"You'll see. Now I have to establish a 'chance.'"

"Why do you get to do all the establishing?" asked Beth truculently.

"Because I know what I'm doing, woman. Be quiet."

Beth subsided, retaining her wariness. It might only be pretend money but he wasn't going to fleece her. He rolled again and it was a two and a one. "Damn," he said. "I threw crabs. A two or a three on chance gives you the win," he explained, making the changes on the score sheet. "Now, oh impatient one, you get your turn. What are you going to wager?"

Beth took the dice box. "I won without doing anything? This is a strange kind of game. I wager a hundred," she said, recklessly seeking to outdo him.

"And I match," he said. "Throw the dice."

Beth rolled two sixes. "There!" she said triumphantly.

"No main," he said laconically. "Has to be five to nine."

"Why?"

"That's the rules. Are you usually this difficult?"

Beth looked down her nose at him. "I am sure I would always be particular over one thousand guineas."

"You're showing your *bourgeoisie*, my dear," he drawled and Beth felt the colour flood her cheeks. She leapt to her feet but he caught her. "Elizabeth, I'm sorry. That was damnably rude."

"You're always damnably rude!" she declared, perilously close to tears. "Let me go, you great ox!"

"Talking of rude . . ." he said, not relaxing his hold. In a deep warm voice that melted her will he said, "Come back and play with me, Elizabeth."

"We have nothing in common," she protested faintly.

"We have two thousand guineas on paper," he replied whimsically, adding, "I'm only a lowly baronet with modest estates and friends in high places, Elizabeth. Play with me."

Beth found herself back across the table, looking at him. "This is not at all wise," she said softly.

He took her small hand and kissed it. "We're not so old surely that we have to be wise all the time." His lips were velvet against her skin, something she'd never experienced before. No one kisses a governess's hand and she and Arthur had never courted in this way. If this was a courtship.

She looked at him, frightened and unsure.

He smiled ruefully and released her. "Roll the dice, Elizabeth."

Relieved to return to the mundane, Beth did so and rolled a nine. "There."

"Good. A main of nine. Now roll the chance."

"And I don't want two or three?" He nodded and Beth concentrated and threw a five and a one. "Is that good?" she asked.

"Fair. The main is nine and the chance is six. Now you throw again. You don't want a nine. A six will win."

Beth threw seven.

"Very good," he said. "Seven is now main. A seven or an eleven will win. Two or three will lose. You keep rolling until you win or lose."

"What a silly game," said Beth and threw two ones to lose. "And to think people risk their fortunes and their homes on this."

"Indeed they do," he said and marked his win.

"It should be against the law," she said.

"It is," he replied and grinned at her. "Don't you feel delightfully wicked?"

Beth did, but it wasn't the dice which were the cause. Discounting the casual meeting at Jane's wedding, she had only known this man for a few days. How could she have come to this pass? For Beth had to acknowledge that she was falling in love—with a man who could bring her nothing but heartache.

Like all lovers through time, however, she pushed aside common sense, determined to grasp her few brief moments of madness.

For all that she called it a silly game, those fictional guineas became real to Beth and she watched the score sheet avidly, rejoicing when she won, fretting when she lost. She had no sense of the passage of time and was startled when Burbage, the Groom of the Chambers, came in to check the room.

Beth felt herself colour and would have leapt to her feet

apologising, but Sir Marius took her hand in a firm grip and she stayed seated, quivering at the thought of her poor lost reputation. She found that though she did not need it, habit made it precious to her.

"It's all right, Burbage," said Sir Marius easily. "We'll lock the windows and extinguish the candles."

"Very good, sir," said the august servant, ruler of the household, as he bowed out.

"He won't gossip, you know," said Sir Marius, still holding her hand. "He's far too self-important for that."

"But what will he *think*?" asked Beth.

"Who cares?"

"I do," said Beth. "You were right, Sir Marius, I am a little bourgeoise." Her bubble of happiness had been popped. Beth only wanted to get away and forget what a fool she had been.

She rose to leave but as she walked past he tugged her into his lap. "Sir Marius!" she protested vigorously.

"Calm down," he said, folding his arms around her. "I'm not going to do anything too terrible but I can't kiss you standing up. It would be dashed uncomfortable."

"Kiss me?" Beth queried, feeling like a child snuggled against his chest.

"Well, I had it in mind to wait a few days but after that fright with Burbage you might start avoiding me. This seems too good an opportunity to miss."

Beth could feel her heart galloping, and strange, forgotten, dangerous sensations stirring up deep within. "And what if I object?" she whispered.

"Do you?"

Beth smiled at him. She felt ridiculously safe. If she said yes, he would let her go . . . but her madness was back in all its glory. There would surely not be that many more occasions in her life to be kissed. She needed something to remind her of this brief, insane delight. "No," she said.

His lips came down, soft and warm upon hers. She felt shy and awkward. It had been a long time and she had only ever kissed one other man. Slowly, though, she relaxed and let her instincts take her. Her hand traced his strong whisker-roughened jaw and crept up into his short, wiry hair. Before he demanded any such thing her tongue slipped between her teeth to lightly brush against his lips. She felt him first tense then relax as he deepened the kiss in response. She shifted to settle more comfortably against his big, solid body and surrendered to all the gloriously swimming sensations . . . Until she became aware of his wandering hand.

Shocked back into her senses, she pushed frantically at his chest. Immediately, he let go of her and she scrambled off him.

They stared at one another as the guttering candles threw mocking shadows on the walls.

He shook his head. "I'm sorry, Elizabeth. I didn't mean . . . I didn't think . . ."

Beth ran from the room.

It was all her fault, she told herself as she rushed to the safety of her bedchamber. All evening she had known where it would lead and ignored the proddings of her conscience. Now he would think her a loose woman. He probably *would* offer her *carte blanche*.

And the terrible thing was that she would have to say no.

=== 10 ===

THE NEXT MORNING Beth awoke to find the heat wave unbroken. A faint headache was tightening her scalp but it was not the sort that prostrated her. She played the coward, however, and lingered in bed until breakfast was over and the gentlemen had hopefully gone off in some activity. When she came cautiously down the stairs to find everything quiet, she took courage enough to peep into the library, scene of both ecstasy and disgrace.

In the daylight it was simply a spacious and dignified room, walled by glass-doored shelves full of leatherbound tomes. How strangely magical and wicked it had seemed in the dark with just that pool of candlelight to break it. The room had been cleaned of course and there was no sign of their occupation. For all she knew Marius had himself returned the dice to the desk.

But then on top of the desk she saw a piece of paper. When she went over she found it was their tally sheet. She smiled to see she had been winning rather substantially. Beginner's luck— or Lord Randal's lucky coin, perhaps—but if they had been playing for real money she would have been some five hundred guineas the richer this morning.

It merely reminded her that she had no place in Sir Marius Fletcher's world. On five hundred guineas she could live frugally for the rest of her life and yet to him it was a casual sum. Nevertheless, she gave in to temptation and folded the paper small to tuck it into the pocket of her day gown.

She went to look for Jane, needing employment to occupy her

mind. She found her in the ballroom, consulting with the house-keeper.

"I have ordered flowers," Jane said anxiously to Beth. "Gold and white. Do you think that will be enough or should we try for something more spectacular such as tents or trellises?"

"I think flowers are always acceptable," said Beth, finding wedding plans a little depressing at the moment. "And it is surely too late to change plans now."

"You are doubtless right," said Jane with a sigh. "But this will be the first grand entertainment at Stenby in so long that I want everything to be perfect." She looked at her friend closely. "Are you all right, Beth?" she asked. "I . . . I didn't really want to abandon you last night but . . ."

Beth moved to put an end to Jane's embarrassment before she started probing. "I just didn't sleep very well because of the heat," she said. "Where is Sophie this morning? I am afraid she was somewhat upset last night."

"Yes," said Jane with a shake of her head. "It reminds me of spring all over again. She was always plunging from ecstasy to the sloughs of despond. I'll go and see if she's in the dismals and persuade her down for some tea." She gave orders for a tea tray and told Beth she would meet her in the Jonquil Salon.

Beth had to ask for directions to this room but when she found it she could see why it had been chosen. On the north side of the house and with a tiled floor it was pleasantly cool. It was also small and intimate. If Sophie was in distress, it would be the best place to both soothe her and draw her out.

The tea tray came and after a few minutes Beth gave in to temptation and helped herself for she was desperate for a cup. It was quite a while before Jane arrived looking vexed. "She's ridden off to the Towers."

"Is that so very bad?" asked Beth. "She doubtless wants to see Lord Randal and there are plenty of people there to act as chaperone if he insists on it."

"And there's Verderan," said Jane with a frown, sipping her tea. "I don't know what happened between them, but I'm sure something did. Beth, I'm sure it's all a megrim—it's probably just this hot weather—but could you possibly go over and keep an eye on her?"

"Jane, what do you fear and what do you expect me to do?"

Jane shook her head. "I have no idea. But I have this prickle of unease and I would feel better to know you are there. I would go myself except that I have the musicians to see about the dances for the ball, and an appointment with Burbage about the icehouse. Our supplies are low."

Beth reflected that at least the errand would get her out of the house and away from Sir Marius. "Of course I'll go," she said, feigning cheerfulness. "A drive will refresh me."

Jane hugged her. "Thank you. You know you don't need to chaperone her precisely. Just make sure she's not up to something disastrous."

Such as a secret tryst with the Dark Angel, supplied Beth silently as she went to collect her bonnet and parasol.

Sophie was indeed involved in a tryst, of sorts, with the Dark Angel, but it was very proper.

She had ridden over mainly to see Randal to tell him she understood. If she had only realised before that her idiotic brother had put a sort of condition on them both, they could have treated the whole thing as a joke. Then she wouldn't have read doubts and indifference into his attempts at good behaviour.

But first she had to see Verderan. She had to put things right and make sure he didn't say a word, ever, to Randal about her shameful behaviour. She just wasn't quite sure how she was going to arrange to be alone with him.

Luck was on her side. When she enquired after Randal she was told he was out. That wasn't good news in the long term but it was better in the short. Further enquiries produced the information that the duke was engaged and the marquess was off on estate business.

Carelessly, Sophie asked, "I wonder if Mr. Verderan is about? I have a message for him."

"I'll enquire, my lady," said the footman and showed her into a comfortable reception room.

Remembering the look in Verderan's eyes when she had seen him last, Sophie paced the room nervously, rehearsing soothing words. When he walked in she knew she would need them. He looked as if he'd like to take a switch to her, or a blade more likely. He came no further than the door and was icily polite.

"You have a message for me, Lady Sophie?"

"Do you expect me to shout across the room?" she demanded, irritated despite her good intentions.

"You don't want to know what I expect from you," he said and it was like a slap in the face.

It took all her courage but Sophie walked a little closer and raised a hand. "Don't shoot yet," she said. "I've come to apologise."

He raised a brow skeptically but she thought he relaxed a little.

"Really," she said quickly. "I was in the wrong, Mr. Verderan. I've been wrong about a lot of things as it happens, though I don't feel it was all my fault. But in your case I was mischievous and unfair. I beg your pardon."

He looked at her steadily. "You surprise me, Lady Sophie. I've rarely heard such a handsome apology and I've heard many. One does, you know," he added idly, "when one has a reputation as a deadly opponent. But since I don't suppose you think even I would go so far as to call you out, I must be impressed. I wonder if I can match it."

He left his defense post by the door and strolled into the room but kept his distance. After a moment he said, "Do you know, I really don't think I can. There is no excuse for my behaviour. I had taken you in dislike, you see, decided that you were quite unworthy of Randal. I even toyed with the idea of seducing you into unfaithfulness but my damnable temper got the better of me and I attacked you instead. I cannot expect your pardon, or that you will ever trust me again, but I have to say that it would be much wiser not to mention the matter to Randal."

Sophie needed no such warning. "I have no intention of saying anything to him," she said. "I . . . I was concerned you might."

"I?" he said in genuine surprise. "You think me suicidal?"

"But it was all my fault."

"I don't think that would weigh with Randal for a moment," he said with glimmer of a smile and turned as if to go.

"You do have my pardon," Sophie said quickly. "And I . . . I hope that you will call me a friend. I will not come between you and Randal."

He turned back and his smile grew and became singularly sweet. "Well, you are bound to, you know. Many of our . . . er . . . activities are likely to be incompatible. But I thank you for your kind intentions. I would be very pleased to consider myself your friend. In fact, I think I may be able to evidence it."

"What do you mean?"

"If you are looking for Randal, I know where he is."

"Alone?" asked Sophie with interest.

"Very. He has taken a rod to a place he called the Magic Pool. Does that mean anything to you?"

Sophie grinned. "It does indeed." Deliberately she walked over and extended her hand. "Thank you, my friend."

He took it and after the briefest hesitation carried it to his lips. "Good hunting, Sophie."

So when Beth rolled up to the Towers in the landaulet a few moments later she found Sophie had just left. The footman assumed she had returned to the Castle. Beth had not passed her but the girl doubtless knew all kinds of shortcuts and there was no point in chasing her.

Beth's headache had not been improved by the drive—to the contrary it had worsened to an alarming degree. She knew she needed to be back in her bed and yet could hardly face the return drive. She was standing rather helplessly in the cool, tiled entrance hall when Mr. Verderan walked out of a small room. She noted that for a wonder, he seemed to be in a good mood.

"Mrs. Hawley," he said with a smile. "Dare I hope you have come to bear-lead me? Randal's gone angling and I abhor handling fish. I find myself devilishly bored."

"I came to bear-lead Sophie," she said tightly. Bright lights were flashing at the edge of her vision.

"Well, she has left and I doubt she will need you for a while," he said, strolling forwards. Then he said more seriously, "Are you unwell, ma'am?"

Beth swayed slightly, or perhaps the world really did tilt. "I think I am," she said. "My head . . ."

She was swung up into strong arms and hazily heard crisp orders. After a little while she was put down on a soft bed in a darkened room. Her bonnet was removed and someone put a

114

wonderful cool cloth on her forehead. She was moved slightly and fingers started to undo the buttons on the back of her gown. She opened alarmed eyes but found her attendant was a middle-aged maid, who murmured soothingly.

Beth saw Mr. Verderan over near the door. "Time for me to leave, ma'am," he said. "I hope you are soon feeling more the thing."

Beth tried to thank him but only the word *angel* came out.

He laughed softly. "Don't place any dependence on it," he said and left.

The maid stripped Beth down to her chemise and gave her a dose of laudanum. Beth tried to worry about Sophie and what she might be up to, but she could only welcome the creeping oblivion when it came.

Jago Haines, Lady Hever's trusted servant, trotted his dun cob along the road whistling a contented little tune. Ten thousand pounds Lady Hever had offered for the killing of Lord Randal Ashby and it seemed finally it was as good as his.

Down at the Three Bells in Setterby he'd struck up an acquaintance with the head groom at the Towers, Mick Zoun. Today he'd taken up Mick's invite to look over the horseflesh there and who should come wandering into the stableyard calling for his favourite mount than Lord Randal Bloody Ashby himself.

Very obligingly, the young rip had chatted to his groom, telling him his plans. Off to a quiet spot on the river to fish, was he? Then that was the place for Jago Haines too.

Just lately he'd been cursing himself for a fool for not taking his chance when the young lordling and his friend had been out with their guns. He'd spotted them and followed, trying to decide what best to do. As they were walking back to the big house he'd had the libertine in his sights as clear as a blackbird in the snow but he'd held his fire. Lady Hever wanted it to look like an accident and that would make his own escape simpler, too.

He was ready to give up on the accident idea, though. What sort of accident does a healthy young nob have? If he'd go swimming maybe Jago could drown him; if he'd stand at the edge of a cliff he could push him. Beyond that, nothing came to mind.

Now, however, things were definitely looking up. For the first time Ashby was away from the house alone. An 'accident' might still be possible and if not Jago would just kill him and make himself scarce. Round here he was Mr. Squires, with red hair and an old-fashioned way of dressing. Give him an hour's start and he'd be clear for sure.

"Something tells me," he said to himself, "it's a funeral not a wedding they'll be having round here next week. And a nice little party for the Haines family, to celebrate."

He turned his horse off towards the river, planning the use of ten thousand pounds.

Sophie cantered along the well-known paths until she was close to the bend in the river that had always been known as the Magic Pool. There were all kinds of stories to account for the name but the unromantic boys such as David and Randal said it was because one could always find fish there, even in the most unpromising weather. For Sophie the name reminded her that this was the spot where she had first realised her love for Randal.

She tethered her horse a good distance away, intending to creep up on her beloved. Apart from anything else, she had few illusions about men and knew he would be annoyed if she scared the fish. She picked her way carefully along a rough path until she saw him.

He was standing on the stony edge of the river, with his creel nearby. He had stripped off his coat, waistcoat, and cravat and looked utterly wonderful in a white shirt, buckskins, and boots. His golden hair was curling wildly in the humid heat. He was lazily flicking a fly over the water but she suspected his mind wasn't on the angling. The heavy weather made it unlikely he'd hook anything, even at the Magic Pool.

With a smile she moved back a little and managed to get out of her boots unaided. She stripped off her stockings and discarded her hat also. She wished she had the nerve to take off her habit as well—for even though it was a summer one it was devilishly hot—but she wasn't at all sure what Randal would do if she went down to him in her shift. Probably not what she wanted him to. She compromised and removed the short spencer jacket, revealing a light lawn bodice.

Picking up her trailing blue skirt she ran swiftly down the slope to where he stood.

He was deep in thought and only turned at the last moment to catch her before she ran into the water.

"Sophie?" he gasped as he staggered.

"Who else?" she asked, taking a firm grip on his shirt so he couldn't escape. "And don't go dashing off. I've not come to torment you. I've just discovered what's really been going on."

He gently loosened her fingers from his shirt and she permitted it. He didn't seem to be preparing for flight.

"Going on?" he asked, stooping to pick up his rod. He began to wind in his line.

Sophie allowed herself a brief adoration of his profile and then forced herself to look away. She had to keep this light, at least for a while. She picked up a smooth round stone, tested the feel of it, then skimmed it over the flat water. "Five," she said triumphantly. "David made you think you had to be the very image of propriety to prove something to him, didn't he, Randal?"

He laid the rod down and turned to face her. "Did he? He only echoed something in my own mind, Sophie."

"And what was that?" she asked, shocked by his serious tone. When she'd finally got it all worked out was he going to start expressing doubts?

He broke eye contact and crouched down to search the stones. "I find it hard to believe I'm good enough, Sophie, strong enough . . . David's right to have doubts. I've played games all my life. I don't even manage my own estates. I let Chelmly do it and just pocket the proceeds. I've always done just what I wanted, satisfied every whim . . ."

He found a stone to suit him and stood to face her. "You've made me see life isn't just games, Sophie, but I don't know if I'm any good at anything else. I know my fatal charm. I did my best to protect you from it." He looked down at the smooth brown pebble, turning it in his beautiful long fingers. "I couldn't let you bind yourself to me unless I was sure I could hold you safe. Perhaps in spite of yourself," he added wryly and turned to spin the stone hard out over the water.

"Seven," he said.

She'd made him see . . . Was he saying he just wanted to play games and viewed her as an end of all that? "Randal," said Sophie desperately. "You don't have to pretend to be noble. If you don't want to marry me just say so and . . ." She grasped her courage, ". . . and we'll go on as we always have done. We'll be friends."

He turned sharply to face her and his eyes seemed to flash blue. "Friends! Sophie, we can never be friends again."

"Why not?" she wailed.

He grasped her shoulders, stiff armed, as if he were holding her away. "Because if I can't touch you," he said desperately, "I'll go mad. And touching isn't enough." Looking straight into her eyes he said, "And if another man ever touched you I'd kill him."

Swallowing, Sophie pushed away the memory of Verderan. She had what she'd sought. Randal wanted her as desperately as she wanted him. Strangely, she found herself nervous—aware of a dangerous force she might not be able to control.

"Can't we be friends and lovers too?" she asked wistfully. "I like playing games."

His grip relaxed a little and he drew her against his body with what sounded like a groan. She could feel the heat of him through two thin layers of cloth and spread her hand on his chest to drink in the wonder of it.

"Perhaps we can," he said softly against her ear. She could feel his fingers working gently at the back of her neck, stroking, cherishing. "But not *just* friends, Sophie. Never that. I've had a summer of that and it's unendurable."

There was honest desperation in his voice. Sophie looked up with a triumphant smile. "Is it over then? The testing time?" she asked. Those fingers were sending singing promises down her spine. She needed, desperately, to be kissed as he'd kissed her at the fair. And for a great deal longer.

He set her sharply away from him, tempering it with a grin. "No, it isn't, minx. Not until next Wednesday." He bent and chose a pebble, passing it to her. "Try and beat my score. You used to be better than that—" He broke off at the sound of a horse approaching.

118

They looked at each other, alarmed, but then laughed. "Even if they think this is improper," said Sophie with a twinkle, raising her skirt to expose her bare ankles, "all they can do is make us get married."

The Marquis of Chelmly came upon a scene of hilarity, leading his horse.

"Randal. Oh good," he said, not appearing to find Sophie's presence, barefoot and bareheaded, of any consequence. "Duke's cast a shoe and I have an important meeting over at Radely. I saw Major back there. Can I take him?"

"Certainly," said Randal. "I'll walk Duke back."

"Thank you." The marquess frowned at Sophie. "There are some sharp stones here, you know. You should be more careful." Then he turned and left. Sophie and Randal started laughing again.

"When his mind's on business," said Randal, "I don't suppose he'd notice a full-fledged orgy."

The word dropped into the sultry air and swam there invitingly. With regret, Sophie realised it wasn't going to lead to appropriate action. Well, this moment was too precious to risk by pushing him.

She turned to the water with her chosen stone. "You challenged me," she reminded him. "What do I get if I beat your score then, my lord?"

He'd gone to lounge against a large, smooth rock, his long strong legs stretched out, his sweat-damp shirt clinging to his torso. All gold and white and splendid. "A kiss," he said softly.

Sophie felt her heart hesitate then start a mad dance. "A proper one?" she enquired breathlessly.

He smiled in a way that raised the temperature a great many degrees. "No, my little flame. A very improper one."

With a little sucked-in breath Sophie turned away from the vision he presented and licked her lips. She fingered the smooth stone and eyed the water. She felt as if this were the most important stone throw of her life. She remembered Randal first teaching her this skill when she'd been about ten—she'd lost a tooth that day and dropped it. He'd hunted amongst the rocks until he found it. It's all in the wrist, he'd told her.

She flexed her wrist a couple of times. With a sinuous flick she skimmed the stone and counted, breath held.

One bounce, two, three, four, five, six, seven . . . eight.

She turned to him in triumph.

They looked at each other across the small, pebbly beach, and Sophie could swear the world held its breath.

"Come here, then," he said softly.

Sophie felt strangely shy and unsteady as she walked over the sandy stones towards him. He held out a hand and she put hers trustingly into it. He drew her to stand between his legs and rested his hands on her slim hips. It seemed the only thing to do was to lay her hands on his shoulders, sleekly muscled under the damp, fine lawn of his shirt.

She could see in his darkened eyes, feel in his hands that he desired her. With helpless impatience at herself Sophie knew even this wasn't enough. Men desired all kinds of women. He'd desired many others in the past and she didn't want to be just another such. He hadn't wanted to marry any of them. Did he truly want to marry her?

She couldn't find the courage to ask. She wanted this kiss. If, despite her hopes, it all went wrong and she had to set him free, she had to have something to remember it all by.

"Why the sudden capitulation?" she asked, her fingers kneading his shoulders with a will of their own.

"Well," he said in a light tone which was belied by the expression in his eyes, "I've been used to considering Chelmly the epitome of virtue and if he wasn't shocked . . ." He pulled her a little tighter to his body and slid her down so she was sitting on one of his legs.

"But his mind was on business," she said lightly to cover her nervousness. Her mind might be nervous but her fingers seemed to have a boldness all their own and were playing amongst the damp edges of his silky hair. "You're hot," she said to fill a silence.

"Extremely," he responded with a thread of humour. One of his hands came to rest burningly against the side of her face and his thumb played against the corner of her mouth.

Sophie knew little of kisses but she mistrusted this hesitation.

Was he going to renege? "You're very slow to pay your debts, my lord," she said tartly.

With a little laugh he pulled her forwards and set his lips to hers. They were soft and gentle, unlike Verderan's . . . Sophie twined herself around him, feeling a magic sweep into her, expanding her and rendering her insubstantial as if she were a bubble floating. And yet she was safe in the cradle of his strong arms.

His tongue teased her lips. The thumb of the hand that cradled her face rubbed softly down her jaw, gently urging her mouth to open to him. For one moment she remembered Verderan and stiffened, but this was Randal and this was wonderful. She welcomed his tongue completely and the soft, tantalizing movements it was making. The taste of him was delicious—hot and spicy. She was fevered and aching but it was the sweetest fever she had ever known.

He pulled his lips away and held her close, crushingly close, burning with a heat that had nothing to do with a summer's day. She heard his ragged breathing and felt the beating of his heart, faster even than her own.

Sophie grasped her courage. "Randal, do you really, really love me?"

He looked at her, dazed. "What?"

"Do you? I have to know. I know you . . . you *want* me, but men can desire women without loving them . . ." She fell to her knees between his legs, pressed hard against him and reached up her hands to frame his face. "Tell me you love me as much as I love you!"

He stopped breathing and stiffened.

"Damnation, Sophie!" he said and pushed her away. He strode to the water's edge. He kneeled and scooped up water to drench his head. For a moment he held his wet hands pressed against his face. Crouched down on the rocky ground Sophie felt herself shrivel. Why hadn't she been able to take the hunger if that was all there was?

He turned, dripping and looking slightly desperate. "How can you ask me that? Sophie, what I feel for you—"

He was cut off by the terrible screaming cry of an injured horse.

"Chelmly!" Randal said and set off at a run.

Sophie ran after him, her trailing skirts and bare feet constantly in her way. She found Randal kneeling by the still figure of his brother while his beautiful grey gelding thrashed in agony nearby. She fell to her knees by his side.

"How bad is it?" she asked.

"I don't know," he gasped. "Bad. He's hit his head. Look to him, Sophie, while I tend to Major."

There was blood on the back of the marquess's head and his skin was pale and clammy, even in the heat. His breathing was shallow and ragged. An icy chill crept into her then she jumped as a shot brought stillness to the woods.

Randal came back, almost as white as his brother, as she supposed she must be. They looked at one another and no words were needed. They clasped hands briefly.

"I'll get help," said Sophie. She wanted to do or say more but there was nothing to the purpose to say or do. She hitched her skirts up high and sprinted back down the path to where she had left her mare. She didn't bother with her boots, hat, or jacket but hauled herself into the saddle and took off at a gallop towards the Towers.

Half an hour later she watched as the cart rolled up to the Towers with Chelmly flat out on a mattress in the back and Randal, still in his shirtsleeves, walking beside. The marquess had not regained consciousness but at least he still lived for Randal was watching his brother as if his very concentration could keep him breathing.

By the time Chelmly was in his bed the doctor had arrived and a large part of the household hovered nearby, whispering anxiously. Sophie wanted to be with Randal but he was in Chelmly's quarters with the doctor. She felt herself shiver despite the dreadful heat and when Verderan put an arm around her she leant gratefully against him.

"It must have been a terrible blow to keep him unconscious so long," she said anxiously.

"I've known people lose their wits for hours and still pull through," Verderan said.

It was kind of him to try to keep her spirits up, but Sophie looked over to where the dowager duchess was sitting in a chair, looking grey and very old and could not feel hopeful. Chloe Stanforth was beside her, holding her hand. Justin stood nearby. Everyone eyed the door to the marquess's suite as if they could see through the oak. No one looked optimistic.

"What of the duke?" Sophie asked Verderan.

"This is his rest time," he replied quietly. "The dowager decided not to wake him until there is some news. The shock . . ."

The shock could kill him, Sophie supplied and another kind of horror crept around her. If Chelmly died, Randal would be the heir to the dukedom of Tyne. She looked around wildly and all she could see was the wealth and power and dignity of it all. The weight, the substance of it, seemed to press down on her soul bringing blackness . . .

She came to her senses in a chair. She felt dizzy and slightly nauseated, and hopelessly feeble to be giving way at such a time.

"I'm going to carry you to a bed," said Verderan.

"Randal . . ." protested Sophie faintly.

"You will be more help to him rested, Sophie."

He swung her up into his arms and carried her away and she didn't resist. At the moment she would be nothing but a burden to Randal.

Verderan left while a maid stripped off her habit and wiped her face and hands with a cool cloth. Perhaps most of her weakness was just the devilish heat . . . but Randal must be as hot and she was deserting him.

Verderan came back and put a glass to her lips.

"I don't need anything," she said but he tipped it down her throat and spluttering, she swallowed it, recognising the bitter taste of laudanum.

"I can't sleep now," she protested.

"Yes, you can," he said. "I'll look after him for you but you must be ready to support him soon, Sophie. If the worst happens, you will have to be strong."

"But I'm not strong," Sophie said muzzily. "I'm a games player too . . ."

"The only way to play games, Sophie, is to win."

He watched while she drifted into sleep then took a moment

to stand looking out of the window, oblivious to the maid taking a watchful seat near the bed.

Verderan recognised the dimension of the tragedy which could befall the Ashbys, befall Randal and Sophie. He had little thought for Chelmly whom he had always thought of as a dull fellow, aware that the dull fellow disliked him intensely; but Chelmly ran the Duchy of Tyne and he stood between Randal and the dukedom. When they were young this had meant Chelmly had been raised to work and responsibility while Randal was encouraged to play, to do anything he wished as long as he didn't cast an envious eye on his brother's expectations.

Verderan looked suddenly at Sophie. Was that what she had meant by being a "games player"? It was either a very perceptive remark or the result of a recent conversation.

Randal hadn't had to be forced into the role, of course. His volatile temperament was suited to the search for the new, to the accepting of purposeless challenges. Had his antipathy to responsibility been inborn, however, or carefully fostered by his father? The duke's younger brother, Lord William, had apparently lusted after the title and honours and it had soured the family. The duke had done his best to avoid the same problem in his own family and had, perhaps, succeeded all too well.

If Chelmly died, would Randal be able to change? Would Sophie, another games player by her own admission, be a help or a hindrance? Before this morning's conversation Verderan would have had little hope but now he thought the young woman on the bed had surprising and untested qualities.

He hoped Randal had too.

=== 11 ===

SOPHIE AWOKE IN a darkened room, confused as to how she came there. In an instant, however, memory returned. The sick misery came with it but not, thank God, the panic.

She sat up slowly, feeling dizzy. The feeling would pass. It was still suffocatingly hot. A window stood open but no breath of air came in to refresh.

A maid rose to her feet and came forward. "Would you like some lemonade, milady. I have some here, still cool."

"Yes, please." Sophie drank gratefully and her mouth began to feel less disgusting.

She was in her chemise. She remembered Verderan. He had been kind and he had said Randal would need her.

She didn't want to even put the question but forced it out. "Is there any news of the marquess?"

"There's no change, milády," said the maid soberly.

No news was good news, Sophie told herself, but still she felt reluctant to leave the sanctuary of this room. Demands could be made of her, demands she was not sure she was able to meet. She needed Randal like she needed cool breezes and soft rain but that wasn't possible. If Chelmly had not recovered, if he was worse, Randal needed her more. But he needed her strong. Better to hide here like a coward than to emerge just to put new burdens upon him.

Resolutely she got out of the bed, stretched, and moved around until she felt more the thing. She drank some more of the lemonade and realised she had eaten no breakfast before dashing off to find Verderan and Randal.

Planning carefully, she sent the maid to fetch quick, simple food, some footwear, and the news.

Sophie dressed in her habit, wondering when she would see her boots, stockings, hat, and jacket again, and what people would think when they were found. She didn't really care but it brought back memories of that kiss. That wonderful kiss and then his anger. Why had he been angry? What had he said? "What I feel for you . . ." What had he been going to say?

All such thoughts seemed irrelevant now with Chelmly in such straits. If the wound proved fatal, Randal's days of carefree adventuring were numbered, married or not. *If* the wound proved fatal . . .

She went to the window. Despite the heat, there was a darkening heaviness to the sky. They were surely building to a storm. She wished it would come, and quickly. Perhaps if it was cooler she could think more clearly.

The smooth croquet lawn was below this window, surrounded by herbaceous borders. Beyond was part of the kitchen garden and she could see one of the orchards. She thought with dread of the succession houses, the fish ponds, the formal gardens and the wilderness . . . It was no different than Stenby, she told herself.

But she had never thought to run Stenby. In fact she remembered teasing Jane about having to undertake such a horrible task. She and Randal had planned to live at the small manor of Fairmeadows, and have a neat house in London. They had been going to travel. Even if he couldn't fight with the army they could travel to Greece, to the Americas, to look for hippopotami in Africa . . .

She pulled herself out of the black thoughts. Chelmly was not dead. He would not die. It wasn't possible. But the picture of the marquess, so still and pale, rose up to argue against her. He could and that would signal a terrible change in all their lives.

When the maid returned, Sophie realised she had tears running down her face and no handkerchief. She wiped them with her fingers.

"It's all right," said the maid anxiously. "There's no change.

Lord Chelmly is holding his own."

The girl laid out a simple meal. Sophie looked at the food with distaste, seeing nothing she could face but then she disciplined herself. If she didn't eat she'd probably faint again and that wasn't going to make Randal's life any easier.

She took up two slices of bread and butter and slapped some chicken between them. She poured herself some tea and managed to wash down about half the food. It was all she could manage.

She stood and put on the slippers the maid had found. They were a little large but once she had tied the laces she knew they would do. In the mirror she thought she looked a wreck but doubted anyone would care today. She also looked pale and almost haggard. She splashed water from the bowl over her face and rubbed at her cheeks. It helped a little, but not much.

At last she ventured out. Was it her imagination that the Towers was ominously silent? It had not been a lively house for years but now the ticking of clocks was the only sound. She walked along deserted corridors and down to the main hall.

A footman was on duty there.

"Do you know where Lord Randal is?" she asked.

"He is in the Adams Room with the doctor, milady," he replied in a muted voice. Sophie could tell there had been no good report of Chelmly's state in the last little while.

Dreading the news she might hear, she went to the cool blue and white room. The doctor and Randal stood talking together near the empty grate. Randal had still not found time to dress and was in his open-necked shirt. A smear of dried blood ran down the sleeve. His features were as pale as the bleached linen.

He sensed her and turned. It was not welcome she saw on his face, or even relief that she was all right. She was another, and distracting strain. Even through her sick misery his strange expression pierced her, and she raised a hand as if to ward off a blow. He had already turned away. Verderan was in the room, standing away from Randal and the doctor, and he came swiftly over to her.

"Chelmly has not recovered consciousness and the doctor fears the worst," he said softly. "The duke has taken it quite well but his health too is a matter for concern. Everything is falling on Randal's shoulders. Are you recovered?"

"As much as possible," said Sophie from an aching throat. "Should I go?" she asked hesitantly.

"No," he said and took her hand firmly. "Of course not. He is bewildered. Too many things are coming at him at once. Just be here."

In a few minutes the doctor bowed and took his leave to go back upstairs to the duke. Randal just stood, staring at nothing.

Verderan and Sophie shared a concerned look and then Sophie took matters into her own hands. She walked forwards and grasped his arm. "What can we do?" she asked.

He looked down at her with a slight frown, but she saw it was bewilderment not rejection. After a moment his expression lightened slightly and he slipped an arm around her and pulled her to him with a sigh.

"Did you hear he's no better?" he asked softly and she nodded.

"Killigrew says he could die at any minute. I can still hardly believe it," he said. "We spoke to him there only minutes before . . ."

"He won't die, Randal," said Sophie, trying to sound certain but hearing her own desperation. "He's always been so strong and healthy. He'll pull through."

"I pray to God," said Randal with a sigh. Without letting go of her he shifted slightly and said, "Ver?" The Dark Angel came over.

"The doctor suspects foul play," Randal said baldly.

Sophie pulled back. "What? But it was a fall from his horse. We were there."

Randal released her and moved restlessly about the room. "Not quite. We got there soon after. Dr. Killigrew says such a head wound could only have been caused by a severe blow from a hard object. Did *you* see any rocks on that path?"

Sophie thought back. It was a dry sandy bridle path and she had noticed no rocks near Chelmly's head. She shook her head.

"Nor did I," said Randal and turned to his friend. "Ver, will you take Justin and go and check? See what there is to be found."

The Dark Angel left swiftly.

Randal turned to face Sophie with a slight bitter smile. "Well, how do you feel about the prospect of being a marchioness?"

"Not too wonderful," she admitted, "but I'll manage, I suppose. Besides, whatever happens I am unlikely to come to that for some time. We can't have the wedding now."

He looked at her sharply. "Yes, we can. This business has brought my father's concern over the succession to fever pitch. The only thing that will hold him together is a grandson."

"With the best will in the world," said Sophie, "that's nine months from now, Randal. A month or so delay will not matter. We can hardly be married with Chelmly at death's door."

"Yes, we can," he said tersely, "though it will have to be a simple affair. I'm sorry you'll have to do without the celebrations but that way we can get it over with."

"Get it over with..." He made it sound like something terrible—a whipping or a tooth-drawing. She couldn't handle this now. "Randal, I don't care about the bridesmaids and dancing but—"

"Good," he said sharply. "Just you and me, Sophie. That's all that matters." It could have been a moving declaration except for the tone.

Sophie forced herself not to squabble with him. She went over to take his fidgeting hand but was arrested when she saw the ring on it. It was heavy gold set with a large piece of obsidian carved with the arms of the Ashby's—the ducal seal which Chelmly always wore.

He followed her eyes. "Disgusting, isn't it? My father took it off Chelmly's hand and forced me to wear it as if he was already dead—" A scratch at the door interrupted him and they turned to see the marquess's secretary, Mr. Tyler. Sophie could see that the sandy-haired man had been crying.

"Yes, Tyler?" said Randal wearily.

"I have prepared the list of those who must be notified of the marquess's condition, my lord. Would you care to scrutinize it?"

Randal waved him away. "No. I'm sure you know better than I who should be told." When the man had left he turned to Sophie. "We'll have to send out couriers to stop the guests from coming to the wedding. Just the family here will attend and we'll have to stay here afterwards, Sophie. I have to look after the duchy for him . . ."

Sophie remembered their tryst for the twenty-eighth at Fair-meadows in the big front bedroom overlooking the rose garden. Oh God, why did such things matter? It was just she and Randal that mattered, as he had said. "If you want it that way, Randal, it will be so. But think on it a bit more," she asked.

"Very well," he said, clearly with little intention of doing so.

Another scratch at the door brought Willerby, the Groom of the Chambers. "Your pardon, my lord, but there is a man here to collect documents the marquess was to have prepared. He says they are of importance."

Randal made an impatient movement but then said, "Put him somewhere and send Mr. Tyler to see what it's all about."

He turned away and ran his fingers through his hair. "I haven't had a moment . . ." he said distractedly. "Can no one do anything without my word?"

"They are as disordered as you are Randal," she said, soothing his hands down from his face. She drew him to a sofa and sat, holding his hand. "I know you don't want all this," she said, "but you have the ability to run the duchy." She tentatively tried for a little humour. "Chelmly will be awfully cross if you let the place go to wrack and ruin."

He gave a slight laugh but then leapt to his feet to wander the room again. "He has no enemies. The doctor suggested a disaf-fected tenant or even a radical but it seems absurd. Who would want to hurt Chelmly?" He stopped dead. "Oh God, Sophie," he whispered. "If he dies, how am I going to cope?"

Before she could try to find an answer, Mr. Tyler was there reporting dryly on an investment which had been planned in a shipping enterprise and the documents which needed to be signed. As the matter was technically business of the estate and not personal to the marquess, he related, Randal could sign.

"Does my father know anything about this?" asked Randal helplessly.

"Only the bare bones, my lord. He does not entirely approve of mercantile ventures."

After a moment Randal said, "Get the man and I'll come and

go over it all with you." He turned to Sophie. "This place is Bedlam. It would be best if you went back to Stenby for now, Sophie. Mrs. Hawley is here with the carriage and I would like you to ride back in it with her."

"Mrs. Hawley?"

"She came seeking you earlier and was overtaken by a sick headache."

"Oh. But I can ride back."

"I'd rather you didn't. If there's a madman about I want you safe. I'll send a pair of armed grooms as well."

He was already moving away and it seemed to Sophie it was mental as well as physical. She was losing him in some way. "When will I see you again?" she asked desperately. "Shall I come over tomorrow?"

He shrugged. "If you wish but it will probably be even worse by then." He turned and left.

Sophie pressed her hands to her face, seeking the strength she needed. It was all very well to understand the pressures which were besetting her beloved, but it didn't make it any easier to handle the fact that he seemed almost a stranger. She had to believe that even if the worst should happen and Randal became the heir to the dukedom the ease would return, the humour come back into life.

Meanwhile it was for her to help as best she could.

She took a decision and sent for Willerby. She noted that despite his stately manner the man was distressed. She supposed the whole household was in a state of turmoil.

"Willerby," she said, "I understand this is a considerable shock to everyone and that you look to Lord Randal to take care of everything. But you mustn't overload him, Willerby."

She saw the man absorb her words. "I see, milady."

"You, Mr. Tyler, Mr. Sedgewick and Mrs. Young must be able to run this place with your eyes closed. Do so. Don't come to him for every little thing."

He bowed. "I understand perfectly, milady. Thank you."

Sophie hoped that would give her beloved a little respite. She went off to find Mrs. Hawley.

A few hours rest had largely dispelled Beth's sickness but she was shocked to see how pale and drawn Sophie looked. It was not unexpected, of course. It was just that Sophie had always seemed a golden child, untouchable by life's harsher winds.

"Oh Sophie," she said. "This must all have been terrible for you." She opened her arms and the girl came into them.

"We were just speaking to him," she said. "And then that happened. And now he might die, Beth. It's not fair!"

Beth tightened her arms, remembering her husband. He'd been a naval officer and had courted death in his profession, but she had never expected him to die. He'd been young and he'd enjoyed life so.

There was nothing adequate to say and so she said the inadequate. "Accidents do happen, my dear."

"It wasn't an accident," said Sophie flatly, pulling away. Tears rolled down her face and she sniffed. "Oh Beth, do you have a handkerchief?"

Beth provided one. "What do you mean, it wasn't an accident?"

Sophie blew her nose. "The doctor thinks someone attacked Chelmly, deliberately tried to kill him."

Beth sat down abruptly in a chair. "It's not possible."

Sophie shrugged. "It happened. Randal wants me to return to Stenby in the carriage and he's sending outriders. It's all quite outlandish, isn't it?"

Beth thought it certainly was and those strange notes came into her mind. But what possible connection could there be between demented notes to Sophie about her marriage and an attack on the Marquess of Chelmly?

As they were preparing to climb into the carriage, Chloe Stanforth came hurrying over with her son in her arms and his nursemaid in tow.

"Sophie," she said breathlessly. "Can you take Stevie and Rosie to Stenby? This is no place for a child and his happy nature is out of order with Chelmly so ill."

Perhaps sensitive to atmosphere, Stevie was sucking his thumb and clinging to his mother's gown looking solemn. Sophie looked at Beth for guidance. Beth could not imagine Jane refusing such a request and nodded.

"Of course," Sophie said and the maid took the child into the carriage.

"Thank you," said Chloe, brushing damp hair distractedly off her face. "This is the most terrible thing . . . I can't believe it. I will send a groom over with some of Stevie's toys and clothes." She looked at Sophie closely for the first time. "I'm so sorry about your wedding," she said.

"Randal wants it to go ahead," Sophie said.

"Next Wednesday! But what if Chelmly should . . ." Chloe stopped herself from uttering the dreaded word. "And why not," she said resolutely. "Whatever happens, Randal needs you more than ever now. Take care of Stevie for me, Sophie, please. I would go with him but I am concerned for Grandmama."

With that she hurried off and Sophie and Beth mounted the steps. "Do you too think it shocking?" Sophie asked Beth a little defiantly.

"To carry on with the wedding?" Beth responded. "I think no purpose would be served by delay, Sophie, and Lord Chelmly would be the first to say so. At times like these we must sometimes go against convention to find the true path."

As she said it, Beth thought of herself and Sir Marius. Did she have the courage to follow her own advice?

Randal was with Chloe and his grandmother when Justin Delamere and Verderan returned from their investigations. He crossed the room halfway to meet them and Verderan placed a turnip-size rock in his hands. It showed damp earth on one side and blood on the other.

"In the path?" asked Randal.

"No," said Justin. "There was a trail of someone leaving the scene and the rock was off there to one side, as if thrown away. It was a planned attack, Randal."

Randal looked down at the rock blankly. "But why?"

"There's no way of knowing yet. But we found something else."

"What?"

"There's a mark on a tree there," said Justin. "A rope was stretched across the path to trip the horse. When Chelmly fell someone tried to finish him off with that."

Even Verderan made a slight movement of protest at this blunt telling. One remembered that Justin Delamere had been a soldier in the thick of the Peninsular War and was no stranger to violence.

"How is he?" asked Justin soberly. "Will he pull through?"

Randal gave a slight gesture of helplessness. "There's no way to tell," he said. "He just lies there. Killigrew refuses to give up hope but even he has to admit that the longer he is unconscious, the worse it looks." He looked down at the blood-stained rock and his hand tightened on it. "I want the man responsible. Come."

He went as if to leave the room but the autocratic voice of his grandmother stopped him. "Randal," said the dowager duchess. "Come here with whatever that is."

After the briefest hesitation he obeyed.

The dowager's eyes took in the stone and needed no explanation. "How could anyone!" she demanded in broken outrage. "How could anyone? Chelmly has never injured anyone."

Chloe Stanforth leant over and put a hand over the older woman's. "They'll find the villain, Grandmama," she said softly and looked up at the three men; her husband, her cousin, and the Dark Angel whom she didn't trust but believed capable of almost anything. "Won't you?"

"Yes," said Randal, "we will."

Men were sent out to search, others to alert all nearby villages, inns and coaching houses. Assistance was called for from the military at Shrewsbury and a Bow Street Runner was summoned from London. Randal, fretting, was left to care for the Towers and support his father while Justin and Verderan rode out to personally supervise matters. Soon David and Marius, alerted by Sophie's recounting of affairs, were assisting.

Sophie and Beth arrived back at Stenby to find Jane already frantically undoing all the complex arrangements for the grand wedding. She accepted the arrival of Master Delamere as a minor inconvenience and arranged for his quartering. This was helped by the fact that the child had fallen asleep on the journey.

"Though a sweet enough child," Jane commented, "he seems to attract trouble."

Beth was surprised to find that Sophie was determined to start learning to run a great house but saw immediately why. She had always thought the girl more capable than she seemed and in her response to impending tragedy, she was showing it. Sophie changed out of her bedraggled habit into her most plain and functional gown and set herself to work. Beth hoped Sophie would never be the Marchioness of Chelmly but she saw no harm in the girl learning management and there was no better prescription for her at the moment than employment.

Three staff members with neat hands had been set to writing the notes to inform the wedding guests of the unfortunate circumstances and the curtailment of the ceremony. Beth and Sophie took the task of supervising and checking these notes against a master list. After a little while, however, Beth saw that this job was hard for Sophie. It focused on the marquess's injury and gave too much time to think. She asked Jane if she had a more active task available.

"Someone should go to the village," Jane said, "and cancel all the orders. It is more suited to a servant but . . ."

Beth shook her head. "They would want to talk about the accident and Sophie needs to get her mind off her problems for a while."

Jane and Beth reviewed all that needed to be done but all the tasks were reminders of the disastrous circumstances and most were administrative. Then one thing came to mind.

"I just remembered. Would you believe that in the middle of all this our mysterious invalid has recovered her memory? She's a Mrs. Haven from over Stone Way. She doesn't know why she was coming to Stenby except that she has been ill since a death in the family. She remembers leaving her coach and servants at Market Drayton and so a message was sent there this morning. Unless she is suffering from delusions, her people should come to collect her tomorrow. Not that we need the space anymore," she added helplessly.

After a moment she pulled herself together. "Mrs. Haven asked to see Sophie before she left," said Jane. "Why don't you suggest that she does that to make sure the woman has all the help she needs to take her leave."

Beth passed on this suggestion and saw Sophie leave her boring task with alacrity.

When Sophie arrived at the small guest room, Mrs. Haven was up and dressed. In her pressed clothes, with her greying hair brushed under a neat laced-trimmed cap, she looked the picture of comfortable respectability. She was sitting by an open window watching the darkening sky and the growing wind but she turned with a smile as Sophie entered.

"How kind of you to come, Lady Sophie." There was something bright about the woman's expression for all it was framed in kindly goodwill. Unpleasantly bright. Sophie thought of the word *avid* or even *gleeful*. Well, why should the lady not be pleased to have her wits back and be set to go home?

Still, Sophie had to admit she couldn't like Mrs. Haven. The woman made her feel uncomfortable but she fought that unreasonable attitude.

She took a seat close to the lady. "I am happy you are feeling well and have remembered yourself, Mrs. Haven."

"Well, so am I, even though the Edith Haven I have remembered is not a happy woman. I was feeling such a burden on you all. I have felt like an interloper, and now I find I am. It is most peculiar. I cannot imagine what drove me here, unless it was that my dear husband and I came to public day here many years ago. It was a happier time."

"You had the newspaper report of my marriage," Sophie reminded her.

"Perhaps that is what put the idea into my mind." The woman's expression became solemn but there was still that glittering eagerness behind it, making Sophie uncomfortable. "I have heard sad news today, my dear," Mrs. Haven said. "May I hope it is untrue?"

"No, it is not untrue," said Sophie. "The Marquess of Chelmly has suffered an accident and is gravely ill."

"The marquess!" exclaimed Mrs. Haven and that gleefulness disappeared. But the woman turned quickly to look out of the window and Sophie felt she could have been mistaken.

"To whom did you think I referred, ma'am?"

"Forgive me," said the woman, looking back. Now she ap-

136

peared truly grieved and Sophie told herself that her earlier reading of the woman's countenance had been in error. "I had heard the injured man was the younger son, the one you are to marry."

Sophie stared. "I would hardly be here talking to you if Lord Randal lay at death's door, Mrs. Haven."

"No, I suppose you wouldn't," said the woman distractedly and looked away again, raising a thin hand to her head. Sophie wondered whether the blow to her head *had* addled her wits. Or perhaps she had always been unbalanced. She felt a distinct urge to flee this room.

Perhaps it was the storm that had created such a disturbance of her nerves. It was coming close and the room had darkened beyond comfortable sight. A sudden gust of wind sent the curtains flapping to knock over a vase. Sophie ran to latch the window and picked up the ornament. Chipped. It would have to go into the target-practice box.

She remembered that carefree evening and felt tears running down her cheeks.

Rain began to splatter the glass. The wind found a gap in the frame and set up a moan.

Sophie blew her nose and made it the opportunity to wipe away the tears. She turned back to the business in hand. The mysterious Mrs. Haven. "Do you perhaps know the marquess, ma'am?" asked Sophie. "You seemed concerned."

"No," said the woman, who had grown more haggard and pale during the interlude. She was clutching at the locket she wore around her neck. "No, of course not. I am a merchant's widow. I do not move in those circles." A flash of lightning made her start. "Pray tell me, what happened to the poor man?"

Sophie decided it was best not to refer to the suspicious aspects of the affair. "He fell from his horse," she said, "and struck his head."

Mrs. Haven looked piercingly at Sophie. "He was perhaps setting his horse at a fence?"

"No," said Sophie but she offered nothing more. Another, brighter flash of lightning lit the gloom, making the older woman's eyes appear wide with emotion. Shock? Alarm? Fear?

"Oh dear, oh dear," said Mrs. Haven. "Truly, in the midst of life are we all in death." Thunder rumbled long and low, closer now to the Towers. "But if he is so ill, your wedding will now be postponed, dear."

"No," said Sophie, looking out as another spear of lightning illumined the dark sky. "Randal wishes it to go ahead on the appointed day but in a simpler manner."

Mrs. Haven released the locket. "You cannot possibly agree to such a thing!"

The crack of thunder was so loud it made them both jump and Sophie rose to her feet, charged by the storm. "That is how he wishes it to be," she said. If Chelmly were to die Randal would need her as never before. She would give her life to ease his path. A hasty, simple wedding was no price at all to pay.

No price at all, in fact, if it meant they were married next week instead of extending their painful waiting. Good heavens, she thought, I must have caught propriety from him to have even considered a delay. Thank goodness he still had retained the common sense to override her.

She watched another flash of lightning and felt her spirits lift a little. Despite everything, they would soon be joined. And Chelmly was young and strong. He would surely recover.

Sophie loved storms. Once she and Randal had been caught in one and they'd run back to Stenby through the streaming rain with lightning and thunder all around, laughing at danger . . .

Mrs. Haven appeared beside her and took her hand. "Oh, my poor child. Do you need refuge? Would you like to come for a visit to my home for a while?"

Sophie came back to the present and dragged her hand out of that dry grasp. "What on earth are you talking about?"

"Oh dear," fluttered Mrs. Haven. "Please don't be angry, Lady Sophie. You have seemed so unhappy about this marriage and now it is being forced with such unseemly haste . . ." She broke off as a ground-shaking rumble of thunder went on and on.

What nonsense she was talking. Sophie had no intention of discussing her personal affairs further with this woman who was clearly unstable. Thank goodness Stenby would see the back of her tomorrow. She moved a few steps away and assumed the dignity of generations of Kyles. "Even if it was so, ma'am, I would hardly wish to run away with a stranger."

"Of course not. Of course not. I just . . ." The woman pressed boney fingers to her head. "Storms. I am afraid of storms. Draw the curtains please, my dear, lest the lightning come in!"

Sophie raised her brows at this unlikely notion but did as the woman asked. As soon as she did so, the storm seemed less a part of the atmosphere in the room and her earlier repugnance towards the woman appeared unreasonable.

Mrs. Haven resumed her seat. "Families are not always a comfort, Lady Sophie," she quietly. "As I know to my cost."

Sophie softened. The woman obviously had suffered in her life and had recently been ill. "My family is all it should be, Mrs. Haven."

"I am reassured then, my dear. As you know, I expect my people and my coach tomorrow. Could I ask that you take breakfast with me and bid me farewell? I have grown so fond of you while I have been here, as if you were the daughter I never had. Or is that too presumptuous, my lady?"

Faced with that, Sophie felt compelled to agree to see the woman off.

She was happy to escape, though, and find her favourite spot—a casement window in the old nursery of Stenby—from which to watch the passing of the storm. She opened the window wide, careless of what rain sprayed in and inhaled the cool, electrified air.

This turbulence was her element. Randal's too. Where was he? Would he be watching the storm approaching the Towers, or would he still be drowning in problems, both great and small? She wished she was with him. Even delaying the wedding until its appointed day now seemed insupportable when they needed each other so.

Perhaps they should run away. All those people—the managers, the stewards—they could earn their keep for once and set him free. She and Randal could elope to Scotland, then run off abroad for a long honeymoon. They could forget the Duchy of Tyne . . .

No matter how hard she tried she couldn't make it work.

Though they were games players, neither she nor Randal had missed the training in responsibility, the *noblesse oblige*. Before today there had been no obligations but now they were inescapable. Unless . . . *until*, she corrected firmly, Chelmly survived, the burden of the Duchy was Randal's to bear, and therefore hers.

It was for her to find ways to make the burden supportable for both of them. The storm began to lessen as it drifted west towards the Towers. Sophie remained at the window, chin on hand, making plans.

=12=

THE MEN WORKED hard all day, but by evening little had been achieved.

It had been discovered that there had been a stranger in the area recently. He had moved from village to village, claiming to be a servant looking for a house to lease for his master and mistress coming home from India. He had been the kind to spend time in the inns talking and had been interested in all the local goings-on. He'd shown no particular curiosity about the marquess or Tyne Towers, but he'd doubtless heard something about him as well as all the other local dignitaries. The man's name had apparently been Squires but he had left the Three Bells at Setterby the day before and not been seen since.

The head groom, Mick Zoun, nervously volunteered the information to Randal that he'd struck up a friendship with the man and that Squires had been in the stables that morning.

"But that was long after the marquess rode out, milord," he assured him. "Squires never showed any curiosity about him or anyone in particular. He looked over the horseflesh and shared a jug of ale, that's all. Then he went on his way. In no hurry at all as far as I could see. I'm sure he could never have had anything to do with such a black deed."

Still, Mr. Squires's name and description were sent out along the roads throughout England. But, as Randal pointed out bitterly, if he was innocent and came forward nothing would have been achieved. If he was guilty the name was surely false, his appearance would have been disguised, and he would have slipped out of the area already and be lost to them.

"But why?" asked Randal of the men as they sat in the library eating a late supper. "If this Squires is our villain he came here days ago and coldly planned to attack my brother. Why?"

"Perhaps," said Justin Delamere, with slight hesitation, "there is something about your brother you don't know."

"I've asked his secretary and his valet," said Randal flatly. "You know what Madame Cornuel is supposed to have said, 'No man is a hero to his valet.' Well, I don't know about hero but Chelmly is close to a saint. There's nothing. No peccadillos, no shady dealings, no gaming, no women . . . As you have all found out the people hereabouts are suitably grateful for prosperity, a caring hand, and an open ear. For heaven's sake," he said, surging to his feet, "if someone was out to kill me it would make more sense."

Through the open window there was a distant roll of thunder. The men all looked at one another.

"He was riding your horse," said Marius at last.

Randal looked around. "Chelmly was mistaken for me?" There was an edge of disbelieving horror in his voice.

"What about that note, Randal?" said Verderan.

"What note?" asked David, instantly alert.

Somewhat reluctantly, Randal produced the letter and the second one he hadn't even shown to Verderan. David pulled out the ones Sophie had received. They were all clearly in the same hand.

The earl leaned back thoughtfully. "He was riding your distinctive grey on the path you would take to get back to the Towers. Could Chelmly be expected to use that path today?"

"I don't know," said Randal. "It seems unlikely. He doesn't ride a circuit or anything. I'd guess that when his horse cast a shoe he headed back to the Towers by the shortest route. When he passed Major where I had him tethered in the shade he decided to ask if he could borrow him. But for heaven's sake. No one has any reason to attack me either."

"These notes mean we have to consider it," said David levelly. "There seems to be a connection to Sophie. Would anyone want to kill you just because you're marrying her? No, that's ridiculous.

Have you made any enemies recently?"

"You should know," said Randal with an edge, "that I've been on my best behaviour for months."

The earl didn't react to the statement. "Before then?"

"Before then was the Season and I spent the quietest couple of months in London I've ever known."

"Let's go back further, then," pursued his friend. "Have you injured anyone?"

"Physically?" snapped Randal. "There was that duel with Jessamy two years back but that was a silly business and I gave him the merest scratch. He doesn't hold it against me. And I haven't won anyone's fortune off them, nor have I stolen any wives, or debauched any daughters. God, I think I'm almost as saintly as Chelmly," he said, thrusting away from the table again. "I suppose *that* augurs well for the future."

"Randal," said Verderan firmly. "Don't fall apart now." He added lightly, "Perhaps our villain was really trying for me. I have enemies behind every bush."

Randal responded with a slight laugh. "But no one with sight could mistake us whereas Chelmly and I are superficially alike." His hand clenched and he pounded lightly against the back of a chair. "Without a motive, we're not going to catch him, are we, so we'll probably never know. And that," he said turning sharply, "I find totally insupportable."

"You've sent for a Runner," said Justin. "The word is out. If Squires shows his face around these parts again he'll be noticed."

But it wasn't very helpful and they all knew it. Randal picked up the letters and searched them again for clues, for hidden meanings. He threw them down in disgust.

He looked stretched tight, as if the slightest thing could snap him. Verderan took it upon himself to call for brandy with the express intention of getting his friend dead drunk.

The other men left Randal with Verderan and the brandy decanter and Randal needed little encouragement to down a number of glasses.

A finger played idly around the rim of his glass as he asked, "What odds would you give of Chelmly recovering, Ver?"

"Favourable," said Verderan firmly.

143

Randal looked up. The brandy was beginning to have its effect but his gaze was unwavering. "The truth, if you please."

Verderan rocked back in his chair then shrugged. "I'm no expert but I've seen more than my share of mayhem. It doesn't look good. I don't like him being out of it for so long but at least he is no worse."

Randal took another deep drink. "I've never valued him as I should. Now I'm faced with filling his shoes I'm in a funk."

"If it comes to that," said Verderan, "you will do as well as he."

Randal gave a short, disbelieving laugh.

Verderan took two large, strangely carved dice out of his pocket. "Very well," he said with a grin. "If you don't want it I'll play you for the dukedom."

"You're on," slurred his friend. "Loser takes all. What are these?" He lifted a die and inspected it under a branch of candles. "Good God. That's outrageous!"

Verderan smiled as he admired the other. "Isn't it. I got them from India. Indian women must be remarkably flexible . . . Perhaps I should try to get hold of one or two. I'll invite you—No, of course not."

"Of course not," said Randal frowning slightly. Verderan admonished himself to watch his tongue. He topped up Randal's glass.

"Do you know that silly chit asked me if I loved her?" Randal muttered, draining it.

"I hope you said yes."

"Of course I did! I told her—That was about the time we heard Major," he said, frowning over the puzzle again. "Do you think those notes had anything to do with it?" he asked.

Verderan realized the process of distracting Randal from his problems would not be easy. He ignored the question and quickly rolled the dice. "Seven," he said.

Randal sat down. "How the deuce do you tell?"

Verderan smiled. "You count the number of visible legs, of course. Are you on?"

"I'm on," said Randal with a grin. "By sunrise I'll have lost every last acre and stone to you."

By sunrise he was safe in his bed, deposited there tenderly by his still steady friend. Verderan took the precaution of forcing Randal to drink as much water as possible before letting him sleep. It was the best preventive for a hangover he knew and though a night's oblivion was prescribed, tomorrow Randal would once again be called on to run the Duchy of Tyne.

Beth was just collecting a candle to make her way up to bed, exhausted after her sickness and then long hours of work, when Sir Marius and Lord Wraybourne walked into the hall.

"Is there any news?" she asked quickly.

"No. Nothing new," said the earl. "Do you know where Jane is?"

"I believe she is in your study at the moment, my lord." The earl went swiftly off in that direction.

Beth and Sir Marius looked at each other in the gloom.

"I'm not going to apologise for last night," he said at last.

"You're not?"

He shook his head. "Now is hardly the time to pursue matters further, Elizabeth. But there are matters to be pursued. You look done in, my dear."

"So do you," she said, finding his rumpled tiredness overwhelmingly endearing.

He came over and brushed her tousled curls back from her brow. "Good-night, my dear."

Beth smiled. "Good-night."

Sophie had spent a restless, sleepless night and was heavy eyed and weary when she reluctantly kept her appointment to breakfast with Mrs. Haven. At least today would see the back of the uninvited guest.

"Sit down, my dear, and let me pour you a cup of tea," said the woman comfortably. "Such a day as you must have had yesterday and little sleep in the night what with the storm and your worries. Drink the tea and you will find it helps."

Sophie relaxed under the gentle fussing. "I didn't sleep very well," she admitted.

"And who could expect you to?" said Edith soothingly. "You are like me, one of the sensitive ones. We take things to heart."

Sophie had never thought of herself as sensitive before but she certainly felt fragile this morning. "Perhaps I wish we could turn the clock back," she said, mostly to herself.

"Ah yes, but it does no good to repine. The future must be faced with courage."

Sophie nodded. "You are right. It is not like me to wilt so."

"If you think of your love, your *true love*, it will strengthen you," said Edith with what seemed to be a genuine tremor in her voice.

"Yes," said Sophie, touched by this romantic feeling in such a dry old thing. "That is true."

The woman leant forwards. "I cannot leave without urging you once more, dear child, to resist this hasty marriage."

All Sophie's kinder feelings evaporated and she assumed an untypical hauteur. "We will not discuss it if you please. How long do you expect your journey to be, Mrs. Haven?"

Edith Hever accepted the rejection. She had not thought the girl could be stiffened to rebellion here in her family home. "About five hours, Lady Sophie, if the roads are not too muddy from the rain."

They discussed roads and travelling as they ate and Edith ran over her plan in her mind, her plan to kidnap Sophie. It would have been better if the girl had come willingly but if trickery was necessary, so be it.

When news was brought that Mrs. Haven's carriage had arrived, she gathered her things together, refusing to let Sophie call for a maid or footman.

Sophie led the way briskly through the passages, anxious to see the last of this unsettling visitor. She came to an abrupt halt at the sight of young Stevie sitting alone on a windowsill.

"Stevie!" she said with exasperation. "What are you doing here?"

He pointed out at Mrs. Haven's coach. "Watch horsey," he said.

"Where on earth is that flighty maid?" asked Sophie, looking around. There was no sign of the girl. Sophie sighed. "Well, young man," she said, "you'll have to come with us and have a closer look at the horses."

She prepared to lift the child down but Mrs. Haven intervened.

"Lady Sophie, do you think that wise? There is still some dampness in the air and children are so very delicate."

Sophie looked skeptically at the sturdy infant. "We can't leave him here," she said. At that moment, the problem was solved by the arrival of a flustered nurse-maid.

"Master Steven! You'll be the death of me, I swear you will!" She bobbed two hasty curtsies. "Begging your pardon, miladies. I only turned my back for an instant. Come with me, you naughty boy!"

The boy pulled back and said, "No." His face began to pucker.

"Well really!" said Mrs. Haven frostily.

Sophie said, "Oh, for heaven's sake. Let him stay and watch the horses, Rosie. I can't abide another screaming session."

Now it was the departing guest who chose to make difficulties. "It is most unwise to indulge children, Lady Sophie," said Mrs. Haven icily. She fixed the maid with a frosty eye. "You must take him back to his quarters immediately. And you," she said, looking at the child, "*will* obey."

Sophie watched his reaction with amazement. For once Stevie set up no objection. Instead, he moved, wide-eyed, to cling to Rosie's skirt. Perhaps they should hire Mrs. Haven to control the child. Then she put the notion out of her head. If Stevie was afraid of Mrs. Haven, she was not surprised. The woman made her feel as if caterpillars were down her back.

She turned to lead the way down the final flight of stairs. With a final commanding glare, Mrs. Haven followed.

Rosie watched her resentfully. "Nasty old trout," she muttered. "What right does she have, may I ask? Tell you what, Master Steven—if you're a *good* boy, you can stop and watch the horseys. How'd you like that?"

The boy nodded.

"Good. Now you stay low-like, so they won't spy you. I just have to collect the laundry basket. I'll be back in a tick." She took two steps and then looked back. "And if you move from this spot, Boney'll come and get you!"

With that she picked up her skirts and hurried off. Stevie turned to watch the coach and horses, resting his chin on the window sill. He saw the nasty old lady come out with her bag. A man stood ready by the coach and swung the door open. The lady stopped and spoke to him then climbed the steps. She turned and beckoned.

Auntie Sophie went close to the coach. She climbed the stairs to kiss the lady good-bye. Stevie was glad he didn't have to kiss the lady good-bye. Then Auntie Sophie sort of fell into the coach. The horses set off. The man swung up behind.

Stevie stretched up to watch the coach as long as he could. When it had disappeared he looked around. He thought about going up the stairs to see what was there. But it might be Boney. Boney had big teeth and claws.

He sat down on the stairs, stuck his thumb in his mouth, and waited for Rosie.

Sophie reached for the door handle. "What are you doing? Let me out!" she cried.

Her hand was knocked away by something hard and cool and when she looked she saw it was a pistol. She stared at Mrs. Haven. "Have you gone mad?"

She had been persuaded to approach the coach to kiss the lady farewell. She had agreed merely to see her the sooner gone. As soon as Sophie had been on the steps she had been pushed in and the coach had taken off.

"No, my dear," said the woman with a smile. "I am not mad. Don't be afraid. We will not hurt you, but I need your help."

Sophie was too affronted and pure bloody angry to be afraid. "If I may say so," she said tersely, "this is no way to go about it. Moreover, ma'am, this is abduction and I'm sure the penalties for that are severe."

Her captor was unimpressed. "You are doubtless right, my dear, but I doubt we will be caught. My name is not Haven, you see, and I do not live near Stone. All I want is to talk to you for a little. Then if you do not agree to help me we will set you down. By the time you have raised the alarm we will be far away."

It was clear to Sophie that her suspicions had been correct— the woman was deranged. But was it some harmless eccentricity or an insanity much more dangerous? "Talk then," she said, watching Mrs. Haven closely.

The woman drooped with sadness. "It is for the sake of my son, my only son, I have come to this pass, Lady Sophie. He is a good lad, my John, strong and honest and true. He loved . . . he loved a darling girl. Oh, you remind me of Polly. She was pretty and lively but with a kind heart and a serious nature beneath her youthful frivolity. My dear John's feelings were reciprocated, of course, and they were to be wed not many weeks past."

"What happened?" asked Sophie, caught despite herself.

"A terrible thing," said the woman, raising her free hand to her face. Sophie eyed the pistol, but by the time she had decided to grab it, the woman's attention was once more upon her.

"Polly was seduced," the woman said. "No, let us put the plain word to it, raped . . . by a rich nobleman who promised her heaven knows what and then cast her aside when he'd used her. Cast her aside to bear a child in shame!"

"That is terrible," said Sophie. "How fortunate she was to have a loving man like your son to give the child a name."

"Give his name to another man's brat?" asked the woman in amazement. "He did no such thing! He had little chance, any-way," she said flatly, "for Polly drowned herself on the day they were to have wed."

Sophie could think of nothing to say. The unknown nobleman was doubtless a villain, but so too were the unforgiving John and his uncharitable mother. "What has this to do with me?" she asked.

The woman looked at her with fire in her eyes. "The seducer, Lady Sophie, was Lord Randal Ashby!"

"What!" exclaimed Sophie in outrage. "That is a lie!" She knew once more Mrs. Haven was mad. She must be to even think such a thing.

The woman seemed taken aback at this. "How can you say so? Even you recounted his abominable attempt at seduction."

"I don't know what you're talking about," said Sophie. Randal had never tried to seduce her, she knew that only too well. Then she remembered Verderan's attack and fleeing to Mrs. Haven's bedchamber. The woman had clearly misunderstood. Had that triggered this whole fantasy?

149

The woman leant forwards. "Don't try to shield him. He no longer is able to terrorize. I *know* him for what he is, my dear, and so does John. I warned my boy to leave it be, not to meddle with those too powerful to touch but he would not. When he heard of your marriage it was the final straw. He knew the monster had to die."

Sophie felt as if she were in a horrifying maze. Randal? A rapist? Terrorizing. *Die*? What was this about Randal dying?

"I sent letters to you," the woman explained. "Letters to encourage you and to warn the libertine." Sophie shrank back. "I followed John," the woman carried on. "I tried to stop him but the strain was too much for me. The accident was the ultimate blow and my poor mind betrayed me. As soon as I regained my wits and heard of the awful events at Tyne Towers I knew—" her voice sank to a whisper—"I knew that John had struck."

Sophie stopped breathing. She felt a chill spread through her body. This woman's son had been responsible for the attack on Chelmly?

Her breath came back, and her wits. "But *Chelmly* was harmed," she protested. "Not Randal."

"So I gather," said the woman bitterly. "Were they alike?"

Dumbly, Sophie nodded. Shivers seemed to be taking over her body at the thought of what might have been. But for that chance exchange of horses Randal could be lying close to death . . . And the assailant was still at large.

"Mrs. Haven," she exclaimed. "We must inform the authorities!"

The pistol in the woman's hand raised to point straight at Sophie's heart. "Hand over my son to the hangman?" cried Mrs. Haven. "Are you *mad*?"

No, but you are, thought Sophie. You and your son both. "What are you going to do then, and why do you need me?"

"I am going to rescue him," said the woman firmly, lowering the firearm. "I will take him out of the country. It is not that I would mind him killing Lord Randal," she said with frightening indifference, "but the risk is too great now. I can only save him, though, if you can convince him you will not marry the debaucher."

150

Sophie put both hands to her head and stared at the woman. "Why? What am I to your son? Why would he pay attention to me?"

"You are just a name," said Mrs. Haven. "But when he read the announcement he was cast into agony. 'This must never be,' he cried, so all the servants heard him. 'Another innocent,' he cried. I could not calm him and it was that very day he disappeared. I guessed what he was about and followed. Now with the hunt up he will have sought refuge in our home but in his mind you and his lovely Polly are as one. He needs to protect you from the debaucher, Lady Sophie. Tell him that the engagement is over, that you know Lord Randal for what he is, and he will come away with me content."

The man sounded as fit for Bedlam as his mother. Sophie remembered her brush with similar madness in Sir Edwin Hever and had no intention of repeating it. "I pity you your son, ma'am," she said firmly, "but I cannot help you. Put me down, if you please. I will have no charges laid against you for this abduction but I will have the country raised to seek your demented son."

Demented? Even as her finger tightened on the trigger, Edith Hever reminded herself that her story had been an invention— sometimes it was hard to keep things clear in her mind—and the girl wasn't talking about Edwin.

But Sophie's attitude was a disappointment. She had thought such a romantic, tragic tale would sway a young thing. She had been sure that a tale of debauchery would finally convince her to reject marriage to Lord Randal.

"Ah, well," Mrs. Haven sighed. "If you insist on going free, I cannot hold you. And perhaps it is better that John free you from Lord Randal one day soon."

"What do you mean?" asked Sophie, fearing she knew.

"Don't be distressed, my dear," said Edith kindly. "If you lack the resolution to refuse the marriage, John will rescue you as soon as possible."

"But—" Sophie bit back the anguished words. She had been about to protested that she didn't *want* to be rescued, except from this woman and her son, but such words would be unwise.

Somehow the woman had the idea that she was disgusted by Randal. That bizarre misapprehension was a weapon if she could see how to use it.

If she refused to help, would they really let her go? It was likely. After all, it would be no easy task to control a healthy young woman for hours. If they released her in an isolated spot, however, then they might well make their escape and she would never have a moment's peace again. Every time Randal left the house she would fear for his safety.

Far better to go along with the woman and hope to trap her deranged son. Better still, Sophie thought, to hope for pursuit and rescue. But when would she be missed? The trouble with having a reputation as a madcap was that no one would question her absence for hours.

If only Stevie and his maid had been watching their departure, the alarm would already have been given. And that was why, she thought suddenly, the woman had been so determined to send them on their way. Now what could she do? Drop something out of the open window to mark the way? She didn't even have a handkerchief and the woman opposite was watching her like a hawk watching a rabbit.

"Very well," said Sophie, trying to sound cooperative. "I will help you. I suppose your son has only acted out of kindness to me. I . . ." The words threatened to choke her. "I have long known that Lord Randal is unsavoury, and cruel in his dealings with women. As you suspect, it is my family who have forced this marriage on me. Randal promised to reform but now I see it is all a sham. I will come and tell your son I intend to cry off. Then you must certainly take your son far away and make sure he never attempts such a thing again. By now the whole country must be raised in search of him. He has tried to murder a peer of the realm."

"Not murderer," said Mrs. Haven sharply. "Say rather he sought to avenge a wrong. He sought to protect an innocent." Despite the sharpness, it was clear she believed every word Sophie had said, and now considered the girl her ally. She even uncocked the pistol and slid it back on top of the portmanteau by her hand.

Sophie eyed it for a moment and then gave up the notion. The one thing she couldn't risk was the escape of Mrs. Haven and her murdering son. She must stay with the woman, appearing to have sympathy with her notions, until she could somehow arrange the capture of them both.

She was in no danger, she told herself. It was merely a matter of telling Mrs. Haven what she wanted to hear. Sophie could lie like a flat fish if it was the price of Randal's safety.

She could not help a slight shiver, however. She felt so alone. Silently she was crying, *Randal come for me.*

Despite the efforts of his upper staff, Randal felt as if he were drowning in details. His father had demanded his presence first thing in the morning and lectured him for two hours on the management of the ducal estate. Randal had only been rescued by the arrival of the doctor who said so much talking was bad for his patient.

Then he had visited Chelmly's room and sat at his bedside, willing him to open his eyes and be himself again.

He was so pale and looked younger and more vulnerable lying still in the bed with his head swathed in bandages. Randal had never realised how much he depended on his older brother, how much he loved him, until now when it seemed he might be taken away.

In recent years they had grown apart for Randal's chosen *milieu* was the social whirl—London, Brighton, the great country houses—while Chelmly's had always been his precious land. When Randal had been young, however, his older brother had been his admired mentor and protector. There were good memories in the farther reaches of his mind and now they made his heart ache.

"Come on, Chelmly," he said softly, ignoring the presence of the valet and nurse. "You can't leave the place to me. I'll make a pig's dinner of it in no time at all."

There was no response from the still figure on the bed. Randal wondered what his brother would think of his intent to go ahead with the wedding. If Chelmly, God forbid, was still at death's door it would be seen as outrageous. Even Sophie had been shocked but, Lord, he needed her more now than ever.

That kiss the other day had shown him, if he needed showing, how fragile his control had grown. He simply could not endure months more of sitting drinking tea with her, playing tennis, riding . . .

And more than her body he needed her company. To lie quietly with Sophie in his arms and talk things over. To lay problems out and solve them together . . .

He had pulled himself together, knowing he was needed elsewhere. He had laid a hand for a moment on his brother's and then left to handle his tasks as best he could. Now he was faced with a mountain of incomprehensible documents. Resolutely he applied himself . . .

There was genteel clearing of the throat.

Randal looked up to see Willerby beside him with papers in his hand. "If you could just approve these expenditures, my lord," the man said apologetically. "They only require a signature."

With a sigh Randal took the lists. The staff kept telling him he need only sign things but he couldn't take the easy way out. He concentrated as he ran his eye over the lists.

The duke and Chelmly liked having a masculine household and after his mother's death Chelmly had taken over supervision of the domestic arrangements as well as those of the estate. Randal wished now they'd brought in some female relative to handle those things. With a touch of devilment he thought that soon he would be able to dump them all in Sophie's lap. Oh, to lay all his troubles and his head as well in Sophie's lap . . .

His thoughts were interrupted by the door opening. In came his grandmother, bent and stiff, but sprightly enough in her own way. Her quick eyes fastened on the lists in front of Randal and she harrumphed.

"Thought so," she said, coming forwards as Randal rose to his feet to assist her. "Forgot Chelmly had taken all this in hand when your mother died. He works so hard and so quietly we never noticed." She picked up the first list and ran her eye over it. "Load of nonsense, of course, but it's mainly your father's fault. Bit of a misogynist. I'll take over all this."

"Grandmama, there's no need—"

"Suspect I've lost the use of my faculties, do you?" she asked sharply.

"Of course not—"

"I'll remind you, you young rascal, that I ran this place for thirty years, most of it before you were born, so don't say I'm not able." Her eyes were sharp and challenging and Randal felt a grin start. He suddenly felt a great deal better about life in general.

"I'd never dare," he said. "But still, Grandmama—"

"If I need young legs," the old woman interrupted, "there's staff galore and Chloe to help me. So go away. I'm sure you can find something else to do."

After a moment he laughed and gave her a warm hug and a kiss. "Thank you, my dear."

"Go along with you," she harrumphed, taking his seat at the desk. "I'd think you should go and see how Sophie's doing. Must all have been a nasty shock."

His eyes twinkled. "Can I take that as an order?"

"Yes. Though what the likelihood is of a jackanapes like you obeying an order, I'd hesitate to say."

"But I'm thoroughly reformed," he responded. "Expect me back at dinnertime." As he walked to the door he said to Willerby, "Have Yorrick sent round. I wish to ride over to the Castle."

The Groom of the Chamber blanched. "But, my lord! The . . . the villain may still be hereabout."

"He has a point," said the duchess, suddenly looking very weary.

Randal stopped with a bitten-back curse. And it was possible that the attack had been meant for him in the first place. He remembered that note which could be interpreted as a clear death threat. "Am I to be a prisoner?" he demanded desperately. "We may never catch the man."

The servant had no answer to such a question.

"Find Mr. Verderan for me, please," Randal said.

A footman was dispatched and Randal moved out into the corridor to await his friend.

In a few minutes the Dark Angel strolled up. "You called, my lord?" he drawled insolently.

Randal burst out laughing. "Gods, Ver, I'm glad you're here."

The two men clasped hands briefly. "Then I must be glad I am," said Verderan. "In what way can I help you?"

"I need advice. Is it reasonable, do you think, for me to ride over to Stenby to see Sophie?"

"Why not?"

"Willerby seems to think the would-be assassin is lurking behind a bush seeking to finish the task."

Verderan gave it serious thought. "I doubt it. This area has been gone over quite thoroughly. It is possible it's a local man, of course, but are you going to lurk in here for the rest of your life?"

Randal could feel the relief spread through him. Such a life would be unendurable. He'd far rather a quick death. "Exactly what I was thinking," he said. "Willing to ride guard?"

"Of course," said Verderan.

Randal laughed and let the madness take him. Not even bothering to change into boots, the two young men went to the stables, commanded horses, and galloped off towards Stenby Castle.

=== 13 ===

By the time they arrived at Stenby Jane and Beth were already wondering where Sophie had disappeared to, though they assumed she had wanted time to herself. Randal's arrival triggered a search. After half an hour of wandering the Castle shouting for her the search moved to the grounds and everyone began to feel uneasy.

"She'll be up a tree," said Randal with a sigh. Beth looked at him and wondered if he believed it. If Sophie was anywhere close to the Castle she would surely have heard her name being called.

They were standing at the base of the terrace steps and Jane and Lord Wraybourne joined them there. In a moment, Sir Marius arrived, shaking his head.

"Could she have ridden out?" Randal asked.

"I checked the stables," Sir Marius said. "No horses have left there at all today."

"What was she wearing?" Randal asked.

Sophie's maid reported that her mistress had dressed that morning in a green sprig muslin gown and silk slippers. No other clothes had gone, not even a bonnet.

"She wouldn't have gone walking without a bonnet and in slippers," said her brother sharply, searching the rolling parkland with his eyes for the hundredth time. "Where the devil is she?"

He was trying to sound irritated, as Randal himself had done, but he sounded worried, and with reason. In view of the attack on Chelmly, there was cause to fear the worst. Those notes that Sophie had received came into Beth's mind but it seemed too farfetched a connection to make.

The search of the grounds was abandoned and they were soon joined by the other men—Verderan, and the Reverend Mortimer Kyle. By silent accord they stayed outside, all still alert for the sight of Sophie strolling across the grass, back from some impulsive errand.

"When was she last seen?" asked Mortimer.

"After her maid dressed her?" asked the earl. "Do you know, Jane?"

"Perhaps we should make further enquiries," said Jane, "but no one has mentioned seeing her since she saw that Haven woman away. She could well have gone for a walk, I suppose."

Randal forced out the question no one else would ask. "Is it possible . . . ?"

"That she's lying somewhere wounded?" completed David calmly. "I don't think so."

"I was going to say 'dead,' " Randal said harshly. "Perhaps this time the maniac was more thorough."

A muscle twitched in Lord Wraybourne's jaw. "I don't think so," he said steadily.

"Is that just blind optimism?" demanded Randal sharply, forcing himself over the subject like someone trying to dig a bullet from his own flesh. "Or do you have logic to it?"

"There is absolutely no reason for anyone to want to harm Sophie," said David firmly.

"There was no reason for anyone to try to kill Chelmly—Damn it. What if it *is* all a plot against me?"

"Why would there be a plot against you?" asked Verderan in a level, drawling voice. "We've established your spotless innocence in the recent past."

Beth flinched from this tone that was perilously close to an insult, but Piers Verderan obviously knew his friend for Randal collected himself. "I don't know why," he said. "But there has to be a connection. The attack on Chelmly. Sophie's disappearance. Those damned notes."

At that moment two people came laughing around the corner and the small figure broke away from his nursemaid to trot towards the men. "Ver!" cried Stevie blissfully.

The Dark Angel cursed softly but moved forwards to stop the boy from joining the somber group. Beth saw the pursuing nursemaid hesitate, obviously more afraid of Verderan than of neglecting her duties. What did she think he was, the devil? More than likely.

Stevie offered his favourite toy for his idol's inspection. It was somewhat faded after its swim. "Horsey," he said.

"We've had this discussion before, brat," said Verderan, not unkindly. "We're all busy here. Go off with your nurse now."

Steve ignored this and pointed towards the porte cochere. "Horsey go," he said, obviously trying to gain Verderan's attention. He cocked his head and offered, "Sophie go horsey." He stuck the horse's hind legs in his mouth and mumbled something else.

They all looked at the child. Were they fools to hope? Stevie couldn't have any useful information to offer, could he? As no one did anything, Beth went forwards and crouched down beside the boy. "Did you see Sophie on a horse, Stevie?"

Stevie shook his head. The back end of the horse was still in his mouth and Beth carefully extracted it. "Did you see Sophie *with* a horse then?"

Stevie moved closer and snuggled against her. "Coachy-horsey," he offered.

"You saw Sophie with a coach and horses?" Beth asked hopefully. Then she remembered that Sophie had seen the accident victim off. That was all the boy was referring to. Stevie nodded his assent and Beth looked up at the others and shrugged hopelessly.

Stevie grabbed her hand. "Sophie wiv ballady, ballady, ballady," he chanted.

They all looked bewildered. "A song?" Jane suggested.

Hope couldn't be dismissed out of hand. Randal beckoned the maid and she came over, nervously pleating her apron. She bobbed a curtsey. "Yes, milord?"

"Did Master Steven see Lady Sophie escort a lady to her coach today?"

"Yes, milord."

"Where did Lady Sophie go after the coach left, Rosie?"

Before the girl could answer, Stevie set up his chant again.

"Wiv ballady, ballady, ballady."

Randal looked up at the maid with impatience. "What the devil is he saying?"

His sharp tone frightened her and she looked around for help, her apron now reduced to a knot. "I'm ... not rightly sure, milord. Sometimes he makes sense, sometimes he don't." She bit her lip and offered, " 'Bad lady,' maybe?"

Randal caught his breath. He picked up Stevie and looked at him as if he might have the answers written across his face. "Why would he call this woman, this Mrs. Haven, a bad lady?" he asked Rosie. "You must have been with him, girl, when he watched the coach leave. What happened?"

"She didn't want him to watch the horses, milord. She told me to take him away. That's doubtless what he means." After a moment she added with real spirit, "She were proper mean about it, and her just a person taken in out of charity!"

Beth saw the disappointment on Randal's face and shared it. For a moment she too had believed that the child might hold the key to Sophie's disappearance. Randal set the boy back on his feet. It was Lord Wraybourne who said to the maid, "But you said he did watch the coach leave."

Rosie began twisting her apron again. "Yes, milord."

"So answer Lord Randal's question. Where did Lady Sophie go when the coach had left?"

The girl's eyes opened wide and she looked as if she might cry. "I wasn't exactly there, milord," she mumbled. She looked up and said quickly. "I went to get the laundry basket. I was only gone for a moment or two and he was safe enough where he was and safe and sound—"

"Be quiet!" Randal cut off the gabble and they all shared his urgency. Logic said this was a wild-goose chase but instinct screamed that Steven Delamere held the key to Sophie's safety.

"How much does a child of this age understand?" Randal asked. They were all childless and shook their heads. Even Beth had little experience with a child of such tender years.

Randal picked the boy up and strolled over to a bench to sit with him in his lap. "Well, Stevie, so you saw the bad lady leave in a coach?"

"Yes," Stevie said with a firm nod of his head.

"And did Sophie leave in the coach too?"

"Yes," said Stevie.

Everyone gasped and Randal looked bemused. Driven by urgency, Beth stepped forwards and sat down beside Randal and the boy. She put the question again. "Lady Sophie got in the coach with the bad lady and they drove away, Stevie?"

"Drove away," said Stevie, smiling at her, seeming pleased to have finally found someone to understand him. Then he added emphatically, "Fast!" He held his horse out and made bouncing motions as he moved it quickly from right to left. "Galloppy, galloppy, galloppy."

"But it makes no sense," said Mortimer softly.

"Sense or not," said David grimly, "I'm setting men to trace that coach." He strode off to put it in hand.

Randal gently put the child in Beth's arms. "See what else you can find out," he said softly.

Beth took a deep breath and asked calmly, "Did Lady Sophie want to go in the coach, Stevie?"

"Wiv ballady," said Stevie agreeable.

"Did Sophie climb in the coach, Stevie?"

Stevie nodded and stuck the horse back in his mouth. Beth looked up the others. "Why would she go with a stranger without a word to anyone?"

At that moment Verderan reclaimed Stevie's attention by picking him up off Beth's lap. The boy took the horse out of his mouth and smiled brilliantly at his idol. Verderan smiled back.

He carried the boy a little way and put him down. He pointed to Beth, still sitting on the bench. "Stevie, you see that lady there. Let's pretend that's the bad lady." He flashed an apologetic smile at Beth. "Let's pretend you're Lady Sophie. Can you show us how she got in the coach?"

Beth looked at Mr. Verderan skeptically. Who did he think Stevie was, the great Kean? The Dark Angel shrugged.

"How did Sophie get in the coach, Stevie?" he asked patiently. "Did she climb up the steps? Was she lifted in?"

It looked as if the questions were getting them nowhere. Then suddenly Stevie spread his arms wide and hurtled forwards into Beth's lap.

"Thrown in," said Randal, surging to his feet. "I'm for following that damned coach."

"We all are," said Sir Marius, "but I think we have to pause and consider matters. It's hours since that coach left and it's possible we may not be able to trace it. We need to find out more."

Piers Verderan came over and took Stevie from Beth. He passed the child on to the maid. "You've been a good boy, Stevie," he said. "Perhaps tomorrow I'll take you up on my horse."

Stevie blissfully watched him over Rosie's shoulder as he was carried away. Beth thought that perhaps Piers Verderan was a rake worth the reforming, but not by her. She found herself instinctively looking over at Sir Marius and he smiled. It was like an embrace and all there could be for them now. More urgent matters were in hand.

Randal imposed an iron control on himself and was attempting to reason it through. "If that woman had some devilish plot against me, why in Hades did she come to Stenby?"

Sir Marius spoke up. "I'm afraid, whatever's going on, you can't lay the attack on Chelmly at her door. She was genuinely ill when we picked her up. There's no chance she crept out, walked five miles, and laid a trap for someone."

"Coincidence?" queried Randal skeptically. "And she could have sent those letters before she left home."

"But what of the one Sophie received at the picnic?" Sir Marius shrugged. "The only matter of importance is who is Mrs. Haven and where is she taking Sophie. The why can be sorted out later."

The earl came back and his expression sharpened when he heard what more had been discovered. "I've sent men out in pairs to check the roads. One to follow the trail of the coach and the other to report back. We should soon know the direction and can follow." He sharp pacing showed the impatience they all felt with just standing. "I'll go odds," he said, "that she's not Mrs. Haven of Stone."

"But who?" asked Randal. "And why Sophie?"

"She came with your wedding announcement in her reticule," Mortimer pointed out.

"Bringing it all back to me," said Randal. "Damnation. No one in the world has cause to bear me this much ill will!"

"Well Sophie has certainly not grievously offended anyone," said Mortimer. "Think again, Randal. Who might you have injured lately?"

"No one," said Randal impatiently. "The only person I've seriously hurt recently is Edwin Hever and no one knows about that."

"They do now," said Lord Wraybourne dryly. "This is to go no further," said the earl sternly, "but the man attacked Sophie. Randal shot him to save her." Jane and Beth shared a look. Jane had told Beth the whole story and that certainly wasn't all of it, but Beth could see why the earl wanted as little of the truth as possible to come out. She couldn't see how that sordid affair could have any bearing on the present problem.

"Could a relative of Hever's be out for revenge?" asked Mortimer dubiously.

Lord Wraybourne dismissed the suggestion. "It was given out as suicide so—"

"Edwin Hever," interrupted Marius. "By all that's holy . . ."

"What?" It was a general question.

"That woman had a locket with her and I thought it reminded me of someone. It reminded me of Edwin Hever with hair."

The earl set off speedily for his library, and they all followed. He grabbed his copy of Debrett's useful tome, *The Peerage of England, Scotland and Ireland*. After a moment he cursed softly, "Hever's mother is called Edith. His home was Marshton Hall in Essex, but it will surely have gone to his heir, a cousin. This doesn't tell us where she will have taken Sophie."

"Or why," said Randal, white and tense. "If she knows the truth, and God knows how, she can only intend to . . . to kill Sophie."

Marius splashed brandy into five glasses and pressed one into Randal's hand. Randal took a long drink. After a moment's hesitation, he put some brandy into two more glasses and offered them to Jane and Beth. Jane shook her head but Beth took hers. It was supposed to be medicinal and at the moment she needed something.

She sipped and felt the spirit burn pure down her throat. It couldn't burn away her fear, however. Those notes and "Mrs. Haven" were all tying together in a terrifying way. They would find Sophie but they would find her dead somewhere by the wayside. She saw that everyone in the room silently shared her fears.

Randal slammed down his empty glass. "We have to follow. Now."

"Not until someone comes back with a direction," said the earl steadily. "I have horses standing ready."

Verderan's cool voice broke the gloomy silence. "We can't all hare off and one lady surely doesn't need five men."

"The question is," said Randal, turning suddenly, "who are you going to get to stay behind? Not me, for one."

"Nor me," said Marius. "I'm the only man here who saw that woman and can recognise her again."

David made a sharp, frustrated motion. "I should claim my place. Sophie is my sister, after all. But someone has to stay behind to handle things here. Randal, you really should stay at the Towers. You could well be needed."

Randal said something very rude and then controlled himself and apologised to Jane and Beth. "They can survive without me for a day. I go."

A scratch on the door ushered Burbage and a breathless groom. "We found the road, milord," he gasped. "Heading Drayton way. Kelly's stayed on the line and he'll leave word behind."

The earl praised the man and dismissed him even as Randal, Verderan, and Marius headed for the door. "Randal, you and Verderan aren't even dressed for riding. Stop to change. I'm sure—" He broke off at Randal's expression. "Take care, then. Remember, someone tried damned hard to kill Chelmly, and there might be a connection." He grasped his friend's hands. "Godspeed, and may you find her safe."

Beth took another longer drink from her glass and silently echoed the prayer.

Sophie would have been pleased to know what was afoot for

she was losing hope. Much of the journey had been passed in silence but occasionally her captor would launch into praise of her dear son John but in a strange way which was not convincing. Did the woman know her son was a maniac and merely try to convince herself otherwise?

Sophie eyed the pistol from time to time, but it was kept close to the woman's hand and far from her own. There were also the two men on the box to consider.

At the first change, Sophie thought of lunging out of the coach into the busy inn yard. But could she make herself understood quickly enough so that the coach would be stopped? If not, the coach would be away at the first word and mad John would be free to hunt Randal. The woman had admitted that Haven was not her real name, and probably John was not the name of her son. How could anyone find them once they were gone?

When the coach rolled away again, she saw her captor smile very warmly. "I see you truly do wish to help us, my dear. I am so pleased. I will have good news for you soon. You will see."

Good news? Sophie deeply distrusted anything this woman thought of as good news.

She hoped they would make a longer stop for food, in which case she might be able to raise the alarm, but it did not happen. They travelled straight through. At one stop the woman called for small beer for them both, but it was brought too quickly to serve Sophie's purpose. She didn't much like the drink even but was glad enough for something to quench her thirst.

Finally as the coach pulled out of Blackbrook the woman seemed to relax. "We are nearly home, my dear," she said. "Now I can tell you the pleasant surprise I have for you."

Sophie braced herself.

"My son is not called John," said the woman fondly, "but Edwin."

Sophie waited. The coach rolled on. "Is that supposed to mean something?"

The woman tutted impatiently. "Edwin, my dear. And my name is not Haven, but Hever!"

Sophie let out a little scream. She could not help it. "Edwin Hever's mother?"

"Yes," said the lady eagerly. "Your darling Edwin. You see. I said it would be a great surprise. I said you were like a daughter to me and so you are. Ever since Edwin first wrote of your love I have longed to clasp you to my bosom."

Sophie shrank away from the woman in horror. Edwin Hever had tried to kill her. Did his mother intend to complete what he had left undone? But the woman was still looking at her with that repulsive fondness. Sophie pulled herself together to use it any way she could.

"I am so confused," she said weakly, and it required little acting. "What of John?"

"Oh, there is no John, Sophie," said Lady Hever gaily. "Was that not a clever story? I almost began to believe in him myself. I have always been good at making up stories."

"So he didn't attack Chelmly," interrupted Sophie, feeling a fool to have been so taken in. But it had all seemed so real.

"No, but my man did," said Lady Hever casually. "I am sorry for it, for I hear the marquess is a good man. Lord Randal was the target. He had to die before he could besmirch you. I am most put out that it was so mishandled." She sat in sour contemplation of the ineptitude of her minions.

And the assassin is still on the loose, hunting Randal, thought Sophie, sitting bolt upright. Not the demented son cowering at home but a hired killer looking to complete his work. She looked more desperately at that tempting pistol. She need to win free and warn Randal of his danger. She stifled a moan of frustration as she saw how impossible it still was.

A glance out of the window showed her they were travelling through open country. Even if she overpowered Lady Hever and escaped from the coach, the two men on the box would run her down in no time.

Edith Hever was too deep in her bitter thoughts to notice Sophie's mood. Sophie quickly slumped down again and tried to appear calm. She must not raise the woman's suspicions.

Lady Hever shrugged. "At least now I have you under my wing that man cannot touch you, my dear. Edwin will be pleased that I have kept you safe for him."

Sophie could feel the hairs on her neck rise. The woman spoke as if her son were still alive. Could he be? No. That at least could not be so.

She forced her mind back to calm. Whatever insanity was going on here, her only chance was to be alert for an opportunity to escape. But she couldn't stop panic fretting at her as she remembered Edwin Hever's spittly voice, his hand tight in her hair as he bent her neck back, shouting abuse at her.

"What do you want of me?" she asked and heard the fear in her own voice.

"Don't be frightened, dear," said Lady Hever soothingly. "You are free of those who would force you into a loveless marriage. I have you safe. I know you are dutiful—how could Edwin's choice be other? If I had told you at Stenby Castle who I was, you would have felt obliged to stay behind and submit to your family's dastardly plans. Now, however, you are free. Edwin's home is your home and we can stay there forever . . . Well, not exactly Edwin's home," she said bitterly. "They took that from me. But I have made Glebe House almost the same. You will see."

Sophie decided she had to try to make this madwoman see sense, but carefully. "I did not plan to marry Edwin," she said straightly.

"I know," said Lady Hever. "He wrote that your family opposed the match and you would not go against them. Though he did hope to persuade you in the end, naughty boy."

Naughty boy. That man had been attacking women for months during the spring and tormenting Jane with lewd whisperings. Sophie swallowed the words that would do more harm than good.

"Lady Hever, they are bound to come after me," she said.

"You need not fear," said the woman who seemed to see everything through her own distorted vision. "They will not know where you are, you see. If they begin to wonder about Mrs. Haven of Stone, they will not find her there. They will never think to look for Lady Hever."

Sophie feared that was true. No one had ever suspected this interpretation of that awful night, or that the uninvited guest at Stenby was Edwin Hever's mother. She began to be afraid again. Lady Hever might not intend to kill her but people could disappear. Could it happen to her? Could she spend the rest of her days locked away with Lady Hever and her dreadful son's memorabilia?

No, she told herself strongly. Randal and David would turn England inside out until they found her.

As if she picked up on the thought, Lady Hever said dreamily, "If they come close we can always move. As long as I have dear Edwin's things it is home. I have them all, you know. His chapbooks and toys, all his clothes since he was a baby. . . . We will never be lonely with all Edwin's things and each other."

Suppressing a shudder, Sophie looked desperately out of the window again. As soon as they reached any sign of civilization she was determined to throw herself from the coach, no matter how dangerous that would be.

Her very life and Randal's depended on it.

Randal and his companions were thundering after them, following the trail of the coach. The groom, Kelly, had left word as promised and the coach had been noted on these quiet roads—by an ostler at an inn, by harvesters in the fields, by a doctor making rounds in a gig. Occasionally they chanced a shortcut. Expert hunters all they took hedge and fence in flying leaps and even thundered through crops, for they would return later to compensate and time was of the essence.

The prime blood horses, however, could not make the whole journey and they had to stop to hire new, less speedy ones. At the Golden Hart, Randal asked about a coach with an old lady and a young, the younger being pretty, with short auburn curls.

"Ay, milord," said the ostler. "One such passed through an hour or so ago."

With this news the pursuit became more pressing. The coach was still far ahead and their pace would now be slower.

Sophie was still waiting for the coach to pass through a sizeable community when it turned in between stone pillars and she felt sick despair. This must be Glebe House. What would happen to her here? Despite Lady Hever's words, Sophie feared her intention was much closer to the Indians who were said to burn a man's wife with his body.

Though she knew it would be wiser to appear compliant, she resisted when Lady Hever tried to draw her out of the coach. Eventually the woman had to call for help to drag her.

"What is the matter with you, dear? This is Edwin's home. You have nothing to fear here."

It looked like Edwin Hever's home, thought Sophie hysterically. Had it been chosen for that reason? It was bleak and slightly misproportioned. The door had been painted a strange shade of brown which was completely wrong with the grey stone. The flowers planted near the drive were straggly because the trees had been allowed to grow to shade them.

Sternly she suppressed both hysteria and panic. Her only chance was to keep calm and be alert for the first opportunity to escape.

"I am sorry," she said as if terrified. "For a moment I thought you had brought me back to Stenby."

This bit of nonsense was accepted without a blink. "Of course not, dear child. Now come inside and you shall sit in the parlour in Edwin's favourite chair while we have a supper. I know you must be hungry."

So Sophie found herself sitting in an uncomfortable wing chair which still held faintly the smell of lavender water. She remembered that Edwin Hever had been wont to drench himself in the stuff. In fact, it had betrayed him in the end.

She couldn't, simply couldn't, stay there. She pushed up out of the chair. "I . . . I feel presumptuous sitting there," she said. "I . . . I would much rather sit here,"—she chose another chair—"and look at it . . . and imagine him there."

Lady Hever patted her shoulder. "Ah, dearest daughter. Did I not say we were alike, so sensitive? How many hours have I sat and done exactly the same thing. I remember his interesting talks about all the things he had done and read of . . ."

Sophie let the voice drone on. Where had the men gone? Were they in on the plot? Was one of them Chelmly's attacker? If she dashed into the hall would one of them be there on guard? She forced herself to stay still. She must wait for a sure opportunity to escape or lose all.

Then her wandering eyes saw the shrine.

On a side wall hung a portrait of Edwin Hever. It was not very good and looked a great deal more like Shakespeare than the baronet. Sophie suspected the itinerant artist who had executed it had been given instructions to make it so. The heavy frame was festooned with billowing black crape and long ends of it trailed to the ground. In front two crystal oil lamps burned.

"Ah," said Lady Hever softly, following the direction of Sophie's appalled gaze. "Is it not a good likeness? I had not a portrait, you know. Mr. Lickmore did it from my miniature with alterations at my instruction." Sophie looked at the woman to catch what could almost be teasing amusement as Lady Hever added, "I have an even better likeness upstairs. You will be quite overcome, I daresay, to see it."

A housekeeper brought the supper and laid it out with the help of a maid. The housekeeper was plump and nervous, the maid looked dullwitted. After assessing them as possible allies Sophie did not attempt an escape. Too risky. When she was shown to a bedchamber, that would be the time. She'd climbed out of many a window in her salad days.

After the poorly cooked food, Lady Hever summoned the strapping young man who had pushed Sophie into the coach. With him as escort, or guard, Sophie endured a guided tour of what amounted to a mausoleum, and a very dirty one at that. Apart from the little shrines to Edwin in this place or that, the house was uncared for. Cobwebs hung in the cornices and mouse droppings scattered the floor.

A study-cum-library was empty of all but a handful of volumes but they, and the shelves they rested on, were dusted.

"Edwin's favourite books," said Lady Hever. "Of course you may read them, dearest Sophie, but you must ask my permission first. I do not like to see his things disturbed."

As they climbed the wide central staircase, Sophie could see all the rectangles on the wall where the previous occupants had hung pictures. None hung there now.

There were five bedchambers on the upper floor but three were completely bare. One, which she was shown briefly, was clearly Lady Hever's and contained another shrine to Edwin, built around an ink sketch of the baronet and a collection of baby toys.

"And now," said Lady Hever almost gaily, "we come to the heart of Glebe House. Dear Edwin's bedchamber!"

Sophie had to remind herself that Edwin Hever had never lived in this place at all. She wondered if Edith Hever remembered.

Unlike the rest of the house, this room was meticulously clean and looked eerily as if its dead occupant were due at any moment. Shaving things stood ready on a stand, soap and towels close by. The bed was turned back and a nightshirt lay ready. An open book lay facedown on a small table, with sheets of paper and a pen beside it. A heavy brass clock ticked ponderously on the mantelpiece and the room reeked of lavender water.

"You may sleep here," said Lady Hever reverently, lovingly patting the prepared pillow. A small cloud of dust exposed the pretence of all this. "I would not allow any other, but you have the right."

Sophie swallowed bile at the thought but reminded herself she had no intention of sleeping in this house at all. She studied the windows and her heart lifted. They were large casements, easy to climb out of, and there even seemed to be a spreading copper beech nearby.

"Thank you," she said with ringing sincerity. "I will be delighted to have this bedchamber."

Lady Hever did embrace her then, and Sophie tried her best not to shrink away. "In fact," she said quickly, "I am very tired. Could I retire now?"

"Of course, child," said the woman, stroking Sophie's hair in a way that made her want to shudder. "But first let me show you his dressing room."

She opened the door and stood back. Sophie walked in and screamed.

=14=

A BALD-HEADED MAN was standing in his dressing room in formal evening dress, clothes stained rusty with blood.

After a breathless second, Sophie stifled any sound behind her hand and waited for her heart rate to slow and gentle so that it wasn't shaking her whole body. She just prayed she wouldn't cry, for that sight had nearly broken her.

The damn thing was dummy.

"Is it not true to life?" asked Lady Hever softly as she went over to gently rearrange the ruffle on the shirt. "I commissioned it from Madame Tussaud in London. It is all made from wax. I had planned to take off these dreadful clothes when he was avenged, but now I don't know . . ." One finger rubbed pensively at a bloodstain.

"I think you should take them off," said Sophie vehemently, recognising the poorly cut evening wear Hever had worn that last night. Thank God she had never seen him with a bullet wound in his head for the memories stirred were already close to unbearable. Part of her was reliving the spittly abuse, Randal's slow movements, and that deafening explosion . . .

"Do you think so?" mused Lady Hever. "And yet they will remind me to persevere until the man who caused his death dies too."

Randal. Randal dead. Before her blurring eyes the figure became Randal splattered with blood. "How did you find out Randal shot him?" she cried.

Edith Hever became as still and pale as the wax dummy. "What?"

Back to earth with a jolt, Sophie realised she had made a dreadful mistake, "Randal was . . . was nearby when he sh—shot himself," Sophie stammered.

Edith stalked over and grasped her arm painfully. "That is not what you said, young lady." She shook Sophie cruelly and then discarded her to fly back to the dummy. She clasped it in her arms. "Lord Randal Ashby *shot* you? Oh Edwin, darling, darling Edwin, you didn't call him out over the foolish girl, did you?"

She released the figure, wild-eyed. "And the rascal cheated, and killed you in cold blood, and all his powerful friends took this way to cover up the crime. *They buried you in unhallowed ground!*" she howled.

Sophie backed up ready to flee and came up against the solid body of the guard. He seemed unaffected by the wild hysteria, almost bored in fact, but he wasn't going to let her out of the door. Sophie turned back to the madwoman.

"No, Lady Hever," said Sophie, desperately trying to penetrate the fogs of unreality around the woman. "No. It was nothing like that. Edwin shot himself."

"I don't believe it," Edith Hever said, suddenly cold as the North Sea as she turned back to Sophie. "I know my son. He had too much respect for his immortal soul to sink to suicide. At last I have the truth. Now what I need to know is *your* part in all this."

Confronted with those malevolent eyes, Sophie backed up again to come up against that solid body. In the face of Edith Hever, the guard almost seemed to be protection.

"How could you?" Lady Hever demanded, stalking towards her. "How could you stand by and allow them to label him a suicide, you spineless tottie?"

Invention escaped Sophie. "He tried to kill me," she said. "Randal saved my life."

Sophie expected denials but the notion of her son as murderer did not shock the woman. Edith Hever just narrowed her pale eyes. "And *why* did he try to kill you? What had you done?"

"Nothing," Sophie shouted. "He was as mad as you are!"

The woman's hand lashed out and cracked on Sophie's face. Though gaunt she was strong. Sophie staggered back with a cry and put a hand to her stinging cheek. Big beefy hands grasped her shoulders.

"Have I been mistaken in you?" the woman hissed, "Were you unfaithful to him?"

Sophie just stood there. Though some form of compliance would be wiser, she simply couldn't anymore. The hands on her shoulders tightened a little and Sophie braced herself for another blow, but the guard just drew her back out of the dreadful room.

For a moment they were alone. Edith could be heard muttering to her son.

"Did he really try to kill you?" asked the young man.

Sophie turned and looked up. "Yes."

"I always thought he was a queer cove," he said and left.

A part of Sophie's mind prompted that this might be a good time to escape, and yet she couldn't. The horror of it all paralysed her.

Edith Hever walked out of the dressing room and shut the door. Her eyes were poisonous as she looked at Sophie. "And what am I to do with you?" she asked.

Before she could come up with a notion, the young man burst back into the room.

"There's a group of riders coming. Da's worried."

Was this rescue? With an icy chill Sophie remembered her careless revelation. Edith Hever would be hell-bent on Randal's destruction now. She dashed to the window to give some kind of warning, but Lady Hever grasped her skirt. "Hold her, Caleb!"

The man did so but demanded, "What the hell's going on?"

"Mind your manners," spat Lady Hever. "We are going to lay poor Edwin's spirit to rest at last. This little trollop preferred a debauched, diseased libertine to my son. She was the cause of his death. They both must die that the sin be wiped clean!"

"Caleb," said Sophie quickly, "she's mad. She wants to kill the son of a duke. The whole of England will turn its hand against you!"

"Your father has already attacked the son of a duke, Caleb," said Edith with a chilly smile. "And he'll hang for it unless you do what I say. Bring her."

Sophie was dragged down stairs and when she tried further

argument with Caleb he tersely said, "Shut up," in a tone she heeded. She had no desire to be knocked unconscious. He was worried, though, and Sophie kept that in mind.

The three men had eventually caught up with Kelly and had to leave him behind, as his horse was spent. From then on the trail of the coach had been more difficult to follow especially once it turned off onto the quiet back roads of Staffordshire. Twice they had been misdirected and lost time. Not far back, however, a grave digger had noted the passing coach.

"Belongs to that crazy Lady Hever," he said with an eloquent spit. "Her as took Glebe House." His directions had been concise and accurate.

Now they rode past the gates of Glebe House without pause and stopped a little way down the road behind a stand of trees to make plans.

The need to race up to the house and wrench Sophie from danger was almost overpowering. Randal already had one of his two pistols out and ready but Verderan put a hand on his arm.

"If there are any men with weapons, we'd best not just ride up there," he said.

"Then we'll approach the house from the back on foot," said Randal coolly. They had to act. Now.

Verderan shook his head. "Despite my reputation as blood-thirsty," he said, "it's been my experience that it's better to try to talk one's way out of these things. Even if she has servants, it's just one old woman we're dealing with. I think I should go up to the house and see what's going on."

"Why you?" asked Randal sharply.

"Well, you can't go. If our suspicions are correct, she knows at least a description of you and they'll shoot on sight. You, Marius, are simply not ruthless enough."

"I beg your pardon?" said Marius coldly.

"One of the penalties of being a large man and honourable is that one learns to pull one's punches. I really can't see you laying a woman flat. I, however, have done so once or twice and won't hesitate to do so again if necessary."

Marius frowned but gave him the point.

"What do we do, then?" asked Randal bitterly. "Just sit here and twiddle our thumbs? God knows what's going on—"

"Fifteen minutes," said Verderan firmly. "If I'm not back in that time, I suggest you find a back entrance and rescue me and Sophie both." With a nonchalant wave of the hand he turned his horse and cantered off to Glebe House.

"One man riding up," said Jago Haines from his position by the dining-room window.

"Is it him?" asked Lady Hever hungrily, but Jago shook his head.

"Nah, it's the dark one. Veryan, or something."

Sophie tensed. It was rescue then. But why was Verderan riding straight into a trap? She was seated in a plain chair and Caleb, as instructed, had his hand firmly in her hair.

"The Dark Angel," said Lady Hever with an unpleasant smile. "Get your wife to show him to the parlour but be prepared. He will be good bait for the other."

So the housekeeper was Jago Haine's wife, Sophie thought. No help there but she hadn't entirely given up on Caleb, who was clearly on edge.

Jago and Lady Hever left, but the door remained slightly open and Sophie could hear what went on.

There was a sharp rap on the door and Mrs. Haines crossed the hall, whining softly to her husband about the pickle they were in. Verderan's crisp voice was heard.

"Good afternoon. I'm looking for Lady Hever and I understand this is her home."

"Could I ask your name, sir?"

"The name is Marshall. If you would ask your mistress for a few minutes of her time."

The door shut and Sophie had to assume Verderan was inside of it, unaware that his identity was already known. Could she call out? But Jago must be nearby with his pistol . . .

Before she could decide, Caleb clasped a beefy hand over her mouth. Not a stupid young man, thought Sophie, and though she wished he washed his hands more frequently she was not totally displeased. It confirmed her opinion that Caleb was a quick thinker. She could work on intelligence better than stupidity, and she had to do something before Verderan was killed in cold blood.

The housekeeper's voice was heard. "Milady will see you, sir. Come this way."

Sophie tried to speak and after a moment Caleb took his hand away. "Sorry about that, miss, but you might have done something silly."

"Caleb," said Sophie. "I am not 'miss.' I am Lady Sophie Kyle, sister of the Earl of Wraybourne. I am betrothed to Lord Randal Ashby, younger son of the Duke of Tyne. Your mistress is mad and has involved you in dangerous matters."

"So?"

Sophie desperately wished he wasn't standing behind her. She couldn't judge his reactions from his slow, country speech.

"So help me now and I will see you all go free," she promised.

"Did my Da really try to kill a marquess?" he asked after a while.

Perhaps stupidity would have been easier. The attempted murder of a high-ranking aristocrat was not going to be overlooked. "Someone did," said Sophie. "Lady Hever says it was your father but there's no proof. If you and your family took off now, you could be free of all—"

"Shut up." He emphasised it by tightening his hand in her hair and clamping his other hand over her mouth again. Sophie heard footsteps in the hall.

"I'm sorry for disturbing you," said Verderan. There was the sound of a blow and a groan.

"Very good, Jago," said Lady Hever. "Bring him in here out of the way."

Jago appeared, dragging an unconscious Verderan. As Caleb removed his hand once more, Sophie worked on keeping her face expressionless.

"It was quite amusing," remarked Lady Hever, "to hear him spin such a farrago of nonsense." She kicked idly at Verderan's limp body, "but I would rather not have had such vileness in Edwin's house. I have heard stories of him." She turned on Sophie. "Your lover too, perhaps?"

Sophie decided it would be much wiser to keep silent.

Lady Hever spat in her face. "Trollop!"

Sophie tried to spit back but fright had dried her mouth.

Cheeks flaming with angry colour, the woman paced the room. "But now *he* will come and I can see him killed. Then Edwin can rest in peace."

She walked over to the shrine and turned up the lamps slightly. "Soon, my darling. Soon," she crooned.

"Da," whispered Caleb urgently. "We'd better to run how. We can get away—"

"Silence!" cried Lady Hever. "You foolish boy. Your father's already in too deep. If he flees now those men will hunt him down. If you handle things properly we can leave here more carefully and there will be money a-plenty for all of you. There were only three riding along the lane. One is here," she pointed to Verderan. "Soon the other two will come. When they are all dead we can leave at our leisure, and your father," she said enticingly, "will have *ten thousand pounds*."

Caleb must have looked a question for the older man gave an unpleasant smile and nodded. "Worth a bit of trouble, ain't it, Caleb boy?" Jago looked down at Verderan, sprawled on the dusty carpet. "I might as well kill him now then," he said. "No point in risking him reviving."

"Very well," said Lady Hever indifferently.

Sophie made a futile movement and cried out as Caleb's hand in her hair held her back. She watched helpless as the man cocked his pistol. Then the door was flung open and Mrs. Haines rushed in, slamming into her husband. The pistol went off and smashed a large piece of plaster out of the opposite wall.

"Daft woman," shouted Jago.

The housekeeper cringed but cried, "Someone just broke through the pantry window, Jago!"

Jago cursed, threw down his useless pistol, and ran out.

Edith shouted, "Go with him, Caleb. I'll guard this silly tottie!"

Caleb, after a hesitation, ran from the room.

As soon as she was released, Sophie leapt to her feet. She did not run towards the door blocked by Edith Hever but back to the shrine. She grabbed a burning lamp, retreated a few steps, and with tremendous relish hurled it in Edwin Hever's sour face.

It smashed. Burning oil drenched the floating crape. Within seconds the portrait was framed by shooting flames.

"No!" howled the woman and ran forwards to save the picture. Sophie hesitated for a moment with a look at Verderan, but then fled towards the door—to be knocked flying when it was flung open by Caleb.

He grabbed her. "Da wants you for a hostage," he said.

"No, Caleb!" Sophie screamed, resisting as best she could.

"Caleb!" shrieked Lady Hever. "Look what she's done!"

Wild-eyed, the woman grabbed a candlestick from the table, lit it at the fiery shrine, and ran forwards. "Burn with him, then!" she cried and Sophie screamed as the flame was thrust to her skirt.

Verderan heard screams. He groaned as he opened his eyes but came to alertness at the sight of leaping flames. He staggered to his feet and saw a young man all over Sophie, and Lady Hever belabouring him with a candlestick.

He threw the woman aside and dragged the attacker off Sophie, but she cried out, "Not him! Watch for Lady Hever!"

He twisted in time to deflect the candlestick from his head. He grabbed it from the demented, gibbering woman and hurled it across the room. Lady Hever went for his eyes with her nails.

"Your house is on fire, if you haven't noticed," he said and gave the woman a mighty shove so that she fell backwards over a chair to the floor.

He looked at Caleb, standing dazed in the middle of flames and mayhem, and knocked him out with a precise blow to the chin. Then he grabbed Sophie and ran out into the hall.

A shot was heard from the back but he ignored it, heading for the front door.

"Randal!" cried Sophie, fighting his hold. She would have run towards the back of the house, but Verderan's grip was steely and he didn't pause.

"Can look after himself," he said as he dragged her out into the fresh air. He didn't head down the drive but into the concealment of the shrubbery. He stopped there, gasping, and put a hand to feel his head. He winced.

"Are you all right?" asked Sophie then looked back through the rhododendrons towards the house. Smoke was beginning to billow from the dining-room window and flames were spreading through the room. She felt sorry for Caleb, who in the end had saved her by putting out the flames.

"No," groaned Verderan. "I am not all right. It is, however, irrelevant. I'm going to call off the attack. You stay here."

He raced off across the drive and down the other side of the house. After a moment, Sophie followed. She realised for the first time that her leg hurt and when she looked she saw it was burned—not badly but painfully. Moreover her skirt was in charred shreds all down one side. She trembled at the thought of what might have happened if Caleb hadn't acted quickly to extinguish the flames.

She looked again at the burning room, wondering if she could go back to her rescuer but abandoned the notion. The room was truly afire. If he hadn't come to his senses and got himself out, he was as good as dead by now.

When a breeze whipped her tattered skirts away from her legs, she gave a moment's thought to modesty. Then she discarded it as being as irrelevant as Verderan's aching head.

As she made her way cautiously down the side of the house she heard Verderan shouting, "Randal, Marius. We're out!" As she came up behind him he said, "Damnation," and climbed through a broken window. Randal and Marius must have progressed into the main part of the house, either that or been captured. The latter seemed unlikely, though, with Caleb probably out of the fight and only Jago against them.

Sophie couldn't face climbing through the window and knew it might be wiser to wait safely outside. She simply couldn't, though. She crept cautiously around to the back of the house and approached the kitchen door. She peeped in.

Mrs. Haines and the maid were sitting in dumb terror at the table. Another shot cracked and Sophie thought she heard a scream. She made her decision and opened the door.

"The house is on fire!" she cried. "Save yourselves!"

The smoke could be smelt and the woman leapt up, wailing. "Oh mercy me! Oh heavens! Come on, Maisie. Save yourself!"

Grabbing a few obviously treasured items, the woman fled past Sophie, the maid stumbling behind her.

When Sophie opened the door into the house, she realised her words had been true. Glebe House was on fire. She had never been involved in a fire before, and it was terrifying how quickly it was spreading. The long passageway leading down to the hall was already swirling with wisps of smoke. She could hear the crackle and roar of flames. Where were the men?

At that moment she saw Randal in the hall and called his name. He ran towards her and caught her into a crushing embrace. "God, Sophie . . ." She held him just as tight. Even in the urgency of the situation she just wanted to hold him and never let him go.

"I'm fine," she assured him. "I'm fine. Let's get out of here."

"The older man's dead but the young one is getting away . . ."

"Let him," she said, coughing as the smoke began to thicken. "He saved me. Let's go, Randal. The house will be down about our ears. Where are the others?"

"Lady Hever went upstairs. Marius followed to try and rescue her and Verderan went to stop him. Come on," he said, heading back to the hall. "It's safe enough yet and they may need help."

The swirling smoke made her cough again but it was up near the ceiling as yet. The dining-room door was shut but beginning to blister. It would not hold much longer. They prudently took a position by the front door. "Ver. Marius," Randal bellowed over the roar of the fire. "Come on!"

In a moment the two men came running down the stairs. "The damned woman's found a pistol somewhere," gasped Verderan. "I finally persuaded our chivalrous baronet she wasn't worth dying for."

Randal swung open the front door and they all ran out, coughing, into the fresh air and sunshine. Flames were shooting out of the dining-room window now. With a *whoosh*, the dining-room door burst open, shooting fire all over the hall.

"Shouldn't we do something?" asked Sophie, still firmly in Randal's arms.

"What?" Randal replied. "When the smoke's noticed someone will probably come, but from what I've seen I think it's better this place be allowed to burn."

"Yes," Sophie said with a shudder, clutching at his strong arms. "She had shrines to Edwin everywhere, and all his things . . . Randal, she even has a full-sized dummy of him in his dressing room—"

She broke off as she saw Lady Hever through the smoke staggering down the stairs with the wax dummy clasped in her arms.

"My God," said Randal, for at this distance, it was frighteningly realistic. It even seemed to move, to lean closer to the woman. Then Sophie realised it was softening in the heat of the fire which was now licking at the stairs themselves. The woman seemed completely unaware of her danger.

Marius moved forwards but Verderan brought him crashing down in an efficient tackle. The two men were fighting over it when Randal set Sophie aside and ran forwards.

"No!" she screamed and grabbed at the tail of his jacket. It slipped through her fingers, and she called after him as he ran towards the flaming house.

Lady Hever looked up and saw them. She dropped the dummy so it sprawled soggily on the smoldering stairs, took a pistol from her pocket and fired. Randal fell into the dirt.

Sophie rushed forwards but he was already scrambling to his feet. "Didn't touch me. Just instinct." He would have gone towards the house again but at that moment the stair carpet caught fire and both Lady Hever and her treasure were engulfed in flames.

Sophie saw Edith Hever, the effigy once more in her arms, scream as the flames reached her. As Edwin melted over his mother, Sophie fainted.

She came to in Randal's arms, in a field far away from smoke and death.

"Where are we?" she asked.

"Half a mile or so away from the fire," he said, stroking her back gently. "We decided it would be simpler not to be around when anyone turned up. He drew her closer and his cherishing hold spoke of his concern and relief that she was safe. She held onto him in the same, eloquent way.

"How did you get hurt?" he asked.

"I set her picture of Edwin on fire so she tried to do the same to me. Caleb saved me."

"Then I hope he won free." He moved her slightly so he could look into her face. He ran his fingers gently down her cheek and rubbed gently at one spot. "You have smut," he said calmly then rested his head against hers. "I've died a thousand deaths since I realised you were missing."

In a moment he carried on more composedly, "Marius has gone to get some kind of carriage for you. Your leg must hurt."

"Yes," she said, becoming aware of the pain.

"Verderan's gone in search of water. We'll bind your leg with cold cloths. Will you be able to bear it like that until we're away from here? If not we'll just go to the nearest village and find a doctor and to hell with the questions."

She'd spent a large part of her childhood being brave at his careless request and the habit held. Verderan soon came back from a nearby farmhouse with a bucket of cold water. He and Randal sacrificed their cravats and Randal laid them, cool and wet, on her leg. The pain eased and she was able to assure him honestly that it was not so bad.

She then told him as much as she knew of Lady Hever's actions and motives. "She was clearly mad," she ended.

Randal sank his head in his hands. "So James is at death's door because Edith Hever thought you were being forced to marry me when you really loved Edwin. And that he had killed himself because of a broken heart . . ." His fingers tightened in his hair. "It doesn't bear thinking of."

"It could be you lying unconscious," she said softly.

He looked up. "It *should* be me."

She took his hand. "You can't expect me to agree with that, Randal."

He reached for her and held her close. She saw Verderan had moved a tactful distance away.

Eventually he said, "What did you mean yesterday when you asked me if I loved you?"

Sophie stirred uncomfortably. "Silliness," she confessed. "With all that's happened since, it seems ridiculous. You'd been behaving so strangely though, ever since we became engaged that I began to think you didn't really want to marry me."

His arms tightened. "You're as mad as Edith Hever," he said.

Sophie shuddered. "Don't jest about it, Randal."

He tilted her face up so she had to look at him. "I'm sorry. But, Sophie, I adore you. What's more I need you in a hundred different ways."

Sophie traced his fine lips. "For kisses?"

He smiled slightly. "Rather more than kisses, minx."

She blushed. "For . . . for bed?"

He cradled her head and a thumb played softly near the corner of her mouth. "Oh, yes, I need you there, little flame. Need you more than you can possibly imagine . . . but more than that too."

"What then?"

His fingers threaded gently among her tangled curls. "For everything, Sophie. For sharing joys and sorrows, for teasing and being teased, for facing problems and celebrating triumphs . . ."

Sophie felt tears of joy as she twisted her head to reverently kiss his hand.

"Of course," said Randal softly, directing her lips to where he most wanted them to be so his breath melded warm with hers, "if we can do all that in bed, so much the better."

Verderan studied a field of cowslips with all the concentration of an ardent botanist as his friend showed Sophie just how much he loved her.

=15=

IT WAS DARK by the time they returned to Stenby Castle in the shabby coach Marius had bought, explaining apologetically that he'd thought it better to do that than to bring along a coachman or postillions. And, he added, he might know someone glad to buy it off him cheap.

They were greeted at the Castle with great relief and no sooner were they in the door than David grasped Randal's arm and said, "We have good news for you too. Chelmly has recovered consciousness."

Randal coloured and a brilliant smile lit up his face. "He will be all right?"

"Killigrew makes no promises—you know how he is—but even he looked cheerful. Not that you're free of work, Randal, for it's clear Chelmly will need a long repairing lease but you probably won't have to wear strawberry leaves."

"If we can get Chelmly married," said Sophie, hugging Randal to share his delight. "More than ever, I am determined on it."

Randal swung her into his arms. "But not for a while. I doubt either of you are up to it and Killigrew has another patient, I fear."

But when Sophie was settled in her bed it was the general opinion that her leg did not need the doctor's care. The cold cloths had been applied throughout the journey and the reddening had lessened. There were only one or two blisters. The housekeeper produced her famous Black Salve and spread it liberally all over the burn, promising that by the next day it would be painless and by the day after, healed.

Then Marius, Randal and Verderan had to tell their story to David, Mortimer, Jane, and Beth.

"Do you know," said David soberly, "this all could be laid at my door. If I hadn't allowed Uncle Henry to involve me in his investigations you wouldn't have killed Edwin Hever and there would have been no attack on Chelmly."

"We can't trace things back like that, David," said Randal. "Hever had to be stopped from his dirty games. Doubtless a lot of his peculiarities could be put on his mother's account. And if Sophie and I had not gone meddling in your business, it all might have turned out differently again."

He and Verderan left to return to Tyne Towers. The Reverend Mortimer had to go to attend to his parish business. The four remaining discussed the macabre events of the past two days.

As the clock struck ten Jane rose to her feet. "It is time for me to retire, I think," she said. When she reached the door she gave a little shiver. "Do you know, I think I am afraid of the dark tonight."

Her husband got quickly to his feet. "I'll escort you." As his arm came comfortingly around her waist he said, "Don't worry, Tiger Eyes. It's all over now." She leaned her head gratefully on his shoulder and they left the room.

Beth only then became aware that she was alone with Sir Marius again. She found herself wishing she could have a gentleman's arm comfortingly around her on such a night. A particular gentleman's arm. She looked at him hesitantly and her nerve failed her.

"I think I too should retire," she said hastily, getting to her feet.

He rose as well. "Not afraid of the dark, Elizabeth?"

In truth, after the story they had heard, the gloomy ancient corridors of Stenby Castle were a frightening prospect but how could she admit it? "Not at all," said Beth firmly.

He chuckled. "A man likes to feel like a knight-errant occasionally, you know. Indulge me and let me escort you to your bedroom."

"Certainly not!" said Beth, knowing her cheeks were flaming.

He grinned, scooped her up and sat down again with her in his lap, easily ignoring her struggles.

"Let me go!" she cried, pounding ineffectually at his enormous chest.

"Don't be silly," he said, unmoved. "I only want to talk to you and you keep running away."

Beth gave up the hopeless struggle. "I do not keep running away. Life has been a little hectic recently, if you haven't noticed."

"I noticed," he rumbled, good-humouredly. "But you've also been running away. Why? Are you afraid of me?"

"Of course not," said Beth attempting to be prim. How could she be prim when she was sitting on his lap, leaning against his big, warm body, with his arms around her?

"Well, you should be afraid," he said. "I could do anything I wanted with you and you'd never be able to stop me."

Beth swallowed. The thought of what he might want to do with her was churning her insides.

"Why aren't you afraid of me, Elizabeth?" he asked softly.

Silence demanded an answer. "You're a good man," she said at last.

"True enough," he admitted and his hand moved up to rest warm against the back of her neck. "So why are you running from me?"

The firm massage of the tightness in her neck and shoulders felt wonderful and Beth sighed and relaxed. "There's nothing for us," she said sadly, "except an affair. And I am determined to resist that temptation."

His hand moved up into her hair and stilled. He tilted her head so she had to look at him. "And is it a temptation?" he asked with a smile of delight.

"Of course not!" she instinctively protested. But then she mirrored his smile. "You know it is. But, Marius, I could not."

The smile widened to a grin. "That's the first time you've used my name like that, Elizabeth. I like the sound of it on your lips. Say it again."

"Marius," breathed Beth helplessly.

His lips gently brushed over hers.

"Oh, Marius . . ."

They settled on hers firmly and the kiss was instantly deep and hungry. Beth moaned a protest even as she reached up to pull him nearer. But then she struggled away.

"No, Marius. Please!" When she had his attention, she gasped. "Please, my dear, don't seduce me. Let me go. You'll forget me soon enough. You'll see. It will be better—"

He silenced her with a hand over her mouth. "Stop babbling, woman." When he took his hand away Beth stayed silent.

"I will not forget you," he said straightly. "It will not be better that way. I will not forget you, Elizabeth Hawley, because I cannot imagine forgetting my own wife."

"Your what?" asked Beth, stunned.

"Wife. I'm going to marry you. So sit back and be seduced."

A hundred emotions surged in Beth, but she gave in to the most pressing and hit him hard on the nose with her fist. He howled and let her go.

"No, no, and no!" she shouted, when she had a sofa between them. "No, I won't be your wife, no, you are not going to marry me, and no, I will not sit back and be seduced, you great, thick-headed ox!"

Though his eyes were watering, he had a besotted grin on his face. "Why not?"

"Why not what?"

"Why won't you marry me?" he asked. "The rest sort of follows from that, I think."

"You think if I agree to marry you, I'll let you seduce me?" asked Beth in outrage.

He stood and loomed over her across the suddenly frail-looking sofa. "Your mind goes more ways at once than a flock of pigeons in a storm. Why," he demanded, "won't you marry me?"

"Because," snapped Beth, "I haven't been asked!" Then she clapped her hand over her mouth at the admission.

He shouted with laughter, grabbed her around the waist, and lifted her bodily over the back to stand on the sofa. He fell to one knee and she had the unusual experience of looking down at him.

"My dearest Elizabeth," he said with teasing sincerity. "You have come to mean the world to me. In a few short days it has become clear to me that my life will be immeasurably the poorer if I cannot share it with you. I delight in your wit and wisdom. I admire your courage and independence. And," he added, his grey eyes full of the promise of passion, "I love the way you blush like a girl and kiss like a woman of the world."

Beth felt her knees weaken and she grasped the nearest support, his broad shoulders.

He slowly rose to his feet so their faces were level. "Marry me, Elizabeth. Please." Before she could summon her wits to answer he added with a grin, "Or I'll sink into a decline and fade away."

She hit him playfully in the chest for his nonsense. He just looked at her, waiting. Beth thought of a hundred things to say, but in the end she just said, "Yes."

He grabbed her and swung her around and around until she was dizzy and crying to be let down. He collapsed into a chair and took up matters where they had recently broken off. Beth waved a warning fist near his nose.

"I will not be seduced, however," she said.

"I was afraid of that," he responded, engulfing her threatening fist in his much larger one. "You throw a good punch for such a tiny little thing."

"Arthur taught me," she said. "He also taught where to hit for the greatest effect."

One eyebrow quirked as he chuckled. "I think I had a lucky escape."

Beth blushed.

"No seduction?" he queried wistfully.

Beth quelled her own desires. "No."

He put her on her feet and stood. "Will you allow me, though, to be a gallant gentleman and escort you to your bedchamber?"

"Of course," said Beth, smiling at him. It had taken a little while for the glory of it to sink in, but now she was aware of happiness filling her to the brim, spilling over to brighten the world. He loved her. She was his. They would be together forever and the world was truly a more wonderful place.

As they passed through the door his hand stroked softly down her spine and she could not help a long, wistful sigh.

"No seduction," she said, hoping she sounded more adamant than she felt.

"It's quite a long way to your bedchamber," he murmured softly as he picked up a waiting lamp to light their way. "Care to lay odds, my darling gambler, on the chance of you changing your mind during such a long journey?"

Beth gulped and just hoped her willpower was up to the task before it.

The next day Jane and her husband were amused and delighted to find that Marius and Beth were engaged to marry and that neither of them was willing to wait very long for the event. Straight after breakfast Marius whisked a starry-eyed Beth off to Shrewsbury to buy a ring.

Jane went to check on Sophie and found her already up but breakfasting in her bedchamber, lying on a daybed.

"I can't move very far without all these bandages falling off my leg," Sophie complained. "I'm going to have to play the invalid for a few days if I want to be healed for the wedding. You will let Randal up, won't you?" she asked anxiously.

"I doubt Wellington's crack troops could keep him away," said Jane dryly. "In truth, most of the inhabitants of the Castle and the Towers have been trying to get you two into an improper situation for weeks. Just for a bit of peace."

The two young women laughed together. "It has all been rather ridiculous, hasn't it?" said Sophie. "But I really did wonder what he felt for me. It's the Ashby charm that's to blame. I do hope none of our children get it." At the thought of children she blushed rosily.

Jane looked a little self-conscious too. "Speaking of children ... By next Easter you and Randal will be aunt and uncle."

"Jane! How wonderful ..."

At that moment the door opened and Randal walked in as if he had every right in the world. The word *wonderful* on Sophie's lips slid easily over to apply to him.

The two were immediately lost in each other and with a smiling shake of the head, Jane left them alone.

Randal came to sit on the edge of the chaise. His hand went

to rest with natural possessiveness on Sophie's hip. She carried his other hand to her lips.

"Hello, minx," he said.

"Hello."

"Does your leg hurt much?"

"Not too much."

Counterpoint to this prosaic conversation their eyes and hearts spoke of love and desire, hunger and unity. His hand burned on her hip. Her fingers twined with his restlessly.

"How is Chelmly," Sophie asked.

"Better than we could have hoped," said Randal with a smile. "He's weak as a kitten and has the devil of a headache, but judging from the questions he was pestering me with, he's lost none of his faculties."

Sophie grinned with relief. "He sounds like the old Chelmly indeed."

Randal smiled thoughtfully. "Not quite. I think you may find him more willing to fall into the matrimonial trap. I suspect the mere notion of the estate being in my feckless hands has scared him out of his misogamy for ever."

"Trap indeed," said Sophie thoughtfully. "Is that how you regard it?"

With a laughing groan he slid down beside her on the chaise and eased her over him. "If it is a trap, minx, there was never a man more willing to be caught. Don't let me hurt you," he said softly.

"You couldn't ever hurt me," she said, laying her head deliciously on his chest, hearing his pounding heart.

"I spanked you once," he said.

"You did not," she replied, without moving.

"You were about six. You tried to pick up a loaded gun."

"I don't remember that, but it sounds as if I deserved it."

"You did. You acted as if I'd hurt you, though. You howled like a banshee."

Sophie giggled. "Probably so you wouldn't hit me anymore. It's the best way. The few times my mother tried to switch me I shrieked so much at the first stroke she lost her nerve."

"And look where it's got you," he said, his hand rubbing softly where the switch might have done its work. "A few proper chastisements and you would have had the sense to marry Trenholme."

Sophie turned slightly so their faces were close. "It's got me heaven, and well you know it. I've wanted you, Randal, since I was a child. When I reached for that gun I was probably just trying to please you. When I howled it was probably just because you were angry. I could never live without you."

She feathered soft kisses on his lips.

"And you've entranced me, little flame," he said, "since you were in your cradle. You were an utterly beautiful baby, you know, even to a young boy who cared nothing for such things. You were a delightfully naughty child and I encouraged and protected you. You followed me around and I loved it. You made me feel like a god." His fingers wandered her back, sending dancing promises throughout her body. "You still do," he said softly.

He surrendered to her teasing and kissed her. The magic was already familiar to Sophie and she no longer wanted gentleness. She reached up to hold him close and taste him, feeling the wonderful shudder go through both of them at the contact. She rubbed against the slight roughness of his clothes. She felt him tense. And then he pushed her away.

"Sophie," he said unsteadily. "We can't do this."

She wanted to protest, but knew he was right. "It hurts," she said.

"Believe me, sweet torment, I know."

He slid from under her and stood, raking a hand through his disordered curls. "Sorry as I am to say it, Sophie, but it's back to propriety until the wedding." He turned back with a beautiful smile. "And this time, minx, can you not tease me to death?"

Sophie grinned in delight. "Did I? You didn't seem to notice."

"Oh, I noticed. The day you left your gown loose at the front and found so many excuses to lean over . . ."

Sophie giggled.

"The way you kirtled your skirt up high whenever we played any kind of sport . . ."

Sophie mischievously began to inch her skirt up her leg. It was enthralling to play this game with him and she couldn't resist.

He sharply tugged her skirt back to her ankles. "Behave yourself, Sophie." His eyes were warmly smiling, though. "The times you brushed up against me when there was room all around . . ." He took a deep breath. "Sophie, I have to go."

By the door he stopped and it was as if he braced himself for a painful task. "Sophie. If you still think it best, we'll postpone the wedding until Chelmly's on his feet again."

Sophie stared at him. They'd surely both expire of starvation. She shook her head and said mischievously, "Don't you dare. Heavens, do a thing like that and they'll think they've reformed us. Let's start by shocking the world so they'll know what to expect."

He laughed with relief. "So be it. We have a tryst then, my fiery angel, a tryst for Wednesday, August the twenty-eighth, in the big front bedchamber at Fairmeadows. The one that looks over the rose gardens and is always full of their perfume . . ." Their eyes met across the room, full of the pain of the brief parting and the promise of endless delight.

"And," said Sophie, "I think we can do without seconds, don't you?"

Author's Note

SOME NORTH AMERICAN readers may be perplexed by the rules of cricket. It does bear some resemblance to baseball, but not very much.

In cricket there are always two batters up, one at each end of a strip of grass called the pitch. The strip of grass is officially 22 yards long and nearly three yards wide.

At each end of the pitch is a wicket. This is a set of three stumps—27 inch high sticks—set in the grass with two small pieces of wood called bails balanced on top. The batter stands in front of the wicket, guarding it with his bat, which is flat and about four inches wide. A bowler from the opposing team throws the ball from one end of the pitch to the other, his main aim being to hit the wicket and dislodge the bails which will get the batter out. The batter is also out if he hits a ball which is caught before it touches the ground. The batter can be out for a number of other strange things but we won't go into that here except for being run out, which will be familiar enough to North Americans.

If the batter hits the ball and is not caught he may score a run if he thinks he can make it. He will run to the other end of the pitch while the batter at that end has to run to his. Either player can be out if the ball reaches the wicket before they do. The batters can continue to run until the ball is returned. Whoever is at the batting end when they stop is the next one to receive the bowling. This is why David and Sophie were each trying to arrange the runs so they would be at the right end.

There is no limit to how many balls a batter may take. He will stay in until he is out or until there is no other batter to be up with him.

A bowler throws the ball six times for an 'over'. Then another player on the fielding side becomes bowler from the other end of the pitch. The identity of the bowler and the end bowled from changes after each over but the same two bowlers can bowl the whole match if they have the stamina.

The wicket keeper is like a catcher in baseball.

The rest of the fielders stand around to stop and, if possible, catch the ball. It should be noted that a cricket ball is solid and very hard and cricketers do not use catching gloves. There are two fielding positions called 'silly mid on' and 'silly mid off' because the injury rate so close to the batter is rather high.

It has always been usual for the batsmen to wear leg and hand protection, and nowadays they also wear helmets. In a casual game, however, this would not be the case and in the regency period the bowlers were still throwing underarm and so the velocity of the ball would have been less dangerous. I'm sure you can understand, however, why Randal was gentle in his bowling to Sophie.

The regency period was an important one for the development of cricket. The game had existed for hundreds of years, but it was during the eighteenth century that it became organized. The White Conduit Club was founded in Islington (a London suburb) but the field where they played was being built upon and so they asked a certain Thomas Lord to find them another site. He found them a location in Marylebone, which is why the ruling body of cricket today is called the Marylebone Cricket Club, even though they no longer play there.

In 1814 Lord found the MCC a new site in St. John's Wood which was called Lord's Cricket Ground, and Lord's has been the center of cricket ever since.

A true cricket match takes a number of days, each team going up twice. Nowadays, as most spectators can't take the time off work, they have one-day matches on Sunday as well. Still, a five-day Test Match can disrupt the flow of British commerce. It's surprising how many cricket enthusiasts have radios, or even miniature television sets, in their desks.

If you visit England and decide to take in a cricket match be prepared for something more leisurely than a baseball match, but just as exciting in its way. Perhaps the best way to enjoy the sport is to track down a village match and sit on the grass with a beer or two for company.

Just take note of one fact, however. If the ball should happen to come your way, you do *not* take it home. A cricket ball has to last a certain length of time and the bowlers are carefully nurturing it until it has just the right degree of wear to produce their most deadly ball—a flipper, a googly or a leg-break, perhaps. Putting the cricket ball in your pocket may land you in the local duck-pond.

I hope you have enjoyed *THE STOLEN BRIDE*. I enjoy hearing from my readers and invite you to write me care of the publisher: Walker and Company.

If you would like to receive details of other Walker Regency Romances, please write to:

The Regency Editor
Walker and Company
720 Fifth Avenue
New York, NY 10019